Terry, Am glad we have kept in touch through the years.

JOURNAL OF DESTINY

Kay Larson

Kay Larson Killen

Publication assistance provided by GSP-Assist,
a service of
Great Spirit Publishing

Great Spirit Publishing

Springfield, Missouri
www.greatspiritpublishing.yolasite.com

ISBN 13-978-1499195835
10-1499195834

Published in USA.

JOURNAL OF DESTINY

Kay Larson

Publication assistance provided by *GSP-Assist*, a service of

Great Spirit Publishing

Great Spirit Publishing
Springfield, Missouri
USA

DEDICATION

To Jack, Barry, and Darwin

for all the right reasons

To Darlys, Jean, Linda, and Marylou

PART I

Chapter 1

Ben Hardisty wasn't old - just sore and bent. The scout was a day's ride ahead of the wagon train and plumb tuckered out. It was time to head back. Ben had found plenty of water and wild game, so the settler's trek could continue at a good pace once everyone was rested up. He had not seen a sign of hostile Indians. The travelers should remain safe as they continued their way into the West.

"Come on, Yonder, you old wooly bugger. Let's get back to some decent food. I'm tired of beans and pemmican," said Ben to the dog that had been at his side for a whole lot of years. He threw his leg over Feather and settled into the creaking saddle. He had ridden more miles in the saddle than he had walked in his boots during the past few years.

* * * * *

Ben had left his family home along the Mississippi River at a young age. The call of the river, and what was beyond, was so strong his parents knew their son would never be happy staying in one place for very long.

"Promise me, son," said his father, "that you won't leave us until after your eighteenth birthday. Promise us that."

His parents stood on the riverbank waving as Ben floated away on a raft he and his father constructed. He was on his way. Ben floated up and down the river until a river boat captain asked if he needed a job: "It's swabbing decks and taking care of passenger needs, but the pay is fair and the food is tolerable."

When he tired of the river, Ben decided to explore further west, by horseback this time. He always made it a point to talk with wagon masters and scouts who were assembling wagon trains. Every now and then one of them allowed him to tag along if he agreed to help with chores.

After several scouting trips back and forth, each time going deeper into the west and with a little more age on him, Ben signed on with a new wagon master leading his first trip. Ben knew the routine having ridden sections of each of the main trails leading to California.

* * * * *

This trip was Ben's last scout. He had a family who needed tending to. Young Clay was nearly a man and needed his Pa as much as Ben needed him. He was missing too many of the growing-up years of his children but good money had lured him to the trail. After this trip he and Sarah figured there should be enough money in the bank to buy a place of their own. He would be through with the trail forever.

It also meant that Sarah could quit her job at the dry goods store and stay home with their two youngest, Adam and Molly. Clay would be finished with school before long. The kids could get to know their old man. As it was, Ben was pretty much a stranger who showed up now and then, stayed just long enough to get everything in an uproar, and then ride off again.

* * * * *

The new wagon master, a young man by the name of Clampton, had sent his scout, Ben, on ahead to search out any trouble spots that might turn up in a day or two. No Indians had been sighted since they left the main wagon train some weeks ago. That train, still headed toward California, was not happy to see so many families leave them to follow the Oregon Trail to the site of their new homes.

Clampton, who had been taught to listen and learn by his father, tempered his eagerness. It was hard for him to allow time for stragglers and sometimes be accused of poor judgment by some of the older men. Nevertheless, everyone was safe and sound. They could find no fault there.

The wagons were in the far country on a trail that led many homesteaders out west. Wagon wheels cut through tall grass and deep into the sod where a thousand teams of oxen, mules and horses had pulled settlers and their families in heavily loaded wagons. A young lad digging his toe into a rut yelled to his friends, "These ruts are so deep they're going to be here for a hundred years, I'll bet."

Clampton knew he could lead his people to a new home in a place called Oregon. He reckoned they weren't all that far from their paradise.

Although there had been little serious illness or major calamity early on, time had been used up fording rivers swollen with melting snow pack and spring rains. Axles and wheel parts that snapped were now quickly replaced by the wheelwright and a crew of men he had trained over the months. Clampton was grateful the wagon train included a harness maker, a smithy, and other skilled people who were always willing to lend a hand.

Horses and oxen that strayed in the night had to be rounded up and herded back. There were none to spare; a difficult climb or two over more mountains still lay ahead.

Since leaving Kansas City there had been two births and a baptism along with sprained ankles and too much sun.

During these few days of rest, Clampton took time to visit with each family. He was not positive everyone fully understood when he had told them there would be nothing waiting for them when they reached Oregon. They would be all alone in the wilderness, miles from any kind of settlement. He had to be sure everyone was still excited and willing to settle in new territory.

Some families were finding the going pretty rough, more than they had bargained for. No one realized clothes and shoes would wear out so quickly. Something was always in need of repair. Many families pitched in with what they could spare to keep everyone in boots. Several youngsters still walked barefoot.

He observed the men and boys bragging to one another about everything they were going to accomplish when they reached their destination. They all had high hopes.

Clampton carefully listened to a few women who were having second thoughts, doubting their ability to care for children in times of illness or injury. "Who will teach them where there are no schools?" they asked. "What if something happens to our husbands? And what about those savages we have heard so much about?"

Because he had no decisive answers, Clampton called the women together and had them share their fears with each other. By the time he was ready to head back to his own campfire, the women fairly convinced themselves everything was going to all right. They agreed to look after one another in times of stress, to keep an eye on all the children, not just their own.

Ben explained to the ladies that because Indians had no resistance to diseases brought to them by the white man whole tribes died from various plagues that swept through their villages. He told them the Paiute were mostly nomads, and the Tillamook were traders, not interested in starting any wars unless they were threatened. Yes, there had been battles over the years, but the U.S. Calvary was there to defend their countrymen. "Don't go looking for trouble," Ben told the group of women. "Just like your children, if you go looking for trouble you are going to find it."

* * * * *

The small wagon train was attacked and silenced before anyone had time to even think about loading a rifle.

Mary was sitting at the campfire softly singing a lullaby to Olivia. It was time for the baby's afternoon nap but she was restless. She looked so much like her daddy with that wild black hair and big brown eyes, just like his.

Mary's lap was full of socks to darn and buttons to replace. Torn pockets and knees out of britches were never-ending. It was the quiet time between high noon and evening supper. Fires were banked and water barrels filled.

This was the first camp the wagon master had ordered since leaving the main wagon train. He told the settlers they would stay as long as it took to restore order to the wagons, relax sore muscles, and care for the animals. They had left the snow and cold behind and were making such steady progress they would arrive at their destination long before winter set in again.

Micah, Mary's husband of just two years, wandered over to the far side of camp where a group of men and boys were standing around scuffing their toes in the dirt, speculating about what they would find in Oregon. Most expected lush, green farmland; others were interested in timber. The younger ones were anxious to see the Pacific Ocean.

Suddenly the circle of wagons was surrounded. The pounding hooves of ponies and war cries filled the air. Arrows found their mark. Canvas covered wagons flamed making it difficult to see through the smoke and dust stirred up by horses.

Everything happened so fast no one had time to defend themselves. All they could do was crawl under wagons for protection or just run and try to find cover. Women screamed for their husbands, babies cried out in fright. Several men ran to save a group of children who were playing just outside the circle of wagons. Frenzied dogs and horses added to the confusion and pulled loose of their tethers.

All of a sudden, the arrows stopped. It grew quiet as the Indians pulled up on their reins. Then, with a bloody cry, they leaped their horses over the wagon tongues and were inside the encampment with tomahawks held high in the air.

* * * * *

While the wagon train was under siege, Ben and Yonder were slowly making their way back to camp. Ben knew Clampton would not break camp before he returned to give him word that the next part of the trip would be safe. They both knew the animals needed a good rest and a belly full of lush green grass before heading out again. Women and children were exhausted from walking miles every day under a hot summer sun. The wagons were no more comfortable to ride in than walking.

Wild berries along the trail were ripe. Ben hoped he had picked enough for pie. The ladies were always clucking at him for never eating enough or always eating on the run. He knew one of them would be pleased to bake him a pie. Yonder ran ahead and scared up a rabbit for their supper. Ben was happy it would be the last meal he'd have to cook for himself out on the trail. They would soon be back with the wagon train.

* * * * *

Slowly and painfully Mary came to. She was not sure where she was or what happened; only that she was on the ground and did not know how she got there. A sharp stab of pain brought back the horror.

When she realized the wagon train was being attacked by Indians, Mary took one last look at Micah across the way before snatching Olivia out of her pine rocker where she had finally fallen asleep. She looked for a safe place to hide and stared right into the face of the enemy. He pulled back on his bow and let go the arrow.

Mary felt the arrow slice into her left side. She held Olivia tightly to her breast but could feel her life-blood flowing away. She looked down and saw her blue dress turning to red. There was no strength to hold her baby tight enough to keep her from being torn out of her arms by a young Indian astride his painted pony. He pushed Mary backwards and snatched the baby. She felt the arrow snap off as she landed on the ground. The last thing Mary heard was crying babies and children screaming for their mamas and papas. Her husband was already dead.

Mary tried to move but hurt all over. When she tried to rise up, the pain in her side was too much. It was so quiet. She thought she could hear someone off in the distance moaning for help.

It took a long time for the pain to ease some. When it did, Mary struggled to stand but her legs would not hold her up. She pulled herself along the ground to where she had last seen Micah running towards her. It seemed to take forever to struggle just a few inches before the pain came back again.

By the time Mary reached Micah, there were only low moans coming from a few who were still barely alive. No one was pleading for help anymore. She saw that Micah had stretched himself over a young boy, protecting the child even in death. She crawled up beside Micah and laid there for a long time struggling to say good-bye to her husband.

Mary struggled to get back to their campsite. The wagon had been pushed over and emptied. A wheel was broken and the canvas tarp burned to ashes. An arrow had pierced the wooden water cask. It had fallen to the ground so Mary could tip it to pour what was left of the water into the palm of her hand. She tried to take a few sips but it hurt to swallow. Her wound was still seeping blood. She knew she had to stop moving around and rest.

* * * * *

Nearly at the end of the ride back to the wagon train, Yonder had run ahead but then slowed. The hackles on his back rose up, he sniffed the air. Ben caught up with him and the two sat still for a minute listening to the quiet. A faint, sickly, sweet smell hung in the air. It was too quiet. The closer they moved toward the wagon train, sweet turned to stench. Buzzards circled overhead.

Ben had seen Indian raids before, but never the devastation that lay before him. He knew that even though many peace treaties had been signed, Indians were still angry at homesteaders who traveled through their hunting grounds. Now they were looking for the new repeater rifles these people carried. With a sick heart Ben urged Feather forward.

With each step made closer to camp, Feather complained. She whinnied and stomped the ground in fear. She could smell blood. Ben saw the wagon train had been caught completely unaware. They had been stalked. "I should have been here," he said out loud. "I should have been here to help fight them off."

The scout slowly slid down from his horse and knelt next to Clampton's body. He bowed his head and apologized to the young ramrod in his new buckskins. "Not on his first trip, please God," Ben prayed, but he knew death had come quickly for his friend.

Ben searched the camp for any sign of life. There was no movement or sounds, no painful groans, no cries for help. Nothing moved but scavenging birds. Bodies lay where they had fallen.

Ben mounted up again to ride over and check the picket line. Feather carefully picked her way through the bodies. Every horse, mule and oxen had either been killed or had run off. Ben was alone, surrounded by death.

Yonder nosed around, sniffing at the drying blood. He sat on his haunches and bayed. Ben urged Feather forward for another look around the campsite. He paused near Micah McCreedy's tipped over wagon where he saw Mary's body stretched out, covered in blood. He wondered what happened to their baby girl.

Ben thought it odd when he noticed a tiny white flag on the ground near Mary's outstretched fingers. Out of curiosity more than anything else, he reached down and pulled the flag out of the ground. A flag is usually a signal, he told himself, and decided to look around some more.

Ben tied Feather to the wagon so the frightened horse would not run off. He picked up a nearby lard tin and pried off the lid. Inside was a roll of money, a belt buckle he recognized as belonging to Mary's husband, and a small leather bound book.

The first thing that went through his mind was that Mary was saying something with the flag and tin of things precious to her. Ben wondered why there was nothing about the baby, Olivia.

Ben removed the white rag from the stick and saw it was an arrow, broken in half. He spread the rag across his knee. "Oh, my Lord," Ben exclaimed when it dawned on him it was a tiny baby dress. It all seemed to mean something, but it was not coming clear to Ben.

After making sure there was no one alive to help, Ben sadly stuffed some food he found into canvas bags, and filled several canteens from the creek alongside the encampment. He put the little pail and flag into one of the bags and tied it over the saddle horn with the others. Ben paused and said good-bye to his fallen friends before he and Yonder headed north, towards Montana and home. He would not be back this way again.

* * * * *

It was a long, lonely journey for a sad man and his old dog. At the first Army fort he came to, Ben reported the Indian attack on the wagon train. The officers informed Ben they were required to file an official report with the authorities. He felt torn apart again answering questions about what he had left behind, three days ride back along the trail.

Before bedding down one night, Ben took the little pail and arrow out of the canvas bag. He had finally come to grips with the massacre and was thinking more clearly. Ben untied the tiny white dress from the shaft of the broken arrow so he could examine it more closely.

Ben removed the belt buckle from the tin and turned it over and over in his hand. It made him wonder what happened to Micah's fancy gold watch he was so proud of.

Next, he removed a stack of money bound in a piece of leather securely tied with a thong. It looked like their life savings intended for a new life in the west. Ben counted out the money and saw he was right about the amount. He stuffed it back in the tin.

Suddenly, a connection flashed through Ben's mind. If Mary was indicating a message to someone through her outstretched fingers near the flag, then too the items inside the tin were placed there on purpose. Ben needed time to think.

Ben spread a blanket on the ground, poked the fire, and laid down resting his head against the old saddle. With light from the flames he leafed through the small book that was also in the pail. He turned to the first pages and began reading. He immediately realized it was written by someone at the end of every day of travel. Each page held the story of a day's journey.

Ben read, turning pages until he came to the end of the writing. There were many more blank pages. Yonder hunkered down at his side and Ben reread the last pages out loud to his dog and the stars above.

There was a signature under the last written line. She knew she did not have the strength to write anything more. Mary's name answered Ben's questions. Now he must answer hers.

* * * * *

June, 1867
Somewhere near the Yellowstone

Wild savages attacked our wagon train. There was no warning. They came silently out of nowhere. Everyone is dead. My darling baby girl, Olivia, was ripped from my arms by one of them. She is gone and I know not her fate. I can only hope and pray they keep her alive.

I am writing this in the hope that one day Olivia, my sweet child, will read these words. It was just days ago that your father and I had you baptized in the Powder River. The water was so cold it took your breath away.

After your name had been pronounced and blessings bestowed upon you, your father tied his leather watch fob around your little neck. He had taken off the gold watch that was a gift from his father when we left Boston, but left the tiny gold four-leaf clover from his mother. You are named for her you know; Grandmother Olivia McCreedy. Your Pa told you the clover would always bring you good luck. You look so much like him. You have the same wild black hair and dark eyes that dance when you are happy.

After the attack, I found your baptism dress among the ruins of our wagon. I could not bear to use it to bandage the wound in my side where the arrow still sucks life from me. The dress was sewn together with such love and devotion to you, our first-born child.

The beautiful sheer white cloth came from the skirt of an afternoon gown I often wore to tea with my mother and aunts. The lace was made by a friend I met on the wagon train. She had many spools of cotton thread and let me choose the color. I stitched the little dress while Iris tatted lace for it.

We spent many hours around the campfire discussing who had been left behind and what was still ahead. What was to be our destiny? Your tiny dress is all I have left of you.

Olivia, my darling child, you and your father fill my thoughts. I could not help him. He died trying to save a small boy but it was too late. If I am ever able, I will come for you but right now my wounds are too deep. Someone will find you. I know that in my heart. I love you, my daughter.

If I am gone and someone finds this journal, swear to my memory you will find our daughter and return her to her grandparents in Boston. My parents are gone, but her father's people, the McCreedys, are a fine family who will want her with them.

If my bones are bleached white, it means Olivia has been with the Indians for a long time. She will know only their ways with no recollection of her father or me. She will not know our language. Let her choose where she wants to be. It is the only gift I can ever give our child.

Mary McCreedy
Wife of Micah McCreedy
and Olivia's mother

* * * * *

Chapter 2

It seemed to Ben it was taking forever to make his way back to his wife and children, who lived in Fort Benton. He was looking forward to their reunion. The massacre was something he would not be able to immediately share with his family. As Ben rode along, his mind could not escape the guilt of not being with the wagon train when it was attacked. He knew he would feel forever sorry for not being able to help anyone who might have survived. He would not collect his wages from this trip. Ben worried how his family would survive without the money, but it was over. He was going home to stay.

Ben read the last pages of Mary's journal more than once by the light from his camp fires. Her words preyed on his mind. Mary had asked for a promise, but Ben felt he just could not keep it right now. He had to get home to his family before he could get involved in hers. His children too had been lost to him for all those years he spent on the trail scouting for wagon trains.

During their long ride home, Ben made sure Feather had plenty of time to rest up. The mare was getting on in years and he knew her feet hurt. Old Yonder was faring a little better, but he was not a pup anymore. He could still scare up a rabbit for their supper now and then; the dog did not spend all day chasing everything that moved like he had in the past.

Ben felt every day in the saddle. Maybe, he hoped, there would be money for a new one after they bought a place in the country, away from town. He hoped and prayed Sarah had managed to save up enough money over the years. His boots were still good for another year.

The last day on the trail, Ben wanted to ride all night to get home. He knew it was a foolish idea. Feather could get real hurt stepping in an unseen hole, or they could slip off a ledge in the dark. He did not sleep much; just laid there watching the moon move across the sky. At dawn, he was mounted and on his way. Even Yonder knew that something good was going to happen today.

* * * * *

For a long time, Ben sat on the rise just beyond the house at the edge of town. It appeared there was no one around. He could take time getting his fill of what lay before him. Home.

Finally the little band of travelers made their way down to the house. Yonder found new energy chasing chickens around the yard while Ben got Feather rubbed down and fed a bucket of oats. He felt almost an intruder as he walked around inspecting the place. The house was not in bad shape. It looked smaller than he remembered. It just needed a few nails here and there and a step replaced. He noticed that the old shed out back had some leaks that he could set the boys to mending. Old tack and tools hung from pegs where he had left them. Poker, the old nag Ben had worn out years ago was still in the corral. She got a handful of oats too.

Inside the house, Ben stowed his gear in the bedroom and stood there taking in the scent of Sarah. He poked his head into each child's room. He shook his head at the mess left behind by three kids already late for school.

Ben caught his toe on the broken step when he went to walk back out to the shed. We will have a big barn at our new place, he thought, with room enough for each horse and tack. He picked up his old saddle and slung it over the fence. He hung Feather's bridle on a peg and stripped off the chaps that had saved him from many a snake bite and cactus thorn. The food he picked up at the site of the massacre for the ride home was long gone.

There was only one canvas bag left. For the last time, he pulled out the roll of money, the belt buckle, Olivia's dress and broken arrow, and Mary's journal. He held the leather book with faded gold trim in his hands and thought yet again how sorry he was that he had not been there to help when the Indians rode in. He thought of Mary and what a struggle it must have been for her to write a message to her daughter to have one day.

Ben silently vowed to see that Olivia would get the journal someday. It may take a long time, but she will have it so she can read it and know what a brave Mother she had. He set the journal down and picked up the roll of money. It was enough to buy a ranch.

No, I could not live with myself if I did that, he thought. This money belongs to Olivia. She will need it to get a place of her own someday.

With that, he jammed everything back into the canvas bag, tied it up tight, and stuffed it where the kids could not find it in the shed. The bag would be there when the time was right.

* * * * *

Ben was sitting at the kitchen table nursing a cup of coffee when he heard his wife and children laughing and talking as they came in the front gate to the house. He got up and stood in the doorway waiting for them to see him.

Tears slid down her cheeks when Sarah saw Ben at the top of the steps. She did not care why he was home so early, just that he was home. The three children could not believe their eyes. Everyone began talking all at once. Ben did not understand a word as he gazed over their heads into the eyes of his wife.

Sarah held back while the children hugged their father and royally welcomed him home. "How long can you stay," asked Molly. "I hope it is forever this time." Ben smiled down at her. "Yes, my daughter, I am here to stay this time." Clay and Adam let out a whoop and a holler, grabbed hold of Sarah's hands and danced a jig around Ben and Molly.

Sarah broke loose of the boys and shyly approached Ben. She put her arms around his neck and said, "Welcome home. We have been waiting for you." As they kissed, the children tittered and ran to the steps to get away from the love birds.

"Are you hungry, cowboy?" asked Sarah. Ben's eyes lit up at the mention of food. He said nothing would please him more than to sit down to a good home cooked meal, topped off with a piece of sour cream and raisin pie for dessert. "That we can do," she assured him. "Let's go inside and see what mischief the children are up to."

"Okay, let's get organized. Clay and Adam, please bring in a bucket of water and wood for the cook stove. See that Yonder is fed and has some water too. Molly, you can bring in the clabbered cream from the well house and get the pie going. Ben, you just sit there and relax while I make a fresh pot of coffee. The children will have a million questions for you, I'm sure."

As their supper was being prepared Ben sipped coffee, watching his family and answered questions they threw at him right and left. Molly wanted to know if he had had enough to eat while he was gone. Ben told her he did get tired of pemmican when he was too far out in front of the wagon train for a meal, but yes, everyone was very nice and often invited him to a campsite to share a meal.

Clay asked if the wagon train had run into any problems or had troubles. Ben took a deep breath and said there were the usual broken wheels and animals that got away from them and had to be rounded up again. He let his answer go at that.

Adam was curious about being on the trail and what he had seen. "Were there any Indians, did you shoot any bear or deer? What was it like crossing the rivers?"

Ben described hunting for deer to feed the people in the wagon train; even a wild turkey or two walked into his line of fire. He could honestly say he had not seen any Indians. Then he went on to describe wheels that had broken and splintered crossing a particularly wide river that was full of boulders.

The children were fascinated listening to him and Sarah occasionally paused to listen. "Let's get back to work. We have got to get supper on the table for this starving man," Sarah teased.

While the family ate their supper, Ben found he had never enjoyed a meal so much as this one. He thought about all he had missed while the children were growing up. Molly looks just like Sarah, he mused. Young Adam was tall and spindly with feet too big. He was not a baby anymore. Adam had already done some bragging about toting water every day and bringing in wood for the cook stove. Clay was built like his father, strong as an ox, but he had his mother's hair and eyes. He wanted to be a scout just like his Pa when he was fully grown.

It was awkward at first. Things did not go well until Ben backed off and let his boys show him what they could do. They were not used to having a father around who insisted they do things his way. They had been on their own too long and had chores divided up between them. Clay had been the man of the house for a long time so he and his Pa butted heads every now and then. Adam finally told the both of them he was sick and tired off all the bickering.

Sarah and Ben also had their small conflicts. They were quickly resolved and never lasted overnight. Sometimes Ben would get a far-away look in his eyes and slip into a mood that no one could penetrate. Everyone learned to avoid him until it passed. No matter how many times they asked what was wrong, or if there was anything any of them could do, his silence was their answer.

Ben was disappointed to find out there was not enough money in the bank to buy a new place out in the country. Sarah swore she tried to watch their expenses, but with three growing children there was a never-ending need for clothes and shoes. Sarah had given up trying to get the boys full at meal times. They were always hungry. There was not enough space for a larger garden that would have helped feed her family.

On top of that, Molly had been bedridden with a fever that just refused to let go of her. Her medicine had dug a hole in the savings.

Ben did not collect his pay for the last scout. Sarah never mentioned the missing wages. She knew her husband well enough to know that something had happened out on the trail. He was too quiet and moody. Ben was not telling tales of his adventures like he usually did when he came home. She had made up her mind to wait until he was ready to talk about it. For now, the family accepted his reason for being home earlier than expected. He simply told them the settlers on the wagon train had found their kingdom. There was no need for them to travel any further.

* * * * *

Eventually, Ben hired on at the stable in town and also helped with the stage coaches coming and going. He liked his work and thought maybe it would be a good idea to build a way-station rather than ranching. The more he thought it out, the more he convinced himself it would be a good life for his family. He was ready to talk it over with Sarah and Clay. He would need Clay's help. One man alone could not handle all the horses they would have to keep corralled. It was at least a two-man job to swap four, six, and eight hitch teams every time a coach came through.

It took a couple of years with both Ben and Sarah working and taking on odd jobs before there was enough money to move his family. Ben could not get a promise from Clay that he would stay at the way-station and help run it.

He said to his Pa: "Now that I'm through with school, there's no reason I can't go in search of whatever is out there. I don't want to live in this town for the rest of my life and work in a store, or a way-station. I can't tell you that I will, Pa."

"More food for thought," Ben said to Sarah when they were trying to make some decisions. "On the other hand, there's Adam. He's a real worker and a homebody unlike Clay who has a real case of wanderlust."

Clay was often late getting home from town school. There was always something new to explore on the other side of the hill, in the woods, or around a corner.

He brought home every kind of bird and mended many broken wings and legs. He even stitched up a few open cuts on furry critters he discovered in need of help.

On weekends, Clay and Poker would disappear over the rise, many times coming back just in time for classes on Monday. Much to the distress of his mother, no matter how often she warned him or asked him to be home by Sunday afternoon, it was impossible for Clay. He took after Ben more than Adam. Pa could not fault the boy for not sticking around. He did the same thing when he was a young boy living on the river.

* * * * *

Ben and Sarah eventually talked themselves out of running a way-station. It would have to be built from the ground up, which would take another year. Even before that happened, it would take a certain amount of time to develop contracts with the stage lines.

There was also the family to consider. Even with three men in the Hardisty family, if anything should happen to any one of them, Sarah and Molly would not be able to do the job. Sarah would always have the cooking and cleaning on top of then having to do a man's work. Molly's health was fragile and always would be after being down so long with the fever. Most certainly, Clay sounded like he would not be around for too long.

In the end, they decided they had not really thought the way station through and considered all aspects of the idea. It was the end of their dream, but like Sarah told him, "Ben, you have always had a dream to have your own ranch. Let's just stick with that goal. I know we can make it come true."

When they told Clay and Adam and Molly they had decided against the way station, but would buy a ranch instead, Adam said it best: "At least we won't have to wrangle all those horses at one time. That kind of scared me because the teams have to be changed in such a hurry. I would not want any of us to get hurt. A horse ranch is better."

Once they had been made aware of the children's feelings toward the way station, they were included in more of the continuing discussions about getting a ranch.

Ben talked to surrounding ranchers to get their ideas about a horse ranch in the area. He explained his idea was to sell horses to the military and keep the stage lines supplied. Eventually, he told them, the ranch would have breeding stock and auction barn.

Ranchers supported his plans and ideas and assured Ben they would be doing business with him. They just hoped his ideas were not too big for one man, and a new rancher at that. They shook his hand and wished him well.

The family liked Ben's ideas and agreed to pitch in and help. They had not been nearly as enthusiastic about the way-station. They groaned when Pa reminded them there would still be chores that had to be done every day.

* * * * *

Ben bought a horse for each member of the family, carefully considering the sizes, how each one would be used on the ranch, and their spirit.

“You had better get used to them before we start in business,” Ben told his children. “We will be spending a lot of time in the saddle, and all of you will have to take your turns until we start making a profit and can hire some help.” He kept reassuring them it would be much easier work than at a way-station. At the same time, he made no promises.

Clay, Adam, and Molly each picked out a saddle. It was the most exciting thing that had ever happened. None of them had ever bought anything in their lives more than a stick of peppermint at the dry-goods store. Neither Ben nor Sarah tried to sway the children to one saddle or the other. They could make up their own mind and the saddle would be theirs.

Ben and Sarah got new saddles too. Sarah asked Ben if he did not need a new pair of boots.

“Next time,” he replied. “It’s time the boys got out of their lace up boots and into some with heels that will help keep them in the saddle. How about you and Molly, don’t you want new boots too?”

“No,” said Sarah, “But we will look at leather gloves. I guess we are more interested in protecting our hands than our feet,” she laughed as she led Molly away.

Ben made arrangements with his old boss at the stable to board the new horses until they could move to a new ranch.

Ben needed the shed out back cleaned up for a place to keep the saddles out of the weather. He made an attempt to move old furniture out of the way but soon gave it up, and asked Clay to help. Ben wanted to get at building the saddle racks, which would take up quite a bit of space.

Ben had been so busy working and getting to know his family that he had all but forgotten about the canvas bag he had hidden when he came home from the trail for the last time. It had been a long time since the massacre. Still, every now and then he would have a nightmare. He pretty much managed to keep it buried deep inside. Sarah never asked, just cooed him back to sleep when he woke with a start, a look of terror in his eyes. She knew that someday he would tell her what happened.

Clay said he would help Pa make room for all the new tack and had a burn pile going in the side yard. He poked around, deciding what could be thrown onto the fire and what might be used at the new ranch. He stacked furniture to the side and asked his mother to come out and make a final decision on what she wanted to keep.

Sarah was shocked at the amount of old furniture she had stored. She started pulling out drawers in case anything had been tucked away but still usable. Anything she removed from a drawer smelled old and musty, so she told Clay to burn anything else he found.

After Sarah had gone back to the house, Clay pulled open the few drawers that were left. He pitched whatever he found into the fire. Clay kept a close watch and raked hot embers back onto the pile. An old dirty canvas bag he tossed landed at the edge of the pile so it was not catching fire. He picked it up to throw it directly onto the flames, but, at the last second, curiosity got the best of him. He opened the bag to see what was inside. Once again the bag was hidden away.

* * * * *

When word got out that Ben was looking to buy a horse ranch, many offers to sell made their way to him. They bought the Flying Star from Old Man Piper. He was anxious to retire and move to town, so had offered the ranch at a good price. Along with the buildings came an excellent reputation. Over the years, Piper had always supplied the best horses and was always willing to deal. That reputation was just as important to Ben as buying the perfect house was to Sarah. When she and Molly stepped into the kitchen on their first inspection of the house, they immediately began planning. There would be no changing their minds.

Molly and Adam had rooms up under the eaves. Clay claimed the bedroom just off the kitchen. "Where I won't disturb anybody with my comings and goings," he explained.

The parent's bedroom overlooked the creek and pastures to the west.

* * * * *

Ben and Clay were keeping an eye on a band of mustangs that had thundered across their pastures early one morning. They could capture several if they made careful plans and could get them headed towards a nearby box canyon. A few horses had been included with the ranch property but not nearly enough to make up a decent herd. What they captured and tamed would be the real beginnings of the Hardisty horse ranch. The men had decided it prudent to also buy a few horses, which would then give them a big enough herd to offer potential buyers. They would eventually invest in some breeding stock.

And then, the money was just about gone. By this time, Ben had all but forgotten about the stash of ready cash in the bag he had hidden. He told Sarah he would have to get on the road soon to let the Army know they were up and running with enough horse flesh to supply any new troops. Clay placed an ad in the local newspaper and their worries were over. Ranchers and businessmen came out to inspect the horses, and satisfy their curiosity about this new horse ranch. Many purchased a horse or two, or traded, and said they would be back again.

Ben was intent on keeping Clay involved as much as possible in running the ranch. He gave his son the responsibility of getting the mustangs broke and ready for sale. He figured that, while still young, Clay might see this could be the life for him rather than out on the trail. The boy still had a tendency to always want to see what was on the other side of the mountain. Lately, however, when he disappeared over a hill, he was more than likely to return with a mustang at the end of his lasso.

Ben and Clay and sometimes Adam rode to their neighbors in all directions, looking for good horses. If neighbors did not have any to sell, they knew someone who did. Sarah and Molly went along, on occasion, to meet the rancher's wives and children. Sarah was interested in quilting bees and holiday celebrations. Molly enjoyed the company of girls, something her brothers just did not understand.

* * * * *

Clay spent a long time thinking about the contents of the canvas bag he saved from a burn pile when the family moved from town. He was tempted to take some of the money and leave. He knew he could not buy anything because his folks would be suspicious where he got money to spend. In the long run, he knew that if something had been that well hidden, it was not meant to be discovered.

Clay was sure it was his Pa who had hidden the bag. He sometimes feared his Pa had robbed someone, and that was why he had come home so early from his last scout. Clay remembered that Pa never talked about that last scout, which made him wonder even more if he was a thief.

Clay never got up the nerve to ask. He buried the bag and its contents deep inside his own trunk, up in his own room. No one ever bothered his stuff, and even if they wanted to, he had a key and kept it locked.

Out on the trail late one night, after the campfire had been banked, Clay and Pa finished the last of the coffee. Yonder chased rabbits in his sleep, and wolves howled at the moon. Clay took a deep breath and said to his father, "Why did you come home early from your last scouting trip? I have wondered about it all these years, and you never talked about it. Can you talk about it now and tell me what happened?"

Totally caught off guard, Ben stared at Clay. Clay waited, never taking his eyes off his father's face. Ben dropped his head into his hands and stared into the fire. "Why do you want to know, son? There was trouble on the trail and I had to leave. It's as simple as that."

"No, it is not," Clay firmly stated. "I don't think it is as simple as that. I found an old canvas bag at the place in town before we moved. I pulled it out of the burn pile. You are the only one who could have hidden it, Pa. There was money in it, lots of money. Did you rob a bank or something like that?"

Ben had put the bag away, along with those awful memories, in a far off place. It all came back to him in a rush of emotion. He looked at Clay, composed himself, and said, "Well, I guess it's time to talk. Let me assure you, son, that first of all, I am not a thief."

"That's a relief to know, Pa. After I found the money I was so afraid the sheriff would show up one day and take you away. I found some other stuff in the bag, too. Then I read the journal. Pa, I want to go find her."

* * * * *

Chapter 3

Pale Moon had often heard the story of how she became daughter of Quaking Tree. She was too young to understand all of the words, but realized she had not arrived like other children in the tribe. Her younger brother had come from inside their Mother.

Quaking Tree always explained, “You arrived in my arms.” Even though she had no recollection of her past, Pale Moon carried something inside that made her want to hear more. Quaking Tree insisted there was no more to it.

Olivia was the better part of a year old when she was first taken from her mother’s arms during an attack on their wagon train. During the two day ride to reach the Indian village, the warrior who stole her made the baby as comfortable as possible. There was little to eat for a young child, so he chewed dried meat until it was soft enough to put in her mouth hoping there was nourishment to keep her alive. He wrapped her in a soft wolf skin. Still, the child cried.

Within sight of the village, women and children ran out to meet the men on their return who showed off trophies held high over their heads of silver candle sticks, pots, pans, bolts of cloth, knives, and guns. Everyone made their way up to the tepee of the chief, who waited.

Everyone gathered to listen to the men boast about the massacre. Cheer after cheer went up when they told how many white men had been killed and how many horses they brought back with them. Olivia was the only white person who had been taken alive. The women had little interest in her.

After the chief had chosen his gifts and given a nod that the rest could be shared with family and friends, Sky In Water sought out Quaking Tree. He had a special gift just for her.

Quaking Tree had lost her only child and her husband. A group of small children were playing along the shore of a river when a section of the bank gave way and two were swept away. Her little girl had not survived.

Quaking Tree's husband was killed on a hunting trip when his horse stumbled and he was trampled by buffalo. Quaking Tree had been a sad, lonely woman for a very long time. Sky In Water tried to be a friend, but she was still too heartbroken.

Sky In Water lost his wife when fever rampaged through their camp. He and his son survived.

When he approached Quaking Tree with the child, she held out her arms. It did not matter that the child's skin was white as snow. She needed to hold a baby in her arms again. Quaking Tree's eyes spoke to Sky In Water. He knew he had made her very happy. He hoped that someday soon she would also welcome him into her arms.

Olivia lost her name. Quaking Tree and Sky In Water argued back and forth on what to call the child. He wanted a fearless name for her that would carry her to new discoveries and adventures. Quaking Tree argued that this was not a man-child. Besides that, her skin was white as the full moon and that held some significance. They called her Pale Moon.

Olivia grew strong with the love and care of Quaking Tree. She was tall and slim with wild black hair her new mother tried to tame with bear grease, but a braid was the best she could do. With her dark hair and eyes, it was easy to forget Pale Moon's skin was pale as a ghost under her deerskin dress.

Pale Moon was accepted by most of the tribe as one of their own, although there were a few who would always resent her for not being turned into a slave. Quaking Tree insisted that Pale Moon was much too young to be anything but a child.

Sky In Water spent more and more time with Quaking Tree after he delivered the baby to her, always with the excuse he was checking on the little girl to make sure she was doing well. He enjoyed the company of Quaking Tree and hoped she would open up to him. He usually came alone because he discovered his little son reminded Quaking Tree of her lost child. The elders kept an eye on the four-year old boy while Sky In Water was away.

* * * * *

The tribe of a few hundred men, women and children, plus their livestock, moved constantly over the years ever in search of food, meat, and good weather. Settlers headed west interfered with the natural ways of the land. All too soon buffalo were not as abundant as they had once been. Attacks on wagon trains did little to discourage white men from invading the plains and forests of the native people. They just kept coming.

Many Army forts were established throughout the west to protect the white man. Trading posts were built to provide wagon trains with supplies and repairs. Hearty mountain men and trappers brought in their hides and furs to trade with fur companies from as far away as New York and Canada, even as far away as England. Many of these men had learned Indian dialects so they could seek out those tribes who had the best pelts in exchange for trinkets and warm blankets.

Occasionally, the tribe camped outside the walls of these posts. They only went inside the gates when invited to trade. Pale Moon was allowed to wander around inside as she posed no threat.

Some of the traders were very interested in the contents of the little deerskin pouch that hung from Pale Moon's belt. They had often observed her dumping out the contents before adding something new. She would pick up each item, sometimes tossing it aside, in place of something new. Mostly, it held a child's treasure of bright feathers, colorful agates and bits and pieces of anything that intrigued Pale Moon. It also held the tiny gold four-leaf clover. This is what the traders wanted.

When Sky In Water had given Quaking Tree the baby, the first thing she did was untie the leather thong from around the child's neck. The little clover charm was removed and tucked away in an old basket. No one knew what it was. An amulet such as this usually held some significance. Quaking Tree did not want anyone to think her child had brought bad luck.

Years later, Pale Moon was snooping around and found the charm hidden in a willow basket. She did not think anyone would miss such a tiny thing, so she took it and hid it in her own pouch. Whenever her curious mother asked to see what Pale Moon had added to her collection, she always pinched the tiny piece of gold between her fingers and shook the rest of the contents onto a blanket.

During those times when Pale Moon was inside one of the posts, she watched the fancy ladies who wore full-skirted colorful gowns. She had a fascination with the colors and frills that could not be denied. She often thought about how much she would like to wear the fancy dresses instead of her deerskin. The shoes they wore seemed sturdy enough so her feet would not ache after a long trek. She imagined her hair coiled in lovely curls under a hat decorated with feathers and lace. Quaking Tree never did anything with Pale Moon's hair but braid it.

As she grew older, Pale Moon played with the youngsters in the tribe, did her few errands and chores, and followed her mother through the woods as she carefully picked various plants and flowers and dug up herbs and roots for her medicine supply. In her own youth, Quaking Tree had been taught cures by the elders of her tribe. She had many baskets of dried petals and roots that she guarded from weather and curious children.

Among her cures, Quaking Tree had a concoction of ingredients, including feverfew that made a man stronger and cured everything from a headache to colic. A tea of hemp seeds cured any wind in the stomach or worms in both man and beast. She told Pale Moon to look for spearmint leaves if she had eaten too much and her stomach hurt. She believed that after cold wet winter a meal of nettles was a perfect tonic.

Pale Moon saved the little baskets she was being taught to weave and kept her own bits of bark and dried leaves in them. She had collected yellow poplar, snake root, burdock, horse radish, sage and mustard seed. She was warned not to experiment with her collection or even taste the dried leaves. Pale Moon always carefully watched Quaking Tree when someone came to her to be treated for an illness or injury. She hoped that one day they would come to her for comfort.

Sky In Water often took his son and Pale Moon for rides across open fields when the moon was bright and stars seemed close enough to touch. He taught Pale Moon how to use the stars to find her way home if she should ever stray too far. He also showed her how water flows, and how to follow it back to where she belonged. "There is nothing to be afraid of in the forests. And never be afraid of the dark. If you let it know you are afraid of it, it will not release you," Sky In Water told the children who were so eager to learn.

It was a happy, carefree time for Pale Moon. She loved her family so much.

* * * * *

Chapter 4

After Ben caught his breath, he told Clay everything that had happened on the last scout with his friend Clampton.

"Son, it was the most terrible thing I ever did see," he said. "Coming up on the massacre too late just made it all the more difficult for me to deal with." Ben slapped his thigh and moaned, "I should have been there. I should have been there!"

"When I got home," he continued, "I hid the bag in the shed. I had read the journal one night along the trail home, and I know it was wrong to hide it. I knew a child was missing."

"At the time, I could have at least told the trappers and miners I met along the way about the missing girl, but I did not even do that. I only told the soldiers at the fort. I just wanted to erase the whole thing for a while. Then it got buried so deep inside that I did not even think about it anymore. I haven't even told your mother about it yet." Ben took a deep breath and said, "Son, I am glad you found that old canvas bag. Now that we have got ourselves pretty much settled in a new home and with business looking good, maybe you and I can take some time to look for Olivia."

Clay knew Ben did not have time to spend time away from the ranch. The place was far too busy for Pa to be gone maybe as long as a month or two. No one would miss though, he told himself. Clay chose his words carefully and explained to Pa that this was something he wanted to do by himself.

"I'm old enough Pa. If you let me go out on the trail, maybe it will satisfy my always having to know what's on the other side of the hill. I will have been there. I will be fine. I'm young and strong. No need to worry about me."

He took a breath, "Besides that, I like being home with you on the ranch Pa. I want to help. It's far better than living in town. Maybe someday I will even be your foreman," Clay teased with a twinkle in his eye.

Ben looked at Clay and smiled. "So you think I'm old and weak, is that it? Let me tell you a thing or two, you young sapling. I can outlast you any day in the saddle."

Clay smiled back, and poured the last cup of coffee.

The campfire died down long before the men had talked themselves out. They argued long and hard, back and forth. Ben finally gave in, and made a deal with Clay.

"When we get back to the ranch, we will explain the whole story to your Ma. If she agrees with you and thinks you're old enough to be away from family and out on the trail, by yourself, for that length of time, I'll go along with the two of you. But, there are rules you will have to follow. There's also the matter of when you can leave, and it won't be anytime real soon."

Clay thought that was fair enough. He did not sleep a wink all night.

* * * * *

By the time Ben and Clay got back to the ranch, Clay was so excited about looking for Olivia he could not stop nattering on and on. Ben was still torn about the whole idea. He knew from reading the journal he had put Olivia's life in jeopardy when he hid it in the shed. He hoped it was not too late to look for her. At the same time, he had doubts his boy was up to the search and would know enough when to come home.

Sarah knew something was up the minute her men came in the back door and hung up their hats. They were too quiet. She always had the fear that someday one of them would come back seriously injured. This time they both looked fine.

"Sit down," she said. "There's fresh coffee and pie. Adam and Molly rode their horses to the neighbors for an afternoon birthday party. It looks like the two of you have something to tell me. Am I right?"

Ben opened the conversation by first apologizing to Sarah. "I'm sorry I did not say a word to you about why I was home early. Thank you for never questioning me about the lost wages. I'm grateful you had enough faith in me to wait for an explanation.

"My story about the wagon train reaching their destination was not exactly true. There was an attack by Indians and everyone was killed while I was out scouting. It was the saddest thing I have ever seen."

"I figured it was something pretty awful," said Sarah. "That's why I left it alone. When your nightmares went away is when I figured you could tell me about what happened. It's been a while, longer than I expected, but now we all know. I'm just sorry for the rough patch you went through by yourself. I wish you had remembered that when things happen, I'm here to share it with you. Good or bad."

Ben smiled at Sarah. She understood him so well. He continued, "There's a canvas bag I brought home from the wagon train. I hid it in the shed, but Clay found it when we moved. Clay brought it up one night out on the trail. And, that conversation led us to this point, here with you."

When Clay picked up the conversation, Sarah had a feeling it was going to be something she did not want to hear. Clay told Sarah what he had found in the bag. He laughed when he said he thought that at first Pa was a thief because of all the money. Then he told her about reading the journal. He said that reading the last words of a dying mother, pleading for someone to save her child who had been taken away by an Indian during the raid was overpowering.

"I know it's been a long time since she wrote the journal, but Ma, I want to go find the little girl. Pa said I could go-if you said I could."

"No," said Sarah. "You are much too young to spend what – maybe two, three, four months on the trail looking for a child who might not even be alive, let alone knowing what she looks like. She's not a baby anymore. Who knows what she looks like? Maybe she's never laid eyes on a white man in the years since she was kidnapped. She will be afraid. Why should she go with you when she finds out you have come to take her home? She is home. Have you given it any thought as to where you would even begin the search? I'm sure you haven't even thought about that. My answer is no."

There was not much argument after Sarah had said her piece. For the time being the men let her be. One day, Clay handed her Mary's journal. He never said a word, but she saw the look in his eyes. Weeks later she finally came around with a lot of what-ifs that she wanted answered before anyone left the ranch. They were a family of good people and would do the right thing.

* * * * *

Clay chose a strong horse from the herd and began training so they would be used to each other by the time he was ready to leave home. Ben spent many hours talking to Clay, advising him to the ways of the trail, what to look for and how to approach anyone he met, especially Indians. This was a time of great unrest between them and the U.S. government.

"Never show fear," said Ben. "But don't be foolish either. Remember that you cannot trust anyone out there in the middle of nowhere."

It was late spring when Clay decided he was ready to leave. His folks thought it was too soon. He needed more time to prepare. He won the argument by pointing out that the trees and bushes had leafed out, rivers had settled into their banks, and the only snow left was high up on the mountains, where he had no intention of riding.

Clay saddled up his new horse, Searcher, said his good-byes and was ready to head out when Ben stopped him. There was one last thing he wanted to tuck into Clay's saddlebag. Mary's journal would go on the trip too.

Clay turned one last time to wave good-bye and there came Yonder. He reined in until Adam and Molly could call the old hound back to them. Clay did not want to leave Yonder behind, but he was just too old and stove-up to travel further than the barnyard anymore.

"Clay is just a boy, Ben. How can we let him go?" cried Sarah as she hung onto Ben's arm trying not to let her son see tears rolling down her cheeks.

"He will be all right," Ben assured her. "When he comes home you will have another grown man in the family. This will be a good experience for him. He's going to meet a lot of new people, including some pretty rough characters. He's going to have to learn how to get along with all of them. We'll see him before long. Clay would not want you to worry yourself sick, so dry those tears and let's send him off with a big smile."

Clay poked Searcher in the ribs. He had no idea when he would see him family again.

* * * * *

Clay's first destination was the Army fort where Pa said he had stopped on his way home after the massacre. He explained to the captain who he was and where he was going. The captain said he remembered his pa.

The captain explained that he had led a troop to the site of the massacre, but had found nothing. "I think we did all we could," he said, "given the circumstances. Adults taken by Indians in a raid rarely escape, and this was a helpless baby."

He suggested Clay go to the site of the wagon train and speak to anyone who was still in the area that might remember something. It would be a good starting point.

"There had been little Indian activity around here lately. Before now, the ones who did show up at the fort were always asked if they knew anything about the baby. None of them ever admitted to knowing anything."

Clay came across a few Indian camps, but was either run off or too scared to approach. Usually, it was children playing in an open area who spotted a strange man on a horse. They ran to tell their fathers, who quickly mounted up. Clay never felt an arrow zing by his head, but he heard plenty of yelling and the thunder of hooves chasing him away. After it happened the second time, he paid more attention to any smoke he spotted in the distance and rode around it. He was not taking any chances.

The two camps he was finally allowed to enter could not help him because he did not understand the language or their signs. He thought himself clever when he decided to offer glass beads to all the children. As they gathered around him, he hoped to spot a white child. But he never did.

* * * * *

According to the map a soldier had drawn for him while he was at the fort, there was a trading post only a few days ride from where he was. Clay would go there to replenish his food supplies and learn what he could. He knew a long time had passed, years, in fact, since the raid and there might not be anyone around who still remembered it. Nevertheless, he had to go. So far, things did not look good. Clay hoped that would change once he got to the post.

Clay easily made friends at the trading post. The young girls were eager to welcome this handsome young stranger. Clay had never paid much attention to the girls back home. He'd known them all his life and did not think any of them special. These girls wore beautiful dresses and smelled so good when they strolled by, flirting with their eyes. He was lured to many dark rooms, but politely backed off. However, temptation finally got the best of him. The world, he thought, after his experience, will never be the same. He considered that he may have to take a second look at some of those girls back home.

Late one night, as Clay was sneaking back to his bedroll, he was beckoned over to a campfire by a group of old worn-out trappers and mountain men. The best part of their day was sitting around the night flames, bragging about their wild adventures in the mountains, on the lakes, and on the rivers. Like the buffalo and beaver, their good old days had disappeared. Many friends who had made their fortunes returned to the east and lived in luxury, never again having to wait out blizzards, rampaging water, or mean Indians. Those who had not been lucky enough to strike it rich were stuck in the west, reliving their past to anyone who would listen.

Clay was curious how the trappers moved around the country, avoiding trouble with the Indians who had been angry with the white man for so long.

A gruff old gent called Long Johns explained, "It was easy to pick up enough of their language to get by. If that did not work, signs were another way to communicate, or a combination of the two. Indians don't know our language any better than we know theirs. It's always a good idea to have a pocketful of beads and a few mirrors in your saddlebags anytime you move away from a fort or trading post." Long Johns laughed and said, "That's a language they all understand."

The men were curious about Clay too. They wanted to know where he had come from and why he was there. They could not believe a mother would let a son as young as Clay leave home to travel all alone.

"It was not easy getting their permission," he explained. "I'm looking for a little girl who was kidnapped some years back during a raid on a wagon train headed to Oregon. She was the only survivor. It's important that she be found, if she's still alive. It happened not too far from here."

"So far," continued Clay, "I haven't had any luck, but then I haven't been on the trail looking very long. I understand it may take some time. I sure would appreciate any information you care to share with me that would make my travels a bit easier."

The old men tumbled their words over each other in their eagerness to tell him what to look for along any trail he chose, to be wary of sounds or unfamiliar noises, what berries he could eat and what would poison him. Clay sat and listened, trying to remember everything they were telling him.

The next day, Clay went looking for Long Johns and found him by the corral saddling up his horse. Long Johns told Clay he had had enough of society for a while. "I need some clean air and space," he said.

Clay took a deep breath and asked if he could travel along for a time. "If you have a mind to, maybe you could teach me some more about the Indians," he hinted.

Long Johns replied, "I would be glad for the company, and to learn you a thing or two, but only for a time. I'm used to being alone and I like it that way."

It was a long time before Clay saw another human being besides Long Johns. It gave him a lot of time to think about the pretty girls he had left behind at the fort.

* * * * *

Chapter 5

Long Johns and Clay headed to his old shack in the woods where they rested, and Long John reminisced some more about his trapping days. When it seemed the old man had run out of tales to tell, Clay asked if he would teach him how to talk Indian. Clay knew he was stretching his luck asking to stay a few more days, but he desperately needed to know enough to approach any Indians he met and not be run off.

Clay had carefully been watching Long Johns trap small game, and cook a good stew or beans for their meals. Some days he even baked fresh bread. He knew Long Johns couldn't read; nor could he write down a recipe on how to mix the bread together.

The two decided the best way for Clay to learn quickly was to spend a day saying Native words, then translating into English. After that, they would try to speak Indian and also use sign language instead of English. Clay spelled out each word phonetically on empty pages in the back of Mary's journal. He practiced saying them each night while his campfire died down.

At the end of a few days he had managed to stretch into a week, it was obvious Long Johns was ready to be alone. Clay said his good-byes and headed in the direction of the long-gone wagon train. Before leaving, he said to Long Johns, "I have to see it for myself.

Maybe someone living around there might recall something, or heard stories passed down about the little white baby gone missing."

Long Johns wished him luck, but not to count on finding anyone. "Too much time has gone by," he said.

* * * * *

There was nothing left at the site of the massacre except a few pieces of broken wagon wheel spokes and shards of dishes he kicked out of the dirt. Bits of leather harness and brass rings looked like they had been picked up at one time or another then tossed into the weeds. It was obvious other settlers had come this way and taken what they could use.

There were no names or dates burned into the wood of crosses placed over graves the Army had dug. This was a sad place. Clay took a deep breath, picked up the reins and began his search once again.

Clay didn't have any luck finding anyone with useful information about the Indian raid. The few people he did run into didn't know any more than Clay had learned from his Pa. Then, one afternoon, he rode up on what looked to be an abandoned shack. As he approached, an old geezer stepped from behind a tree with his gun leveled at Clay's chest. Cautious greetings were called out before Clay was invited to climb down from Searcher. Staring each other in the eye, man and boy shook hands.

Clay discovered the old man had a mind like a bear trap. Nothing got by this guy, even though Clay thought he looked to be close to a hundred years old. Percy Longacre was so grateful for some company he invited Clay to share a pot of squirrel stew. One thing led to another. Percy's stories went on and on, and before long Clay was bedded down beside the campfire still listening to Percy ramble on as he fell asleep.

The next day, Clay woke up to the sound of Percy still talking. He was only half listening when he thought he heard Percy say something about an Indian girl with curly hair. "Strangest thing I ever saw," said Percy.

"Wait, wait, wait. What did you just say, Percy? Repeat what you just said about the Indian girl."

Percy had to think for a minute what he had been talking about. "Oh yes," he said. "A year or so back, it was early fall as I remember. I was visiting with some Indians who came through on their way to wintering grounds to the south of here. They spent a day and a night down by the creek, and left early the next morning. Before they started out I gave all the youngsters some trinkets. I always keep a supply in my shack. You never know when you might need to trade yourself out of a tight situation.

"The young-uns played in the creek and got pretty wet trying to catch trout for breakfast. There was a squaw with them. When the kids climbed out of the water, she lined up the little girls and braided their hair. I noticed the hair on one of the girls was curly, wavy sort of. Very odd, I'm thinking, but gave it no never mind. It was just odd."

What a stroke of luck, thought Clay. It had to be Olivia. It was too bad so much time had passed. Clay was too excited to listen to any more of the old man's tales. He asked Percy if he knew where the tribe might now be, if they had camp grounds they moved to and from over the years. He lit out at daybreak.

* * * * *

For the next month Clay wound around the western mountains, always in search of someone who could tell him where to find more Indians. A few camps still chased him off while others made him welcome. Even though none offered any information about the girl, Clay felt they were not telling him everything they knew. Occasionally, some friendlies would tell him something that sounded right, but then send him off in the wrong direction.

I hope they have a real good laugh at my expense, thought Clay. I must really look like a greenhorn.

More than once, he traveled for days in one direction expecting to find a camp, only to discover they were long gone. Clay was learning a lot about living in the wild. He was growing up, and wising up, every day. He learned to be more direct with his questions and, most importantly, to offer more in trade for information.

His survival skills had improved so much that he seldom went hungry or thirsty. He treated Searcher with care, always checking for sore feet and saddle blisters. Clay wished he had a dog along on the trip. His mind kept wandering back to all those pretty girls back at the fort, who smelled so good, and when he would see them again. He needed someone to talk to.

After going a particularly long time with no human contact, Clay thought he had come to the end of his trail and would have to head back towards home. Where was everybody, he wondered. It was the middle of summer; too soon to be headed to winter encampments. Indian raids were few and far between, so he knew the tribes were holed up somewhere.

* * * * *

There came a day Clay thought he would go insane if he didn't find someone to talk to. And just like that, his luck changed. He had been following old trails through the woods for two days, but now, looking ahead, he could see a clearing.

He approached what looked to be an old deserted Army outpost. He was sure it was the snicker of horses he could hear coming from inside the walls. Clay stayed on the edge of the woods, waiting to see what would happen. He didn't spy any soldiers patrolling from the parapet, yet he could hear a yell every now and then from inside. It wasn't as deserted as it first seemed, but, he was convinced the Army had been long gone.

Several young Indians finally rode out of the stockade. Clay moseyed Searcher out of the trees headed to where he would cross their path. He prepared himself to flee if any of them made a threatening move. As they neared each other, one of the riders spotted Clay and shouted at him. Clay held up his hands showing he held no weapons.

No need to be afraid, he kept saying over and over to himself. I just hope they are friendly, Searcher.

One of the young Indians motioned for Clay to get off his horse. The Indians circled him with their ponies. Carefully, Clay reached for the journal in which he had written down words he hoped they could understand.

They watched in silence as he began making hand signals, and saying a few words. When they realized they could communicate, the men came off their horses and sat on the ground. Clay joined them, continuing to say a few words. One of them appeared to be the leader and he spoke to Clay. Clay offered a handful of beads, giving himself time to translate the words. This was his first experience sitting down on a blanket with a group of braves for a palaver.

The young man told Clay he and his friends discovered the abandoned fort long ago. When they had nothing better to do, a bunch of them would mount up, ride over and go through the empty rooms. They showed him belt buckles and buttons attached to their necklaces. The metal needles and spoons they found were given to the elders. For themselves, they kept anything that was shiny.

Clay was invited to ride along back to their camp. He felt confident enough after spending the afternoon with the group they would not kill him. He accepted their offer. He had not yet mentioned the missing child.

* * * * *

Everyone mounted up and rode across a wide open clearing in front of the stockade before heading into the pine forest that crawled its way up and down the mountainside. Eventually, the horses spread out into single file as they walked the narrow path leading down into a canyon where Clay could see smoke rising in the air. Shouts went back and forth as the men got closer. By the time they slid off their ponies everyone had gathered to greet the stranger.

Some of the younger children, who had never seen a white man, edged forward and reached out to touch him arms and legs. His new friends shoved the children away, and led him to a camp fire where they could get food.

That night Clay slept soundly on a pile of soft hides.

This is the best sleep I've had since leaving home, he thought. I sure don't look forward to sleeping on the hard ground again after this.

He awoke to the sound of children running by on their way to the creek. It was time to get up and start a new day of his adventure. The first thing Clay did was find his new friends and ask if he would be allowed to talk to their chief.

When word came back the chief would like to talk with him, Clay stuck some bolts of bright fabric he carried for trade under his arm. He offered the cloth to the chief, who accepted it with a smile and a motion to sit down.

Again, using hand signals and the words he had memorized, Clay answered questions as best he could. The chief was interested in where Clay had come from, how far away and how many moons ago. "Why are you here?" asked the chief.

Clay retrieved Mary's journal from his back pocket and held it up. "This is why I am here," he replied. Saying just enough words to get the idea across, he told the chief he was looking for a young girl who had been kidnapped by Indians.

"In this book," Clay continued, "a mother wrote about a raid on a wagon train. She tells us her baby was taken, and hoped that one day the girl will be returned to her white family. I am searching for the girl."

"Is this girl your family?" asked the now suspicious chief.

Clay was beginning to feel uneasy. He was not sure the chief believed his story, but he continued anyway. "The girl is not my family," he admitted. "I am searching for her, and when I find her, I will ask her if she wants to return to her white family. If she chooses to stay with the Indians, I will leave her and go home alone. But, if she tells me she would like to be with her white family, I will take her with me.

"There is also something else I must consider. If I find the right tribe, will they be friendly toward me, or will they kill me like they did everyone on that wagon train?"

The chief considered Clay's story for several minutes, keeping Clay on pins and needles. Clay didn't know if he should leave without another word, or risk waiting for a reply. He did not feel threatened, or that he would be killed, but he had the distinct feeling the chief did not want him around.

Finally, the chief spoke. "There is no such child with us. My warriors have told me they once saw a young girl with black hair that was different." He made a waving motion with the flat of his hand. "She was with a band further to the south at the time." He said no more, just stared at Clay until Clay stood up and walked away.

Clay left early the next day. The old chief gave him directions to where he thought the tribe who had Olivia was camped.

As a parting gift, Clay's new friends tied one of the camp dogs to his saddle horn. Earlier, he mentioned he wished he had his old dog along so he would have someone to talk to. The young braves laughed and thought it very strange that white men talked to their dogs. Clay tried to explain the meaning of having a pet. Dogs were food as far as they were concerned. In honor of his friends, Clay named his new pal Warrior.

Clay and Warrior eventually became good friends. Once he understood, the dog was happy with all the attention he received, and tried his hardest to please. Back at camp, no one paid any attention to the pack of dogs. With no soft buffalo hides to sleep on, Clay was pleased when Warrior finally curled up next to him at night, and shared some body heat. At times when Clay thought the wilderness would drive him crazy, Warrior listened until Clay calmed down again.

Clay got lost twice during his search for the tribe he hoped had Olivia. Warrior was no help. The dog didn't want to go back to his old tribe, and had no skill to sniff his way to a new one. Clay would have sworn it was a month of Sundays before he finally found what he was looking for.

Clay and Warrior camped across the river from a large gathering of tepees, just to let them know he was there. When the children went down to the river bank, Warrior ran to play in the water with them. At first the children were afraid, but soon realized he was not a threat. When Clay walked near the river to call the dog back to camp, he quickly scanned faces of the children hoping to see a white girl with dark hair.

Clay knew that if Olivia was with this tribe, they were the ones who had killed her parents and everyone else on the wagon train. Although he feared for his life, Clay had been told by many men along the trail that Indians raids were nearly a thing of the past. Those tribes who had fought for rifles were now armed. Regular wagon train routes were well-established and rarely abandoned to cut across Indian territory. Of course, they had reminded him it probably wouldn't take much to get them upset over a foolish mistake made by any white person. Just be careful, they admonished. Don't go looking for trouble.

At last, Clay felt confident enough to approach the village when he thought he had given them enough opportunity to watch and see that he meant no harm. Clay crossed the river on Searcher, with Warrior close behind. As soon as he was spotted, several men confronted him. He explained as best he could that he needed to speak with their great chief. The men were slow in reacting, but when Clay offered a handful of mirrors, one of them ran to tell the chief a white man had approached and that he was unarmed.

When Clay explained why he was there, the chief became reluctant to talk about any of the children. He paraded a small group of youngsters in front of Clay, proving there was not a white child among them.

Clay went back to his camp on the other side of the river to watch and wait. He kept an eye on all the children who came to play in the water. There was still no sign of Olivia. From all descriptions and given locations, he was convinced this was the tribe that had her.

One late afternoon, a young warrior rode across the river to Clay's camp. When he dismounted, Clay handed him a handful of colored beads. The Indian didn't have much to say, it seemed like he was checking on Clay to see why he had not moved on. He never returned. And Clay waited some more.

* * * * *

Quaking Tree waded across the river to Clay's camp. She carried a berry basket so no one would suspect what she was really up to. Quaking Tree had heard that the white man across the river had come in search of a white child. She always knew this day would come.

"My name is Quaking Tree, and I have a child. You have not seen her at the river because she is not allowed to go there unless I am with her."

"And why would that be?" asked Clay.

"Because I once lost another child to the river."

He invited Quaking Tree to sit, and introduced himself. "Why did you wade across the river to tell me you have a child?" Clay asked.

"Because," replied Quaking Tree, "my child is white, like you. My husband, Sky In Water, brought her to me many moons ago. It was the beginning of a new life for all of us."

Clay listened to her story, trying not to betray his emotions. Finally, Quaking Tree asked, "Why do you want to take my child away?"

Clay explained that his father, the scout for a wagon train her tribe had massacred, had discovered one of the babies had been taken by a warrior.

"Before she died," said Clay, "the mother wrote down what had happened. She said her baby was stolen out of her arms. There is a short description of the baby, along with a plea that someone search for her girl and return her to her family.

"When my Pa returned to the wagon train, he saw that everyone was dead. He found a small pail packed with some personal items. That's when he learned the baby had survived the massacre. It's all written down in this book."

Quaking Tree reached for the book Clay held out to her. She took it, but did not open it. Quaking Tree nodded her head, and handed it back.

* * * * *

After that, Quaking Tree returned to Clay's camp but never with her daughter. Teetering on the edge of frustration, Clay asked if he could at least see the child, even if it was from across the river. When Quaking Tree finally agreed, he asked that, as a special favor, her hair not be braided. She didn't know why, but she suspected it was because of her daughter's wavy hair, so unlike that of the other Indian children.

Clay and Pale Moon stared at each other for a long time across the river, across years. Pale Moon had no idea why the white man camping on the other side of the river stared at her, with her hair all fluffy and blowing in the wind. Her mother had told her to go to the river, all alone, not to go in the water and just stand there until she heard a signal to return. She would explain later.

Pale Moon was full of questions when she returned to her mother. Quaking Tree held her baby as tears ran down her cheeks. Quaking Tree knew she was scaring Pale Moon, but still could not answer all of her questions.

Clay had second thoughts about what he was doing. Lots of children, he told himself, even adults, had been taken by Indians over the years and kept as slaves. How do I know Pale Moon is the right child? She couldn't be the only one captured who happened to have dark wavy hair. Whatever I do, I cannot take the wrong child. I need more proof.

Then he reminded himself that maybe Quaking Tree would not allow him to take her child, even if it was positively proved she was Olivia.

Clay decided he could not let himself get ahead of what might or might not happen. If this girl is not Olivia, I will move on, he told himself. If it is Olivia, and Quaking Tree will not let me take her, so be it. We can inform her grandparents where she is and that she is safe. They will be reassured that someone has actually seen her.

Clay was getting nervous, afraid he had made a huge mistake. How was he ever going to prove to anyone that Quaking Tree's child was the one he had searched for, for such a long time? He thought about breaking camp and riding away. He could go home and tell Pa that Olivia had vanished into the wilderness. But she had not.

The next time Quaking Tree returned to Clay's camp, he began throwing a barrage of questions at her so fast that she couldn't understand anything he was trying to say. She waited until he finished ranting, and then told him to say one thing at a time. He explained to her he had thoughts about Pale Moon being the wrong one, not the child he had come looking for at all. "This whole trip has been a waste of time and I'm ready to go home," he said.

It gave Quaking Tree a thread of hope. I could let him go, she thought, and Pale Moon would be mine forever.

Quaking Tree asked Clay to read Mary's words in the book. He retrieved the leather book from a saddlebag and showed it once again to Quaking Tree. He read a few pages and explained it was the day-to-day story of a wagon train traveling westward. When she nodded her head that she understood, Clay skipped to the last few pages Mary had written and read them to Quaking Tree. She silently listened. Now she knew, without a doubt, that Pale Moon was Olivia. Not saying a word, she stood up. Clay watched as she waded back across the river, wondering what was going on in her mind.

* * * * *

Warrior licked Clay's nose until he finally woke up. He was startled to find Quaking Tree and Pale Moon standing there waiting for him to open his eyes.

"This is Pale Moon," said Quaking Tree. "She is who you have come for."

* * * * *

Chapter 6

"Why are you telling me this, Quaking Tree? Why would you give up your child? How can you even prove to me this child is Olivia? You could say nothing and keep her forever. Why are you telling me this?" Clay was shocked and mystified at the words Quaking Tree spoke.

Quaking Tree slowly shook her head, and waiting until Clay calmed down. He had a wild look in his eyes. She could not tell if it was from excitement or fear. Was he excited to have found Olivia and could go home now? Or, was he fearful his quest had been in vain, and he would go home alone?

Clay had taken an immediate liking to Quaking Tree. If it was true he had found Olivia, he would feel terrible about taking the child away from her. I could turn and walk away, he thought to himself, but I have come this far. Either way, I need to know.

Quaking Tree touched Pale Moon lightly on the shoulder to move her towards Clay. Pale Moon had talked with white men many times when the tribe visited posts. She took two steps forward. Clay hunkered down to her level so they could talk eye to eye. Pale Moon wasn't afraid of Clay because he didn't seem, to her, like any of the men at the post.

"How old are you Pale Moon?"

She looked at her mother, who repeated what Clay had asked. Pale Moon shook her head, indicating she did not understand.

Quaking Tree spread a blanket on the ground and motioned for everyone to sit. Clay and Quaking Tree made idle conversation while Warrior and Pale Moon played. They tried to include Pale Moon, but she was so reluctant. When her mother told the man her daughter could run swift as a deer and swim like a tadpole, Pale Moon relaxed and sat down on the blanket. Warrior stayed close by her side.

Pale Moon was feeling more at ease with Clay. With the help of her mother, she told him she had been keeping an eye on an eagle's nest waiting for the babies to hatch. Quaking Tree told Clay that she had caught Pale Moon cadging bits of meat and gut from kills hunters brought back to camp. She followed Pale Moon and discovered that she laid out the pieces out for the eagles to find and eat.

In their conversation that morning, there was no indication that Pale Moon didn't think of herself as an Indian. She told Clay about visiting trading posts and how much she liked watching the ladies in their fancy dresses and shoes. She asked Clay if he knew anyone who wore such clothes. When he told her that his sister and mother both had fancy dresses to wear on special occasions, her eyes lit up. "Can you get me some?" she asked, having overcome her shyness.

Clay laughed and said, "Would you like to come with me and choose some for yourself?"

Pale Moon vehemently shook her head and grabbed her Mother's hand. She could not think about ever leaving her mother. Quaking Tree realized his question had scared Pale Moon. To distract her, she asked the child to show Clay the treasures she kept in the little deerskin pouch tied around her waist.

Pale Moon slowly undid the knot and emptied the contents of her pouch onto the blanket, carefully pinching the bottom of the pouch so the gold four-leaf clover would not fall out. She explained where she had found each colorful pebble and feather, and how the piece of bark looked like an animal if you held it a certain way. She was disappointed to see the beautiful flower she picked had turned brown and fallen to pieces.

With a finger, she rolled over a piece of eggshell so Clay could see the beautiful blue color. She held out a tiny mirror to Clay, and motioned for him to look into it.

Clay asked who had given her the mirror. "An old man in the woods gave it to me many moons ago when we rested near his camp," she said.

"Is that everything, Pale Moon?" asked Quaking Tree. Pale Moon looked at her mother, lowered her eyes and nodded yes, that was all.

"Are you sure?" Quaking Tree frequently inspected the contents of Pale Moon's pouch to make sure she didn't pick up anything that would harm her or give her a rash. She knew Pale Moon had taken the tiny piece of gold and was hiding it from her.

Pale Moon let loose of the bag where she had been pinching it tightly between her fingers. She laid the bag on the blanket. Quaking Tree reached over to pick it up and gave the pouch a slight shake. Clay thought it was a gold nugget that fell out, but his fingers picked up a tiny gold four-leaf clover. He dropped it like it was on fire.

"I know about this," he said to Quaking Tree. "Her mother wrote it down that when they named her Olivia, her father threaded the piece on a string or something and tied it around their daughter's neck. It's meant to bring good luck."

Pale Moon's eyes flew to Quaking Tree, afraid she was about to be punished for taking and hiding the tiny bit of gold. Quaking Tree looked at Clay, who stared back at her, dumbfounded.

Quaking Tree motioned for Pale Moon to pick up her things and help fold the blanket. It was time to leave. After they were gone, Clay knew Quaking Tree would be back. Both of them needed time to think about what had just transpired. Clay now knew he had his proof. Quaking Tree was sure of it.

* * * * *

Quaking Tree remained quiet for so long that finally Pale Moon asked if she was going to be punished for taking the gold charm. "No," said Quaking Tree. "It's yours."

Pale Moon wanted to know how her mother knew she had been carrying it in her leather pouch for such a long time, always careful never to show it to anyone after the traders tried to grab it away from her.

"A mother knows everything about her child," explained Quaking Tree.

Her answer was not enough to satisfy the little girl. "What is this stone? Why did you hide it from me if it is mine?" she asked.

"Tonight, just before it is time to sleep, I will tell you. Maybe it will awaken a wonderful dream for you. It is a long story. Even though you will not understand all of it, you must listen carefully. At the end, remember that we are a family; you, me, your little brother, and Sky In Water. We will take care of each other forever. There is nothing to be afraid of. Ever."

* * * * *

Pale Moon did not move far from the tepee the rest of the day. Her stomach ached, and she could barely swallow food. Her baby brother cried and cried, even when she tried to make him happy again. At last, he exhausted himself and fell asleep. When Sky In Water returned from taking care of the horses, Pale Moon curled up next to him and they napped on a blanket in the shade.

Quaking Tree was distracted thinking about what she would say to Pale Moon. She knew in her heart she had to do the right thing, but what was right for the child? Would it be so bad to keep the girl, and watch her grow into a young woman? Pale Moon's true family was gone. It was strangers who wanted to take care of her now.

Quaking Tree finally convinced herself the white man had no business taking Pale Moon away.

Then she began doubting herself again. Quaking Tree talked to herself saying, I know what she will go through when the time comes; when Pale Moon discovers she is not one of us. Someone will say something to hurt her feelings, or the children will begin teasing her about the pale skin under her dress. Eventually, the boys will have nothing to do with her.

"What am I to do?" Quaking Tree asked the trees and the river and the sky. "What am I to do with this child?"

* * * * *

Sky In Water noticed a change in both Quaking Tree and Pale Moon when he returned from rounding up several horses that had gotten loose from their tethers. It wasn't like Pale Moon to get so close to him rather than her mother. After the child had fallen asleep on the blanket, he asked Quaking Tree what had happened.

"I always thought this might happen and now it has," she explained. "A white man is here, camped on the other side of the riverbank. He has come searching for Pale Moon. He calls her Olivia. He has a book that tells everything about our child.

"This man," she continued, "who is called Clay, says Pale Moon's white mother wrote in a book, before she died of injuries, about that raid on the wagon train many moons ago. It says the baby's father had tied something around her neck during a special naming ceremony just days before the attack.

"It also says her baby was snatched from her arms during the raid. Are you the one who stole her, Sky In Water? Or are you the warrior who rescued the baby when you brought her to me?

"When you handed Pale Moon to me, I removed the amulet and hid it away. If it was meant to protect from harm, it didn't work for those people, did it? Even though I thought it might bring trouble to our tribe, it belongs to Pale Moon so I did not throw it away. Maybe someday, when she is older, and knows she is not truly one of us, it will mean something to her. It is the only thing left of her life before she came to us. The whole story is in the book, Pale Moon's story.

"Today, the white man saw that little piece of gold. Pale Moon had found where I had hidden it in a basket. Even though she has no idea what it is, she put it in her own pouch. When I made her show him what she kept in the pouch, it was the proof he needed to make sure Pale Moon is the child he is seeking. I am sorry she ever found it."

Sky In Water listened to the grief in Quaking Tree's voice. Having Pale Moon was a joyful thing for her, and losing her would be heartbreak all over again.

"I am the one who took the baby and brought her to you, Quaking Tree. I watched you mourn too long for the child you lost. I hoped a baby would bring you back to us again. I will be sorry, too, if the child leaves us. What do you want me to do?"

* * * * *

Clay was surprised when he saw a man accompanying Quaking Tree and Pale Moon on the other side of the river. Quaking Tree had a papoose strapped to her back. After they waded over to him, Quaking Tree introduced her family and explained why they all come back to see him again. "We have come to talk about Pale Moon," said Quaking Tree. "My husband wants to hear, for himself, what you have to say about her."

Quaking Tree asked Clay to read from the book again. Words they did not understand Clay worked out in sign language. Sky In Water stared at Quaking Tree, frightened by what he was hearing. He would not allow this man to take their child and break the heart of Quaking Tree. Pale Moon did not understand what was about to happen to her and her family.

"She must go with you," said Quaking Tree. "It will make my heart sad, but she must be with her true family. I thought I had convinced myself to not let her go, but after listening again to her mother's words, I have to."

To be fair, Clay said that Pale Moon did not have to go with him. "Listen again to what the book says - that if Olivia is found long after the raid, she should be given the choice of where she wants to live. I am just trying to fulfill Mary's wishes."

"No. She must go. Now. Before she finds out somehow she is not an Indian, and starts to ask many questions. She is young enough. She will forget all about us, and have a good life with her grandparents in this place called Boston. With us, there is nothing but a constant struggle for food, always on the move. There is always the fear we will not live long enough to see our hair go white.

"What can we tell her when the taunting begins? There are some who still think she should be a slave. What happens when she is old enough to suffer? You must take her."

"How do you know all this will happen?" asked Clay. "She's been here all her life. Doesn't everyone accept her by now?"

"No," replied Quaking Tree. "Those who are resentful will never let you forget."

"You don't know that, Quaking Tree!" Clay countered.

"Yes, I do," she said.

"How do you know?"

Quaking Tree stood up, and pulled down the shoulder of the soft suede leather dress she wore.

Clay could not believe what he saw. He stared at Quaking Tree, unable to speak. The white of her skin under the dark leather dress was startling to his eyes.

"So, this is how you know her life will be miserable if she is not returned to her grandparents," said Clay. "I had no idea you were a white woman. When where you stolen away? Why didn't you go back?" he asked.

Quaking Tree looked down as if ashamed. Clay could see tears forming in her eyes. She quietly murmured, “No one came for me.”

* * * * *

Chapter 7

Quaking Tree and Pale Moon stood on the riverbank watching as Clay rode away from them. He never turned around to wave good-bye. They were not sure he even realized they were there. Quaking Tree sensed they would see him again one day.

Clay spent a troubled night pacing in front of his campfire. He talked to Warrior about his predicament, convincing himself that leaving was the only thing to do. He felt guilty about letting Mary McCreedy down by not rescuing her baby.

Mostly, it preyed on his mind that he was letting his own pa down. Clay had promised he would find Olivia and bring her back. Now, having found her, he could not do it. Not right now. He was sure Pale Moon, if she was older and given the choice, would have chosen to stay with her Indian family. He tried to grant Mary's wish that she had written so clearly in her journal, but had failed.

Two good things that came out of his trip was that now they knew Mary's daughter was in good health and where she could be found.

Clay had used up his curiosity about always wanting to explore what was over the next rise, across the river, or through the trees to the other side. After such a long time on the trail, he couldn't wait to get home and settle in. He wasn't interested in leaving the ranch again for a long time. The season was changing, and fall was closing in. The trees would be in full color by the time he got home, and then the snows would come.

Considering how far he had ridden away from the ranch, it didn't take Clay nearly as long to return. He rode steadily through late summer rain, and watched aspens begin to turn from green to yellow and orange. He could smell fall and felt the air begin to cool.

Each day he talked to Warrior, his new dog, about the good life they would have in just a short time. "There are all kinds of things for you to do at the ranch," he told Warrior. "You can chase a few chickens, get acquainted with Yonder, help round up the horses, and sleep without fear. Just stay away from the porcupines, please."

* * * * *

As Clay approached the creek that ran through several pastures, he reined up. He sat there for a few minutes taking it all in. He gave up the lonesomeness he had felt for so long. He didn't think anyone had spotted him so he took his time riding around the stables to the far side where he could get a good look at the house.

There she was on the porch, watering baskets of ferns she had asked Clay to hang from hooks in the ceiling. Warrior moved forward, and gave a yip when he saw the chickens pecking in the yard. Sarah turned and saw a stranger on horseback. She yelled to Adam, "Quick, run, get your Pa. There's a stranger riding in."

Sarah was used to strangers hanging out down by the barns. They were usually ranchers or territorial soldiers looking for horses. This man didn't have that look about him, and he was headed directly to the house. He rode low in the saddle and seemed weary. Sarah hoped his dog wasn't mean.

As Clay neared the house, Sarah realized he was beginning to look familiar. Clay stepped down out of the stirrups and said, "It's me, Ma. I'm home."

"Oh, my goodness! Clay! Clay! Clay!" Sarah flew into the arms of her son and hung on for dear life. She was not about to let him go away again.

Clay had grown so much he was a head taller than his mother. As they clung together, he bent his head and breathed in the sweet scent of her hair. Warrior was jealous and nosed his way between the two of them. Mother and son broke apart and patted him on the head. Satisfied, Warrior went back to the matter of the chickens.

Meanwhile, Adam had found Pa in a shed repairing harnesses.

"You'd better come quickly, Pa. Ma needs you. Someone rode in and we don't know who it is. He's up by the house."

Ben put down his tools, and ran behind Adam back to the house. He recognized Searcher right away. His boy had come home.

The two men stood there clasping hands until Ben pulled Clay into his arms and patted him on the back, the way men do. When Adam realized his big brother had come back he ran into the house to fetch Molly.

"Come see who's here!" he yelled at the foot of the steps, not wanting to waste any time looking for his sister.

Sarah got her family settled around the kitchen table, and put a pot of coffee on to boil. Everyone was so full of questions that Clay couldn't pick out one to answer. The first thing Molly wanted to know was where the girl had gone, because she didn't see her in the house. Adam, of course, was curious about the people he had met. "Did you see any robbers get hanged?" he asked.

Ma and Pa asked if he was all right, not sick or hurt in any way that needed attention. Clay just listened to the wonderful sound of their voices. He could not believe he was finally home.

* * * * *

Adam and Molly soon went outside to get acquainted with Warrior. Ben and Sarah now had their chance to talk with Clay alone. "Didn't you find her?" asked Ben.

"Yes, I found her, but she needs to stay where she is at least for a while longer," Clay replied. "It was a hard decision to make leaving her behind, and I knew you would be disappointed, but it was something that had to be. We'll get her back. For now, her Indian family needs a little more time together.

"You know the part in Mary's journal where it says to let Olivia make up her own mind where she wants to be? Well, I made that decision for her. She's still too young to leave the only family she has ever known."

"How is that, Clay?" asked Ben. "When we read that journal, we vowed to get Olivia back, and see that she returns to her grandparents back east. What went so wrong that you couldn't uphold the promise? I don't understand."

"Like I said, Pa, she is too young to even know what the question meant. The only white people she has ever been around are at trading posts, and they are few and far between. Those people are merchants, trappers and traders. She has no concept of a white family.

"I was introduced to the man who is the father in her family. He never actually said a word to me, and I never spoke directly to him. His name is Sky In Water. He and Quaking Tree live together with their son and Pale Moon/Olivia. Quaking Tree told me he is the man who gave her the baby, so we know he was at the raid. I don't know for sure if he is the one who snatched her out of Mary's arms."

"What kind of life does the child have?" asked Sarah. "Are they good to her? I've heard such awful stories of what Indians do to anyone they capture. Is Olivia a slave? Does she remember anything at all from before the massacre?"

"No, she isn't a slave," Clay assured his mother. "Sky In Water gave Olivia to Quaking Tree because Quaking Tree had lost both her daughter and her husband. She told me she got her life back when Sky In Water handed the little girl to her. Now they are a family and Olivia even has a new baby brother."

"But why didn't you bring her home?" Ben asked again. He still couldn't believe Clay had ridden home alone without the child.

"Quaking Tree actually made up my mind for me," said Clay. "After I had read the last page of Mary's journal to her, Quaking Tree insisted I take Pale Moon with me. She knew right away that Olivia, the baby she had been given, was the child in the book. She later proved it to me when I was full of doubt.

"Earlier, it had occurred to me that maybe I was not rescuing the right child. Lots of them are kidnapped, and who was I to just ride up and take one back? You taught me better than that. Now I knew for certain who she was.

"Quaking Tree told me that one day the tribe would turn on Pale Moon. They would tease her about her pale skin - that's how she got her name, by the way - and insist that she be a slave like the rest of the captives. Then she would be ignored. No one would come near her. It was obvious to me Quaking Tree loves Pale Moon enough to make the sacrifice of losing her, if it meant a better life for her child.

"You would not believe what happened next," continued Clay. "I was a little perplexed about the whole situation. Quaking Tree wasn't making it any easier for me. That last page in Mary's journal kept running through my mind, but something held me back. Frankly, I didn't know what to do.

"Finally, Quaking Tree stood up in front of me, and Sky In Water, their baby, and Pale Moon, and showed me the color of her skin underneath her dress. She's white, Pa. She's white! She told us everything."

"Well, I am glad you are home, boy. But you aren't a boy anymore, Clay. Look at the size of you. Didn't I tell you, Sarah, a man would come home to you? Didn't I tell you that?"

Adam and Molly came slamming in the back door and into the kitchen for more chocolate cake. "We like your dog," said Adam. "What's his name? Did you find him on the trail? He sure does like our chickens."

"Tonight, after supper, I will tell you all about Warrior," Clay promised. "Right now I need to wash up and lie down on that soft featherbed I know is just waiting for me in my old room. I'm so tired I can't keep my eyes open a minute longer. The story I have to tell you is very long, so goodnight until later."

* * * * *

Chapter 8

Adam and Molly would not give their big brother a moment of peace. Adam especially wanted to hear everything about Clay's adventure, but mostly the trouble he got into. Molly was interested in Olivia. She was fascinated when Clay told her that Olivia didn't know she was anything other than an Indian. "How can that be?" she asked. "Doesn't she look different and act different from them?"

Clay told her that, no, Olivia was taken at such an early age she had no recollection of anything other than always being with her tribe.

Clay was glad when the kids high-tailed it off to school the next day and he had a few hours to work himself back into the ranch. At first, Pa talked a mile a minute about everything that had been going on at the ranch while Clay was gone. He finally got it all said and settled down enough to let Clay do some talking. There was so much to tell on both sides.

It got into a routine where Pa did his talking during the day, explaining everything about the ranch and how business was going. He definitely wanted Clay to take over managing the place someday. Pa needed to make sure he understood everything from doctoring horses to paying the bills.

In the evening, after supper dishes had been cleared away, the family sat around the table with their coffee and dessert and listened to Clay tell one story after another. He skipped the one about meeting all the pretty girls. His mother winched every time he told them about his close calls or being run off by Indians. She never said anything, just thanked the good Lord her son was home all in one piece.

It didn't take long before it seemed to Clay like his trip had happened ages ago. There were still the chores that never went away. He hated that part and tried to talk Pa into hiring extra hands. Pa knew Clay was just being lazy. Sarah wasn't so sure.

When Sarah questioned his attitude toward Clay, Ben explained: "Right now his muscles are sore and he's exhausted from his time on the trail. The day he is out there and working without one of us having to get him out of bed every darn morning is the day he becomes a rancher. Time is all it takes, not another hired hand."

While Clay had been gone and Ben was doing everything by himself, with a little help from Adam and Sarah, the horse ranch thrived. The Army proved to be a good, constant source of income. People were coming to the Hardistys in search of finely bred horses to pull their carriages and wagons. A perfectly matched pair was expensive but highly prized. Ben made sure he always had plenty of teams on hand. Folks liked to have a choice when it came to horseflesh.

Cowboys came from neighboring ranches wanting a strong mustang that could be ridden from sunup to sundown. Ben rode far and wide in search of breeding stock. The Hardisty reputation was proving to be priceless, thanks to Ben's tireless efforts to supply nothing but the best. He was always willing to dicker if a potential buyer did not have quite the money for what he wanted. Rarely did anyone go away disappointed.

Ben decided to take one more trip in search of wild horses, before the snow began to fall. When Clay was gone, Ben put up a map on the wall in his stable office where he marked each sighting. There didn't seem to be any established pattern, but Ben got really good at second guessing. When he did ride out to see if he was right, it wouldn't be long before mustangs showed up.

"Saddle up. Let's get out of here before it gets any colder and we decide to stay home," Ben called to Clay.

Adam was making a nuisance of himself wanting to go along. "I never get to do anything," he whined. "When I get bigger and you guys ask me to do something, think about what my answer is going to be to you." He stomped off to the house. Ben and Clay smiled to each other as they mounted up, and headed toward the hills.

* * * * *

There were no horses at the first location so the men headed off deeper into the hills. It was cold, camping in this weather. Ben tended to build a 'white man's fire,' as Clay called it; a fire so big and hot they couldn't get near it. Ben got a little ticked at Clay for complaining and told him, "Go build your own fire, then." So Clay did. A small fire, just like the Indians taught him, small yet with some heat in it. Now he could get up close and soak in the warmth rather than moving back from heat, hot in front and cold on the behind. He fed it small twigs and branches through the dark evening then banked it so he could sleep close, and still absorb heat from the embers. Two nights later, Ben sheepishly asked Clay to teach him how to make an Indian fire.

Ben and Clay managed to herd back about a dozen horses. They didn't want too many in case they had to be fed over winter when horse trading slowed down. Sarah was always glad to see her men folk come riding in, whether they trailed horses or not. The first one out of the house to greet them was always Adam. He never stayed mad long. Molly stayed behind and watched from the windows. Ever since she had gotten sick that one year, she didn't always feel good when the weather got cold. She liked to sit near the kitchen stove with her books and writing tablets.

* * * * *

Spring came and business was better than ever. Up until now, the two Hardisty men could handle everything. It was now at the point where they would have to hire some extra hands. Adam was growing bigger and taller but still didn't have any heft to him. He was always a willing worker, but until he got some meat on his bones and developed more muscles he tended to play out too soon. Ben and Clay often discussed Adam's role in running the horse ranch.

"If he stays skinny, he won't be much good in the saddle," said Clay. "I learned that out on the trail. It takes stamina to do what we do. I doubt if he will ever amount to much in the size department. He takes after Ma's side of the family, not yours."

"We have to give him a chance, son," Ben replied. "He's still a growing kid."

"I've got an idea," said Clay. "I've been doing a lot of thinking about how to share the work load. What about moving a desk and chair into your office for Adam and letting him learn how to do the paperwork? If he starts now he will have it learned by the time he's out of school and can work for us full time. It would be one less thing to worry about. Ma and Molly, neither one, are good with figures. Someone has to do it and I don't want to. Do you?"

Ben thought the idea over for a minute then agreed. "I think it's a great idea. It is the perfect job for Adam. We'll discuss it with him tonight after supper. I know he will never be a born-in-the saddle rancher like you and me."

First, they let Sarah in on the new plan. "Nothing would please me, or Adam, more than him being a part of running the ranch," said Sarah. "How did you ever come up with this idea?"

Neither man thought it would be a good idea to tell her they did not want her puny son taming mustangs. "He's good at math," said Pa, and let it go at that.

* * * * *

Adam could not believe what he was hearing. First, Ma was picking on him for eating so much and not putting any meat on his bones. "Where does all that food go?" she asked. "To your brain instead of your stomach? You are going to be a tall drink of water someday, just like your Grandpa Lucas."

Adam didn't know what to make of it. Then Clay did a little teasing about Adams's inability to hoist more than a dozen pitchforks of hay before he was panting like a dog in the hot sun.

Molly didn't have anything to say. She listened and wondered why all of a sudden everyone was being mean to her brother. She made herself ready to defend him when she saw he had enough of the teasing.

"Son," said Pa, "we're just joshing with you."

Adam squinched his eyes shut, balled his hands into fists, and hoped for the best.

"Adam, how would you like to become an official working partner in the ranch?"

"What's a working partner? You're asking me to be some kind of partner?

"Calm down, calm down, Adam," Pa laughed. "I said, Clay and I would like you to learn how to do the paperwork for the ranch. It's a very important job. It involves paying the bills, learning how to order supplies we need, figuring out how much feed a horse needs and ordering vet supplies. Things like that. It's a big, huge job that neither Clay nor I really have time to do. We think you are up to it. You are really good with numbers. What do you say?"

Clay watched Adam's face.

"You want me? You want me to help run the ranch?" Adam stammered.

"Yep," said Clay. "You will even have your own desk in the office, right next to Pa's. We will get you some new pencils, a box of erasers, and all the journals you need to keep track of our money and all the other records we need. Are you ready?"

When Adam recovered from being so surprised he asked, "When do I go to work? Do I have to go to school tomorrow? Can I have my own chair too? Does this mean I don't have to do chores anymore?"

"No, son, none of us are that lucky," Pa answered. "Along with your regular chores, you now have this new job. I will warn you though, if it gets in the way of your school work, we will discuss it and probably make some adjustments. Is that agreeable to you?"

Adam shook his head in agreement.

* * * * *

The next day, Sarah and Molly were getting ready to ride into town for provisions when Ben walked up and asked Sarah to bring back a can of paint. Molly asked if there was a particular color he wanted.

"Pure white," said Ben. "Oh, and better bring a wide bristle paint brush too."

After they had returned from town with the supplies, he perched a ladder against the wall of the huge stable, and painted a new ranch brand high above the double doors. Under the "ABC Horse Ranch" he painted "Hardisty and Sons" in smaller letters.

Adam pondered that "ABC" quite a while before it dawned on him what it stood for. Now that he was being treated with some respect, he was not about to allow himself to act like a kid and ask Pa or his big brother for an explanation.

Ben and Clay just let him stew. When he did figure it out, Adam was thankful he had not opened his mouth to tell them what a dumb brand he thought it was at first.

"I got it! I got it!" he yelled as he ran in with an armful of wood for the cook stove. "Ma, you know what the ABC Pa painted on the barn is for?"

"No. No idea. I can't figure it out myself, and Pa won't tell me," she smiled at her young son.

"It's for us partners, Adam, Ben, and Clay. Got it? Got it? ABC. Where's everyone? I have to tell them I figured it out. Oh man, this is really something," he yelled as he slammed out the back door, headed to the barn.

* * * * *

Chapter 9

It seemed to Clay there were endless, mind-numbing chores repeated, day after day. Hours in the saddle gave him plenty of time to think and his mind wandered. He thought mostly about the pretty girls he had left behind at the fort, the old coots he had met along the way, and his warrior friends. He missed the adventure, but at the same time was glad to be home. He tried to convince himself it was not all that tedious.

Eventually, the rhythm of the ranch caught up with Clay. He looked forward to each new day. He came around to thinking that he wanted to live on the ranch and run it for his family when Pa got too old to sit in a saddle. That time may be years away, he thought, but what way of life is better than this? He thought about how much his Ma and Pa loved the ranch, and how they worked together to make it a success, not only for themselves, but for himself, and Adam and Molly.

Clay was no longer so eager to know what was on the other side of the hill. His trip into Indian country had showed him more than enough. Scouting trips into the hills looking for mustangs got him away for a day or two, and filled any need he had to satisfy his curiosity about what lay beyond. He was learning to value his family and all they meant to him.

There was one thing he decided to do something about right now. Clay needed to take a second look at those girls in town. "Maybe they aren't as plain and dumb as I used to think they were," he told himself.

And that's how Clay ended up at his first dance. Unbeknownst to him, the church was having its annual box social. Everyone in town was there to bid on picnic lunches that all the young girls had packed.

The ranch was doing well, so Clay had money to spend. Instead of carrying beads and other small trinkets in his pockets, he now carried some "jingle," as he liked to call it.

Adam and Molly took the opportunity to do a little teasing of their own while Clay was getting ready to go the dance. Molly asked if he was going to fall in love and kiss the girl when no one was looking. Adam made fun of his fancy clothes and all the time Clay spent on shining his boots.

Both of them pinched their nose following him through the house, "You smell so sweet," cooed Molly. "Don't go out to the stable because the horses will run away from you," she laughed. Adam said he thought Clay smelled like a field of flowers, not the brother who spent his days with animals.

Clay stood inside the doorway watching the dancing before he ventured over to stand closer to the fiddle player. Girls smiled at him as they twirled past in their long colorful dresses. He began paying more attention to their faces figuring out if he recognized them or not. He was surprised to see how pretty they all were.

By the time he had circled the room, spoke to friends, got clapped on the back in greeting, and took more than one secret sip, he had worked up enough gumption to ask a pretty girl in a blue dress to dance with him. After that first dance, it was easy for him to ask another girl, then another and another to dance.

During a break in the dancing the bidding began. A particularly large fancy box was offered up by the auctioneer. Clay knew it had been put together by a girl who knew the way to a man's heart; lots of food. Clay reminded himself there was no commitment other than sharing what was inside, maybe dancing a couple reels with the girl, and that would be it.

The decorated boxes were placed on a table; the girls who had put them together were not allowed anywhere near. The biggest and prettiest box was always held for the last, which made the bidding fast and furious. It took every cent of Clay's jingle to win the box and the girl. When she stepped out of the crowd Clay recognized her. She was Abigail, the teacher's daughter.

He did not know it at the time, but Clay had just met his future bride.

* * * * *

All the men were out of the house when Molly spied a bunch of riders headed across the far pastures. By the time they were near the creek, she saw they were Indians. Scared out of her wits she ran to find Ma, then ran out to the barn to warn Pa they were about to be attacked. Ben and Clay grabbed rifles. They yelled at Adam to get to the house to protect the women as best he could.

It was a noisy bunch of warriors, chasing a small herd of ponies that leaped their horses over the creek, putting the fear of God into Ben. It was just what they intended to happen when the young men came in sight of Clay's home. Pa raised his rifle and held a bead on the one in the lead. Clay aimed, and recognized who he had in his sights. He pushed Ben's gun away from his shoulder and said, "This is OK, Pa. I know these guys."

The Indian in Pa's bead jumped down and grabbed hold of Clay. Clay put his arms around the tawny muscled man and lifted him off the ground. The rest of the gang surrounded Clay all talking at once. He motioned for them to slow down and give him time to figure out what they were saying. It had been a long time, and he had forgotten most of the Indian words he had learned. Hand signals came easier.

Clay yelled to Pa that he was all right, not to be worried about what was going on. Pa stood there stunned, not knowing what to do. He finally set his rifle down and stepped back to watch his son. What in the world happened out there, he wondered, that would bring a gang of Indian roughnecks out of the woods looking for Clay? I hope they don't mean any trouble, he prayed.

Pa turned to watch the ponies that had finally settled down and were grazing on sweet pasture grass. He wondered why the Indians were herding horses and where they were headed.

One of the first things the Indians wanted to know was if Clay had eaten his dog yet. "No," laughed Clay. "Would you like to shake hands with Warrior? Let's go find him."

As it turned out, their chief remembered Clay asking if the tribe had extra horses to trade for blankets or whatever else they needed. He explained to the chief that his family had recently bought a horse ranch and needed more stock.

At the time, the tribe had none to spare. Each year the chief traded some off, but never enough to reduce the herd to where a man or two couldn't take care of them. Recently, the herd had grown to the point where there were too many to handle.

The pack of wild teenagers who had brought Clay into their camp was now a pack of wild young men with too much energy for their own good. From lack of anything to do they were getting themselves into trouble.

The last time the gang made trouble for everyone, the chief suggested they round up some of the extra horses and take them to Clay.

"That will keep them out of our hair for a good long time," he told the elders. Everyone in camp encouraged their sons to take the chief up his offer. The chief told them they could trade for any personal items they wanted, but first they had to trade for warm blankets and tools for the tribe.

The young men were anxious to go but no one knew exactly where Clay lived. Montana Territory was a big place. The Indians didn't want to wear out their horses riding all over to look for a phantom ranch. They sent two of the younger members of the band to the trading post with instructions to find out all anyone could remember about Clay and where he came from. In a few days, the boys returned with a map showing the general area where Clay could be found. Clay had made a lasting impression on a lot of people who thought him very brave to go into the wilderness alone looking for a young girl.

Clay and Pa indicated to the Indians they were welcome to set up camp right where they were, in the pasture. The fences would keep their horses in, and the creek was nearby.

"How did they find the ranch?" Pa asked Clay at the supper table. Clay told them they had followed a map until it ran out, and then explored until they saw ranch buildings. "They didn't go to town and ask where we lived because they were all too aware of the mistrust. They were in our area for a couple of days looking for me. Now, here they are!"

Ben and Clay dickered all afternoon with the natives, who drove a hard bargain. When everyone was satisfied with their trades, Sarah offered to take the wagon to town and pick up everything needed for the trade. She had no desire to stay around any longer than necessary where those savages were concerned. She took Molly with her. She couldn't budge Adam from all the excitement.

Sarah picked out bright bolts of cloth, pots and pans, and hammers, among other items. Molly picked out colorful shirts, and a couple of cowboy hats that were special requests.

That night, around the campfire, old friends and old memories were shared with Clay's family. Sarah and Molly were not so sure about the experience, but Ben, and especially Adam, and Clay had the time of their lives.

"These are the Indians I told you about, Ma. Remember? I said they were going through an abandoned fort looking for anything they could find when I stumbled across them. They won't hurt you. They know you belong to me," he assured her.

"Right," she said. "You just keep reminding them, would you please?"

She was glad to see them headed back across the creek the next day.

It didn't take long before neighboring ranchers had heard about the visit a band of Indians had made to the -ABC-. Many suspected the worst and made a trip out to the ranch to talk with Ben and Clay. They wanted to see themselves no harm had been done.

When the excitement was over, everyone in the territory knew the story about Clay's search for Olivia.

* * * * *

Chapter 10

As time went by, the Hardisty horse ranch became, more or less, the social center of the county. Hands were hired and fired, mustangs tamed and sold, horses bred and traded. Many community events were held at the -ABC-.

Ben was so grateful to the community for their support that he was more than willing to open some of the pastures for weekend church fairs and school activities. After he cleared several picnic areas under the big oaks, Ben had his men build a small race track. Weekend traffic on the new road to the track was buggy after buggy during summer racing season. It was hard to beat the Hardisty horses, but people came from far and wide to try. Visitors tended to have better luck with harness racing. Clay took it upon himself to make sure word got out about racing weekends. Everyone was given a fair chance to win.

Sarah and Molly joined in the fun and made many new friends. They sat and visited with the women while their men and boys raced the horses and told tall tales.

* * * * *

Clay proposed marriage to Abigail, much to the delight of his mother. Abigail had turned Clay's head, and he never looked at any of the other pretty girls after their first dance. The couple talked about a wedding in the future, which was a disappointment for Ma but pleased Pa. He needed more time with Clay teaching him all he could about running the ranch. Adam and Molly did not know about having their teacher's daughter for a sister.

The couple knew, as did everyone, that they were a perfect match. They made no definite wedding plans, other than to wait a year. Both of them had things to do, and places to go before they settled in and started a family, as they explained to everyone who was eager for a wedding.

Abby explained to her future mother-in-law that she wanted to go back east one more time before getting married. She had plans and made a list of special things for the wedding and their new home. Ma didn't argue with her about a delayed wedding day. She was curious about the items Abby wanted for her new home.

When Clay objected to her being gone for such a long time, Abby promised, "After this trip, we will always travel together. Wherever I may go, you go too, and I with you."

Clay had been thinking a lot about settling down and having a family. Both he and Abigail wanted a houseful of kids. On a Sunday afternoon they walked across one of the pastures and picked out a spot on the other side of the creek where their new house would be built. "Of course," said Clay to Abigail. "But first, we have to get permission from Pa and Ma to build here."

"It's such an ideal location," said Abigail. "When you take over managing the ranch it's not so far away that you couldn't get over there at the first sign of trouble, or whatever."

Abigail said to Clay, "Even though I have always lived in town, I want to spend the rest of my life in the country, right here at this spot with you, Clay."

Ben happily signed over the land by the creek to Clay. Ma said, "That was the first step on the way to this first marriage in our family. I can't wait for the next step. Any hint, Abigail? A year is a long time to wait when you are in love."

Abigail and Clay looked at each other, avoiding answers. They didn't tell anyone how many evenings they rode to the site to plan where the living room, kitchen, and lots of bedrooms would be located in their new house. Ben explained to Abigail, "If Ma knew, she wouldn't give us a minute of peace."

* * * * *

Clay had Olivia on his mind again. "It's time to do something about that child," he told his folks. "I want to take another trip before I get married, mainly to make sure she is doing well and not sick or in harm's way. I have no idea if she will come back with me or not. I'll be surprised if she does, but we can always hope she will."

No one had mentioned Olivia in a long time. It seemed that, once again, the Hardistys had hidden her away. Clay wasn't even sure how much Abigail knew about the history of Olivia.

Clay and Ben talked about another trip. Both were anxious to close Mary's journal once and for all. "I hate to just abandon Olivia," said Ben. "Especially if it is meant for us to see that she gets to her grandparents."

Clay agreed, "She deserves a chance to at least meet with her grandparents. That's all we can do. This time, I think she is old enough to make some choices. I would make sure she clearly understands her relationship to them. It will be overwhelming simply because there is so much involved she has never had the opportunity to experience. She's lived in the wild all her life and we would be sending her to a city of thousands of people. It's a big decision."

Clay and Abigail sat on a huge rock, not far from where their house would be built. It was just before twilight. They sat, listening to the gurgle of the creek and birds twittering as they nested for the evening.

He said, "I have a story to tell you. I don't know how much you know about me going to look for a little girl that was stolen from her mother by Indians, so here's what happened."

Abigail listened in awe as Clay spoke. She didn't have much to say. Her only question was to ask how long he had been away.

Clay had thought to bring Mary's journal with him, and he handed it to Abigail. "This is the journal that tells the story," said Clay. "I want you to read it, and try to understand why I need to go one more time and try and find her." He proceeded to tell Abigail everything that had transpired since the journal had been found.

"You have to go. You know that, don't you?" said Abigail. "Go now. Bring her home and we will see that she gets to her family in Boston. If she doesn't want to go we can keep her here. We have to give her all the opportunities in life she's missing."

"What if she wants to stay with her Indian family? I can't force her to come with me, can I?" asked Clay.

"We can't answer those questions, Clay. If you want to bring this story to a close, you have to go. If she stays, it's the end of the story. If she comes out with you, it seems to me that there will be another chapter. One written by the Hardisty family, and then it will go on from there until Olivia is writing her own story."

The final decision called for a family counsel. Adam was practically the age Clay had been when he looked for Olivia the first time. But Adam wasn't Clay and still didn't like to get too far away from home.

"Adam," said Clay, "how would you like to tag along on this trip? Think of the adventure you would have. You might even meet some more Indians."

"No, thanks," replied Adam. "For one thing, I'm too busy around here and have school to go to. Could I ask a favor though? If I give you an empty book would you write down everything that happens? Like a diary, something that happened each day you are gone."

As much as Ben wanted to make the trip this time, his wife and children would not allow him to go. Neither would his sore knees, so he let the matter drop and concentrated on Clay. Let the boy go, he thought to himself.

He finally was satisfied with decisions made when he said to Sarah, "Clay will bring Olivia back, and then I'll be the one who sees to it she gets to her grandparents in Boston. Both of us will have fulfilled Mary's wish."

"I may be a married foreman someday," Clay reminded his father. "But that day isn't here yet, so I'm still footloose and fancy free. The hired hands can pick up the slack while I'm gone and, with any luck, I won't be away too long this time."

* * * * *

For the second time, Clay was ready to set out just after spring had settled down and summer was about to blossom. Everyone got involved in his trip this time. It was driving him crazy. Instructions and advice from Pa were never-ending. He had to promise Ma that he would eat and sleep enough and try to keep dry. "Yes, yes, I know, I know," he repeated to everyone over and over again.

Adam handed Clay one of the farm bookkeeping journals he had not yet used to take along. "Remember to write down everything, and I do mean everything," said Adam.

"I want to read about a real adventure, not those dime novels anymore, so make it good!"

Molly packed two of her outgrown dresses and shoes for Olivia. She made sure to include a brightly colored one she knew Olivia would like because it had been one of her favorites. "It will be like having a sister when you get back," she said to Clay with such a happy look on her face.

Clay thanked Molly for her thoughtfulness and for remembering that Olivia had asked if he could get her a pretty dress. Clay didn't want to disappoint her by reminding her that he would be bringing home an Indian who did not know how to speak English.

"You will be a good big sister to her," he said. "And one day she will tell you how much she loves that."

Abigail cried, kissed Clay good-bye, and cried some more. "I will see you soon. Do not be a hero," she pleaded. "Come home to me and bring that little girl with you, you hear?"

Clay climbed up on Searcher, whistled for Warrior, and they started down the road. "This is the last time I'm going down this trail alone," he remarked to Warrior. "When we come back this time, it will be to a whole new life."

* * * * *

Chapter 11

There was something in the air. Change was in the air, and it was scaring Pale Moon. It made the hair on her arms stand on end. She had the feeling she was waiting for something to happen. She had no idea what she was waiting for.

Pale Moon asked Quaking Tree and Sky In Water, "What is happening? I feel funny, not sick or anything like that. It's more like I am waiting for something and I don't know what it is. Do you feel it too?"

They had no good answers. There was nothing to say to satisfy her wariness. Quaking Tree actually did understand what her child was feeling, but kept it to herself. There was no reason to alarm Pale Moon right now.

Quaking Tree felt there was time enough to discuss Clay with Pale Moon, and see how much she remembered about the white man from his first trip to find her. It had been many moons since Clay had come to take Pale Moon away.

Quaking Tree asked Sky In Water if he remembered Clay. "I think he is on his way to us again," she told him. "I am worried it won't be so easy this time. He will ask her if she wants to find her white family. Then what will we do? What will she do? I know I have to talk to her about it. It's hard to know what to say."

Sky In Water told Quaking Tree he thought of Pale Moon as a member of their family, including his older son and their new son, Red Morning. He will not be willing to let go of Pale Moon, thought Quaking Tree, and I will be caught in the middle.

Pale Moon was old enough that her feelings were easily hurt. As many times as Quaking Tree said, "Don't pay attention to that little band of terrors. Find some new friends." It was easier said than done. It was difficult to ignore the taunts and rocks that came flying close to her face. Still her parents told her, "Ignore the bad ones. When they get tired of you not reacting, they will leave you alone."

The taunting had grown worse and spread from the youngsters to older children, and finally to several women who still thought that Pale Moon should be a salve, not a daughter of the tribe. "It was bad enough," one of them moaned to the chief, "that Quaking Tree was not their slave, and now this girl, too!"

Many in the tribe were satisfied that Quaking Tree could take care of their ills with her potions and salves. This was not the work for a slave, they argued with those who did not agree. "Quaking Tree has a special calling to heal and make our sick babies well," a young mother reminded them. "This tribe needs her, and we will need Pale Moon when Quaking Tree is too old. She is already teaching her daughter how to mix potions and teas."

The chief appeared not willing to do anything about the situation. He knew it would eventually take care of itself. "Be patient," he told the angry women. "Let her be a child for now."

Quaking Tree had told the chief long ago that one day Clay, the white man, would be back for Pale Moon. He would take the child back to her white family. When that happened, she told him, she never expected to see Pale Moon again.

Life was getting more and more miserable for Pale Moon. It seemed her friends and enemies changed every day. Eventually, she gave up and stayed close to their campfire. She looked after Red Morning and did her chores.

“I am so happy to see you spending more time with your little brother,” Quaking Tree told Pale Moon. “Someday, you will look back on the days spent with him as a very special time.”

Quaking Tree taught her how to prepare simple meals and take care of her own hair and clothes. Pale Moon was eager to learn and listened carefully to instructions.

Quaking Tree showed her how to dry beans by stringing them on a length of sinew and hanging them in the sun to dry. She often roasted corn in a pot over the fire, and then beat the kernels to break them off the cob. While the corn was roasting, Quaking Tree said to Pale Moon, “Corn needs a special basket to keep it dry. I am going to teach you how to make such a basket. You should have it finished by the time all the corn is ready to be stored.”

Whenever Sky In Water went out hunting, and knew he would be gone for several days, he asked Pale Moon to wrap bits of corn in a piece of leather. He explained to her; “When I stop hunting because I am hungry, I mash the corn and drop it in a water tight basket full of water. First, I put a very hot stone that has been placed near the campfire into the basket. The heat from the stone makes the water hot enough to soften the corn. Sometimes I add wild onions and even some berries.”

Pale Moon watched Quaking Tree roast birds and small animals over an open fire for their meals. Her mother boiled pieces of venison or bear, opossum, and ground hog that Sky In Water brought home from his hunting trips. She and Pale Moon spent many hours crushing corn between rocks into a fine cornmeal. The boiled meat was especially good when some cornmeal was mixed in to thicken the stew.

Pale Moon’s favorite drink was hot tea sweetened with honey. “Let me show you how to make your favorite tea,” said Quaking Tree. Just like Sky In Water had told her how to heat water, Quaking Tree put rocks in the fire, then put them in a tightly woven basket full of water from the creek. When the water was heated, Pale Moon sprinkled in crushed peppermint leaves and stirred them around. It always smelled so good.

Sky In Water taught Pale Moon how to approach a bee hive without getting stung. "If you know where there is a hive full of bees, and also full of honey, make a bundle of dry weeds and set it on fire. It should make lots of smoke. Be very quiet, and walk slowly up to the hive," he explained. "Stand there until they get used to you being there. Then wave the smoke in the air so it drifts toward the hives. Bees dislike smoke and they will fly away. That is when you reach in and get all the honey you can."

Pale Moon had done some exploring on her own and found several dead trees where bees had made their hives. She never ran out of sweetness for her peppermint tea.

Quaking Tree and Pale Moon spent many hours together discussing what it is like to be a wife and mother, and how things would always be different for Pale Moon. "Many things are changing for you right now," Quaking Tree said. "And it will be that way for many moons to come. This is your time for growing up and becoming a woman, your own person. One day, maybe you will be a wife and mother to sons and daughters. Embrace the changes as they occur and enjoy life with your family."

So many things were beginning to make some sense to Pale Moon; especially after Quaking Tree explained what she had gone through as a white youngster living among Indians

It was early spring. The tribe packed up and got ready to migrate back to one of their favorite summer camping spots. They had not been back for a few years, so it was time. With no one living there, game and berries would be plentiful, along with many fish in the river and, hopefully, a garden area that had not been grown over too much with weeds. For these farmer Indians, land was of utmost importance. Over hundreds of years, they had learned how to care for it and nurture it so it would always feed them well.

It was up to the women to dismantle the tepees, fold up all the pieces, and pack them onto travois. A horse was then harnessed to the travois, which was a stretcher made of two long poles, crisscrossed with smaller poles or leather straps. Everything a family owned was loaded onto the travois and pulled along the ground to a new camp site.

It took many days traveling from winter camp to summer camp, but everyone had done it so often that reassembling tepees again took little time. Within a few days of arriving at the camp along the river, it seemed they had never been away.

The women started right in on their garden plots so the ground would be ready to plant at the next full moon. Precious seeds were saved and guarded from year to year. The children fished and caught enough that they could begin hanging some out in the sun to dry.

Camp was a busy place until everyone was satisfied there was enough food on hand, clothes to wear, and shelter for all. Only then did they relax and take some time to visit and pick berries. The men were gone nearly every day either hunting or scouting the surrounding area for anything they thought should not be there.

* * * * *

Clay was well on his way. He figured he should be at the Indian camp in a few day's ride. He did not have it in his head the possibility the clan would have moved away from their camp where he had found them the first time. He assumed that was where he was supposed to go. It was fate alone that had brought the Indians back to the old camp after all these years, where Clay would find them once again.

It was driving Clay to distraction having to watch the trail and constantly call Warrior so he would not run off and get himself lost. At night camp, Warrior got extra jerky to gnaw on, "…..for being such a good boy," encouraged Clay while he petted Warrior.

When they first started out, Warrior was reluctant to follow beyond the pastures he knew as home. He remembered that anywhere else was a life of misery. By the third day out, Warrior was following right along without stopping every hundred paces and looking back toward home.

In another four days, they approached the river where Clay had camped such a long time ago. "You can rest easy now, Warrior," Clay called. "The camp should be just ahead, across the river." But, as they neared, Clay didn't see any camp fire smoke, and it worried him.

"Oh, my gosh, what if they aren't here?" he cried to Warrior. "I didn't think about them moving to a different camp. It never occurred to me when we started out that we might not find them. Oh Lord, please let them be here."

Clay was more than disappointed not to find the Indian camp. There was nothing to do but keep following the river in hopes of finding the tribe. He finally spotted smoke drifting over tree tops. He let out a whoop and a holler that set Warrior to barking. Searcher picked up the pace a little.

This time, he camped further away from the tepees, thinking it would give him more opportunity to hide if he got himself into trouble. In case it was not the tribe he was looking for, he had to be ever vigilant.

Clay let some days drift by, allowing the Indians to find him and get used to the idea there was a white man camped nearby. If this was the camp he was looking for, he had no idea if they would remember him, or not.

Clay didn't think any of the men on ponies had gotten close enough to recognize him. He constantly reminded himself not to make any sudden moves, reach for a weapon, or threaten in any way when he felt their presence, even though he had not seen them yet. They did not trust any white man. This he knew. Too many promises had been broken. Too many of them had not returned home.

* * * * *

When Quaking Tree heard there was a white man camped across the river, she knew it must be Clay. “I cannot avoid it any longer,” she said to Sky In Water. “I have to talk to Pale Moon, and tell her everything this time.”

She sighed thinking how she would deal with her husband. Both Clay and Sky In Water knew the role each had played, so far, in the life of Pale Moon.

Quaking Tree knew neither one would easily give her up.

* * * * *

Chapter 12

"Pale Moon, come sit beside me," called Quaking Tree. "Leave your brother there. I want to talk to you."

From the tone of her mother's voice, Pale Moon knew it would be another serious conversation, like many they had been having of late. With each passing moon Quaking Tree had been telling her about her own life in the village, and also more about how Pale Moon became her daughter.

"Sit down. I need to tell you something very important. Listen to what I have to say because at the end you will have to tell me what you want to do. It's a lot to think about and time has run out, so be a big girl and listen carefully. If you don't understand something, ask me to stop and I will explain until you do. You need to understand every single word of what I am about to tell you."

Pale Moon sat on the blanket opposite her mother and looked into her eyes. She had no idea what to expect. It made her fearful.

"There is a white man camped across the river. He was here once before, many moons ago, when you were much younger. I doubt you would even remember him, but his name is Clay. Do you remember anything at all? Do you remember seeing a white man near camp?"

Pale Moon slowly shook her head, but in the back of her mind she faintly remembered standing on the river bank. A man had stared at her until she ran back to her mother in fright. She timidly asked, "Is it the same white man who stared at me down by the river who has come back?"

"Yes. It is the same man," replied Quaking Tree. "It is very hard to tell you what I have to, now that he is here again. He's here for a reason, and it involves you. I know you have no idea who he is, but he knows all about you.

"Pale Moon, you know you are different from the other children in the tribe. Up to now, I have avoided telling you the whole truth whenever you have asked why your hair is wavy and your skin is not as dark as theirs. Are you ready to listen? It is a long, complicated story."

Quaking Tree told Pale Moon the whole story of how she had come to the Indians. This time, she included every detail she could think of, leaving nothing out. Pale Moon stopped her more than once to have her mother explain something she did not understand. Quaking Tree answered every question Pale Moon had asked in the past but always managed to evade until now.

Quaking Tree saved Pale Moon's name to the last. Tears slid down her cheeks when she told Pale Moon that she had once been called Olivia. Olivia McCreedy.

"It is a name given to you in the sight of their God," said Quaking Tree. "Clay told me you were named for your white grandmother.

"Now, he has come to take you back to his family and then to your grandparents. Your real grandparents are white people who live in a wood house in a town much, much bigger than any fort or stockade or trading post you have ever seen. Bigger than ten of our tribes all gathered together."

Pale Moon became frightened when she heard her mother tell her she could be taken away. "I won't go! I won't go!" she sobbed. Quaking Tree took her daughter in her arms. She took the small shaking hands in her own and said soothing words, but there was no end to the child's tears.

"Now, let me tell you something else. It is all about me this time. It is something I have never told you before. I came to this tribe exactly like you came to me."

Pale Moon stared at Quaking Tree in disbelief. "How can that be?" she asked. "I don't believe you. You are just saying this to make me feel better."

Quaking Tree continued, "Many moons ago, this tribe you and I are a part of raided a trading post. My family was there. My white family, just like you had at one time. We were there buying provisions when Indians attacked the post. One of the warriors swept me off my feet as I ran for shelter. He carried me off and I became his wife. When he was killed in a buffalo stampede, I stayed with the tribe. I had no other place to go.

"I do not remember my white name," Quaking Tree said. "It has been too long. All I know is that when I was kidnapped and brought to this tribe, I was so scared I shook like an aspen tree. That is how I got my Indian name, Quaking Tree. I tried for so long to sing and recite what I could remember of the white man's words, but too soon they were gone."

Pale Moon smiled at the thought of her mother shaking like a leaf in the wind. "How did I get my name?" she asked.

"We call you Pale Moon because of the color of your skin under your dress. It is the same color of the moon when it is full and all the stars are out."

Pale Moon began to calm down and steady herself. Her hands had stopped shaking and her tears had dried. She became very quiet, snuggled in the arms of her mother.

"I know you have a lot to think about," said Quaking Tree. "Let's just sit here while you put it together. I will answer any questions you have, and I will be truthful. I won't leave anything out this time."

Pale Moon sat quietly, thinking. She finally asked, "How will I talk with the white man?" she asked. "How will I answer the questions you say he is going to ask me? I am scared to tell him I don't want to go with him. I don't want him to hurt me."

"You will understand each other," replied Quaking Tree. "Do not even think about it and it will come. Do not be afraid to ask your own questions. Always tell the truth when he asks something. You will understand everything. Listen carefully, like you are listening to me now."

Questions began popping into Pale Moon's mind. "Mother, can't you come with me? Do you want me to leave you and Sky In Water, to leave Red Morning? Or do you want me to stay with you forever?

"Oh, how can I even think of leaving? I won't. I want to see Red Morning grow up to become the fiercest warrior in our tribe. I want to stay with you forever. You are my family. I don't know those other people you talk about."

Quaking Tree, being truthful with Pale Moon, said, "When Clay was here before to take you away, I told him to take you. He left without you. I really don't know why. One morning he was just gone, and you were still with us."

"I had told him the day would come when you would be an outcast and now that time is here. It isn't going to change. There will always be those in our tribe who want you to be their slave. They do not like the fact that I was never a slave, and now you…it is too much for them. They will always expect the worst from you, which means you must always give your best. Sometimes that is a very hard thing to do. Sometimes it is impossible to take one more minute of the torture they put you through.

"I do not want you to grow up, like I did, with more enemies than friends. With more expected of you when you have no more to give. I want you to be with your family. But only you can decide which family that will be. It is your decision. I cannot make it for you."

* * * * *

Pale Moon had a lot to think about. Quaking Tree told her there was no hurry. She should take her time and think it through before making up her mind. There was an unanswered question, but Pale Moon waited a few days before going back to Quaking Tree. She knew how upset her mother was and it was affecting Red Morning and Sky In Water too.

She finally asked, "Why didn't the man take me with him when he was here before?"

"I think it was because he knew how precious you are to me. He just wanted us to have a few more years together."

Pale Moon had sleepless nights while she thought about the decision she faced. Finally, she was ready to cross the river and talk to the white man, the man who held her destiny in his hands.

* * * * *

Chapter 13

Pale Moon told her mother she was ready to meet Clay. They walked hand in hand to his camp. He was waiting.

"Do you recognize Pale Moon, Clay? She has grown as tall as the spruce since you have been gone. We have talked about your last visit to our village. Pale Moon does not remember you. The only thing she told me she can recall is someone looking at her from across the river."

"It is good to see you again, Quaking Tree," Clay greeted. "And it's nice to see you too, Pale Moon. You have grown so much."

Clay looked at Quaking Tree finding it hard to believe that no one in her family had ever come for her. He invited Quaking Tree and Pale Moon to sit on a blanket in front of his breakfast fire.

Pale Moon was jittery and nervous. She didn't move until Warrior walked up and nuzzled her hand, wanting a head scratch.

"Welcome to my fire," said Clay. "I'm sorry there is nothing left to eat, but I can pour some coffee." Quaking Tree shook her head no. Pale Moon was too busy with Warrior to think about eating.

"I have gifts for both of you," he smiled as he handed Quaking Tree a necklace of garnet stones. "This is very beautiful. I shall be proud to wear such fine beads," said Quaking Tree.

Clay told her, “The red stones are from the ranch where I live. I found them in the stream that runs through the woods and across a pasture.”

“I have something for Pale Moon too. My brother, Adam, made it just for you.” Pale Moon reached out, hesitating in taking the braided leather belt Clay held in his hand. She looked at her mother for approval. Quaking Tree nodded her head and said, “Go ahead, take it. It is a gift from Clay and his brother.”

Pale Moon shyly reached for the belt and carefully examined it. It was braided in a fashion she had never seen before. “Thank you for this gift. Look, it just fits around me!”

“I have something else for you, too. Clay walked over to his saddle lying on the ground near the camp fire. He reached into a saddle bag and pulled out a bundle of bright cloth.

“This is for you, Pale Moon,” smiled Clay. “I told my little sister, Molly, how much you liked the bright colored dresses ladies at the post wear. She wants you to have one of hers. She also sent along a pair of shoes, with hopes they will not hurt your feet.”

Pale Moon reached out and held the dress, marveling at the colors. As much as she was fascinated by the dress, she made no move to slip it over her head. She was so bewildered; she could find no words to say to Clay about this gift.

Pale Moon tugged off a moccasin, slipped her foot into a shoe, and stood up. It pinched her toes and made her face squinch up. Pale Moon shook the shoe off. She handed both items back to Clay.

“I prefer my moccasins,” she said, totally ignoring the colorful dress.

Clay was puzzled by her reaction to the clothes. He looked at Quaking Tree, but she only shrugged her shoulders. She had no idea what was going through Pale Moon’s mind.

Clay did as Pale Moon requested and never mentioned the dress and shoes again. He handed her several strings of pretty beads. She accepted these with a smile.

The three of them spent the afternoon talked about trivial things. Clay told them he used to know a lot more Indian words but had forgotten so many of them. "They are slowly coming back to me," he said, "but if you could use the hand signals too, it will help me understand."

Each time Quaking Tree and Pale Moon walked to Clay's camp over the next few days, they began asking each other deeper, more searching questions, and expected full answers in return. Their comfort level improved as well as their communication. They rarely had to use hand signals anymore to help Clay get their message.

Pale Moon asked, "Where did you come from? Is it many moons away from here?" She then told Clay she did not know the word ranch. "What is that?"

Clay explained, "A ranch is like a huge camp but without so many people. Just one family lives on it. They stay there, not moving around like your tribe does with each new season. Houses are built of wood rather than animal skins and lodge poles. They are big and strong to keep out the wind and the cold. Each person has a separate room where they sleep. There are even separate houses but we call them barns, for all the animals."

Clay asked Pale Moon what she thought about living in one place where she could watch the seasons change without having to go outside, but instead look through a window. Pale Moon was so mystified she didn't know what to say. She sat quietly, mulling over the strange words Clay kept saying. "Room, window?" said Pale Moon.

"A room," he said, "is a place by itself that is just yours and no one else shares it. Pale Moon liked that idea. She laughed when Clay told her she could climb up to the rooms on top of the house to sleep. "Just like climbing a tree to peek into a bird nest."

That didn't make any sense at all to Pale Moon. She decided he must be teasing her.

* * * * *

Back at their tepee, Pale Moon and Quaking Tree had more long talks. Her beginnings with the tribe were coming to her more clearly now. She better understood what had happened when she was a tiny baby.

Pale Moon's feelings about fitting in with a third family, and this time among white people, gave her much to think about. She pondered what her life would be like if she stayed with Quaking Tree and Sky In Water. She knew that much of the time it would be a life of ridicule and scorn, but at least she would be with someone she knew and trusted. They would always take care of her and protect her. She kept all these thoughts to herself. As much as she would like to be told what to do, no one could answer them for her.

She asked herself if it would be worse if she left. Pale Moon doubted it. Clay told her his family would never think of her as a slave, nor treat her as one. He said a war had been fought and won, over just that thing. There were to be no more slaves, ever.

"Should I stay, or leave with Clay?" she asked herself a hundred times a day. No one could make the decision for her.

* * * * *

Pale Moon woke with a start. She had dreamed all night long, but the dream did not frighten her this time. No one was teasing her or calling her bad names. No rocks came flying through the air, and no one was whipping willow switches against the backs of her legs.

Pale Moon dreamed of soft spoken people who lived by themselves away from any settlement. She dreamed of Clay who was never upset with her and gave her presents instead of harsh words. She awoke knowing she would be free of torment from this time on.

* * * * *

Chapter 14

Sky In Water and Quaking Tree were talking quietly when Pale Moon rose from her nest of soft furs. Sky In Water had an unhappy look on his face, but he then smiled at Pale Moon as she moved towards him. Pale Moon sat down, looked into her mother's eyes and said, "It is time for me to go."

Quaking Tree nodded. She knew it was the right decision. Sky In Water picked up Red Morning and stomped away from the campfire.

"We will walk to Clay's camp after you have eaten some food and say good-bye to your baby brother. I hope you will always remember him. He is so young now that he may not remember exactly what you look like when he gets older, but he will always be your little brother.

"You must also talk to Sky In Water. He does not want you to leave. Maybe you can help him understand your thoughts about why it is time for you to go. He will not like it, and he may try to talk you out of it."

It took all of the girl's courage to walk away from the familiar campsite. She took nothing with her but the little pouch of treasures she had collected over the years.

Quaking Tree carried a soft suede dress she made for Pale Moon and a pair of moccasins with precious beads sewn into a favorite design.

Pale Moon held Red Morning one last time, and held Sky In Water's hand for a long time, afraid to say anything or she would cry. Pale Moon gave a lock of dark curly hair to her mother.

"Take care, my daughter. Promise you will come back some day before Red Morning does not recognize you. I will never forget our life together."

* * * * *

Silently, the family waded across the river to Clay's camp. Clay stood up as they neared. He knew from the look on their faces a decision had been made. He held his breath.

Pale Moon said to Clay, "I want to go with you to find my white family."

At that, Quaking Tree finally let the tears slide down her cheeks. Sky In Water spun around and ran back across the river. Pale Moon threw her arms around her mother and held on as if she would never let go. Quaking Tree forced the tiny arms away, whispering with a small smile, "It is time to go. It is time to find your place in a new world. Always remember us. We love you. That will never change."

Clay watched, wondering if he was doing the right thing. How can I tear them apart? he asked himself. They are life itself to each other, and now here I am, ruining everything for them.

"Let's get ready to leave," Clay abruptly said to change the somber mood. But he took lots of time packing his saddle bags and cleaning up camp. He wanted to give Pale Moon enough time to change her mind if she was having any second thoughts. He asked if she had anything she wanted to put in a saddlebag. She gave him her new clothes.

Just as Clay reached down to grab Pale Moon's arm to swing her up onto Searcher's back they heard a loud splashing coming from the river. Sky In Water came charging out of the water and up the bank to where they stood.

"Oh no," said Clay. "Quaking Tree, didn't you explain to him why I was here and what might happen? He looks mad enough to tear my head off."

Sky In Water slid from his horse, picked up Pale Moon and gave her a fierce hug. He set the child down and glared at Clay.

"Now see here," said Clay. "I didn't come here to make any trouble. This is something Pale Moon's family asked us to do. If she decides later on that she doesn't want to stay with us, I will bring her back to you. That is a promise. I swear."

Sky In Water stared at Clay. He had thought long and hard about Pale Moon leaving them. He loved this child. His guilt about stealing her when she was a baby had long since passed. She had brought love and joy to his life. He would be forever grateful to this child who had brought Quaking Tree to him, and then a son. He stood his ground not saying a word.

Sky In Water had reluctantly agreed with Quaking Tree that Pale Moon should leave. He could not bear to hear the bad names she was called. After many years, sometimes Quaking Tree still had to endure being called nasty names because she was not a slave. He didn't want that for his daughter.

"It is not good for the child and it will not change with time," Sky In Water said to his wife. "We must see that Pale Moon is treated with respect, and she will be with her white family.

Suddenly, Sky In Water whistled as loudly as he could. A pure white pony came charging up the river bank, walked straight to Pale Moon and nudged her shoulder.

"She is for you," said Sky In Water. "I have trained her so she will be gentle and patient with you. She will take you to your new family."

Sky In Water turned and without another word or looking back he disappeared into the willows along the river. Pale Moon opened her mouth to thank Sky In Water for such a wonderful gift, but he was gone.

Clay hoisted Pale Moon onto the back of the pony. She grabbed its mane and hung on. Quaking Tree walked up to the pony and held out a blanket.

"This is to make your ride home more comfortable, Pale Moon. I hope you never forget us." Then she too turned and walked back across the river, never once looking back.

* * * * *

Chapter 15

Tears slid down her cheeks as Clay and Pale Moon began their way back along the trail which would take them home to Montana and the ranch. It was all she could do not to kick the pony in its ribs and gallop back to her mother. They rode only a few miles and already Pale Moon missed her family. Clay left her alone in her misery. He could not think of anything to say that would make it better for her. I wish Ma was here, he thought, she would know what to say.

Pale Moon had never been on a horse for any length of time. When they finally stopped after the first day's ride, she was stiff and sore. Clay tried to kid her about her legs being so stiff but he couldn't get a smile out of Pale Moon. As soon as Clay had fixed them something to eat, she curled up in front of the fire with Warrior stretched out alongside her and fell sound asleep.

There were times when Pale Moon felt so homesick she sobbed and moaned for her family. Clay was kind and gentle, letting her cry it out before mounting up and riding any further. He was anxious to get home and let his ma take over.

For sure, he told himself, this is my last long trip to the other side of the mountain. I am never coming back this way again. If Pale Moon wants to go back to her Indian family, someone else is going to have to take her.

To break the monotony of the ride, and because Pale Moon didn‘t say anything unless spoken to, Clay sometimes would babble on about nothing. "I can't wait to get back to the ranch," Clay told Pale Moon. "You'll be surprised how beautiful it is. Pa didn't clear-cut when he put in the pastures, so there is plenty of woods all around the house. The family is going to be so happy to see you after all this time. I'll bet the first thing Ma fixes for us to eat is fried chicken and an apple pie. We have our own apple trees, you know. We can eat apples even in the middle of winter." Pale Moon looked at him sideways, thinking he boasted too much.

Pale Moon and Warrior made best friends with each other. They were in cahoots and got into mischief. It seemed to Clay he was constantly reminding the two of them to settle down. Her tears dried up, and Pale Moon began talking to him around the campfire each night.

Clay swore he could smell chicken frying the closer they got to the ranch. He asked Pale Moon if she could smell anything. "No, only the horses!" she replied.

* * * * *

Clay purposely didn't tell Pale Moon how long it would take for them to get to Montana. It would be a long enough ride without her counting the days and nights, and then being disappointed if they were delayed because of the weather or any other calamity. He hoped it would come as a nice surprise for her when they finally got to the end of the trail.

As they were sitting around the campfire one night, Clay asked, "Would you like to know anything about your new family? Aren't you curious about what your life is going to be like? Pale Moon shook her head. She wanted to know everything but didn't know how or what to ask.

I don't want him to think I am slow in the head, she thought, but I really would like to know about sleeping up in the air. Clay had never mentioned stairs leading up to the bedrooms again. Pale Moon listened to him babble on about the ranch. He didn't talk much about stuff a girl would be interested in hearing.

In the middle of a bright, sunny afternoon, after spending many days in the saddle, they walked out of the woods. Clay had a huge smile on his face. Pale Moon asked, "Is this Montana?" The clearing before them was pasture land surrounded by trees. Mountains rose up in the distance. It looked very much like places where her tribe had lived from season to season. The only differences were the fences outlining each pasture.

The two mounted up again; one returning to be married, the other to begin an entirely new life. Olivia was about to begin her journey of destiny.

* * * * *

Part II

Chapter 16

In a panic, her heart throbbing, Pale Moon pulled her horse to a stop. As far as she could see, fences were going in all directions. There would be no freedom here, she thought. She wondered, is this how white people live all penned up never going anyplace? Never leaving to find more food or fish, or get away from the cold? I should not have come. I'm not going to like it here. She opened her mouth to tell Clay, but he was gone.

Clay could not wait any longer. He let out a whoop and a holler and galloped across the pastures. His horse flew over a fence before he reined in to make sure Pale Moon was behind him. He was trying so hard to make it seem like a good thing to be here. When he looked back at her, it was obvious she didn't think so. Tears were swimming in Pale Moon's eyes again.

Clay turned and started back to Pale Moon. She poked her pony in the ribs. She wasn't about to try jumping a fence like Clay just did, but she couldn't find a place to get out on the other side. There were too many fences. She felt trapped. Clay watched the look of panic on her face. He went to her rescue.

Clay climbed down from Searcher, and motioned for her to ride over to the gate he held open. She took her own sweet time. Clay was tired, sick of the trail, and about out of patience with Pale Moon.

I have to remember to be patient with her, he thought, but this attitude may drive me crazy. If she thinks things have to go her way all the time, she's got another think coming. I'll have to warn the folks about this. Maybe suggest we let it ride and then gradually ease it around some. Clay shook his head as he finally closed the gate behind Pale Moon. Then, side by side they road toward the ranch house.

Warrior knew this was going to be a good day. He had missed his chickens. There weren't many animals to chase all the while they were gone. Anything that did come near the campground Clay either chased them off or took a shot at. Warrior was constantly warned to sit or stay and leave those animals alone. Warrior still wondered what it was about a skunk that Clay was forever warning him. Warrior spotted a hen scratching in the dust and took off in pursuit.

"We are home, Pale Moon. Look at Warrior chase his chickens. He never does them any harm, but Ma swears his chasing stops them from laying eggs," laughed Clay.

Pale Moon stared straight ahead. She was so frightened she could not find her voice. Adam came running out of the barn to see what all the commotion was about.

"They're home, they're here!" he yelled as he ran to the house to fetch Ma and Molly. He couldn't take his eyes off the beautiful girl on the snow white horse. Pa rode up to meet them on a horse he had been working with in one of the corrals, a big grin on his face. "It's good to see you, son. I saw you coming across the pasture. So, this is Pale Moon. Welcome to your new home, young lady. May we call you Olivia?"

Pale Moon was afraid to come down off her horse. She was surrounded by white people. Nothing looked familiar. They were all talking at once. Clay was acting like a fool dancing around, throwing his arms around the women and lifting them in the air. The small boy jumped on Clay's back and hung on.

The old man took the reins from Olivia. He walked her horse over to a big shady willow tree in the front yard. "Adam?" he called. "Would you get a bucket of water and a pocketful of oats for the horses?"

When the pony lifted its head from the bucket, Ben looked up at Olivia and held out his arms. "Come down from there and let's get you cooled off too." He smiled. Olivia slid into his arms. Ben felt her body trembling.

"Let's go meet the rest of the family and drink some cool lemonade," said Ben. He put his hand across her shoulders, coaxing Olivia towards Molly and Sarah. Clay stood back, watching.

Olivia dug in her heels. It was too much. There were too many people making too much noise. They kept trying to touch her. She didn't like that at all. Clay saw her distress and went to her rescue. "Come on, Olivia," he said as he took her hand and led her up the steps to the porch. He motioned for the family to stay behind, to give them a minute alone. Pale Moon looked like her heart was going to bounce out of her chest.

Clay opened the screen door. The spring squeaked and Olivia jumped. This was a new noise. She had no idea where it came from. Clay put his arms on her shoulders and more or less marched her through the doorway, into the house. Olivia immediately felt penned in. She tried to turn and head back out the door, but Clay held on and walked her a few more steps into the kitchen. "This is it, your new house. Better get used to it because you are not going to live outside any longer."

Clay led Olivia through the kitchen to the parlor. He pointed to a rocking chair. Olivia shook her head no. She was not interested in sitting down and letting those people surround her again. As scared as she was, all she really wanted to do was walk through the entire house. She finally found her voice, "I want to see the room that is high like a nest in a tree, and how to get there. I want to see where I can be all by myself."

"You are right. In your own bedroom no one will bother you unless you want them to enter. Let's go. I'll show you where you will sleep tonight."

Olivia thought it would be the perfect place to be right now.

"Remember, I told you about climbing some stairs to a place all your own. Here they are."

Olivia didn't know about this. Stairs, he called them. Clay instructed her, "You just take a step up from one to the next. With each step, we will rise up a little further until we come to another floor. That's where the bedrooms are. Just like birds fly up to their nest high in a tree."

It did not make any sense to her but she took a step anyway. She motioned for Clay to go ahead and lead the way. She held onto the back of his shirt all the way up to the landing. She felt light-headed, afraid to let go.

"Now that we are here, let's find your room, shall we?" asked Clay. He opened a door. Olivia looked inside.

"See, someone stays in this room already," said Clay. "Look at all the books and toys in here. That thing by the window is called an easel. Molly uses it when she paints her pictures. Your room is over here, on the other side of the hall. Let's go take a look."

Clay opened another door, surprised at what he saw. He sat down on the bed and beckoned to Olivia. She went to him, her eyes darting around the room. It looked like someone lived in this room, too. There was a beautiful quilt on the bed with dolls perched on the pillows. Spinning tops and jacks and a tiny rubber ball sat on a shelf along one wall. There were boxes of puzzles, and books, and a pile of tiny new dresses for the baby dolls. It all meant nothing to Olivia. She had no idea what anything was or how it was used. Once again, Olivia was speechless. Clay could see her bewilderment.

Sarah and Molly had spent hours putting the perfect room together for Olivia. They had even finished a quilt for her bed while

Clay was gone. They wanted Olivia to feel welcome when she got home. Adam and Molly put toys they had outgrown on the shelves.

Olivia climbed up on the bed next to Clay and leaned against him. She was exhausted. Clay bounced up and down making the iron springs deliver another strange sound. Pale Moon leaped off the bed shouting, "There is a bad spirit hiding in here. Do you hear it? We have to get away!"

Clay laughed. He got down on his knees to look under the bed. He pulled Olivia toward him, and said. "See, there is nothing evil hiding under the bed."

Olivia replied, "Just because you can't see it doesn't mean it's not there."

"Would you like to stay here for a while?" he asked. "I'll go back down the stairs and wait for you. Take your time. Look at everything. There is no hurry. We are home now so you can relax and get used to your new space. Remember what I told you. There are no evil spirits, nothing is evil in this whole house."

Clay left the door ajar and thumped down the stairs. Olivia was now alone, totally bewildered. Her family crowded her thoughts, all she wanted to do was go back to the riverbank and never leave them again, ever.

Olivia finally moved. She walked over to the window, pulled back on the lacy curtains, and looked out. It felt like her head would spin off her shoulders. She had never been so high in the air in her life. She felt like she could fly like a bird. She reached forward to spread her arms and banged into the window glass.

Olivia walked back to the bed, climbed up, and bounced like Clay had done. She wasn't heavy enough to make much of a noise, but it helped her realize it was only a sound and somehow she was making it. Olivia yawned and laid her head down. She fell asleep and was famished when she woke up hours later.

* * * * *

Chapter 17

While Clay was taking Olivia through the house, the rest of the family moved inside to the kitchen to all talk at once. Sarah poured fresh coffee. Molly placed a platter of freshly baked cookies on the table. When Clay came in from upstairs, he said, “Ma, I have never smelled or tasted anything better than your sugar cookies. Have you seen Abigail?” Clay asked.

“Not lately,” said Ma. “Abby just returned from her trip back East a few days ago. We haven’t been to town yet to welcome her home.”

“How was your trip in the wilderness this time?” asked Pa.

“Much easier,” replied Clay. “No big surprises this time, because I was better prepared. I didn’t go hungry or get hurt. It was a good trip. Just a very long one.”

Adam asked, “Did you have any real adventures along the trail? Did you meet any desperados, any gunslingers or mountain men? I hope you wrote everything down, Clay. I want to read your journal.”

Clay chuckled and said that no, he had not run into any scoundrels, and yes, he wrote something in his journal every night he camped. “It might be a little boring for an adventuresome guy like you,” he teased.

Adam went on, “Did you know I’m working full time for Pa this summer? Bookkeeping is easy. Pa lets me ride into town with him.

We go to the bank and do some real business, not just pretend stuff. That's so I can learn."

Molly asked if Olivia liked the dresses and shoes she had sent along. "I don't know," Clay told her. "It was just too much for her to take in, what with her leaving, getting the new pony, saying good-bye to everyone and everything she ever knew. She looked at the dresses and tried on the shoes. But, she was back in her moccasins in no time.

"In a few days, after she is rested up, why don't you spend some time in her room with her? Introduce her to some of your girlie stuff. Right now, she has no idea where she is, or what's going on around her. We have to give her time to adjust.

"We are going to have to be patient with her," explained Clay. "Pale Moon needs to feel she will be a real member of our family. She's missing her mother and baby brother a whole lot right now. It's going to be a tough job. I imagine it will take a lot of time and a lot of patience. If she starts balking at anything we'll just have to try harder. But we are committed to this and need to do a good job. We can do this!"

"Yes," everyone agreed, and began making plans how they were going to deal with this frightened little creature that was now a part of the family.

* * * * *

Olivia came down the stairs after the family had eaten supper. Sarah and Molly were just finishing up the dishes when they heard the stairs creak. Turning, Molly saw Olivia standing in the middle of the kitchen looking miserable. Molly knew that look.

She took Olivia's hand and led her outside, down a path to another smaller building. Molly held the door open and motioned for Olivia to go inside. She refused to budge. What kind of place is this, she wondered? It's dark and stinky, and there are bugs. Olivia shivered at the thought.

Molly stepped inside the tiny room, turned around, lifted her skirts and sat down. Olivia was totally bewildered until she heard the tinkle of water. She smiled at Molly and repeated what Molly had just done. Olivia made hand signals to Molly indicating this was much better than walking into the woods or high brush to find a private place.

The only drawback, as far as she could see, besides the bugs and spiders, was the distance between this tiny house and her room. It would seem even longer in the dark. Little did she know Molly also had a solution for that problem too!

When they returned to the house, Olivia smelled something so good it made her smile. Sarah had warmed up leftovers for her. "Sit down and have some supper, Olivia."

Everything on the plate looked strange, but Olivia ate it all, with her fingers. She rubbed her tummy to show Sarah how good it tasted. On their long trip, Clay had fixed nothing but stew and sometimes he gave her a handful of pemmican if she was lucky.

Sarah exchanged glances with Molly when Olivia scooped up the food in her fingers. "That's something else we have to be patient about," Sarah whispered to Molly.

"Tomorrow we are going to celebrate," Sarah told Olivia when she had cleaned her plate. "We will have fried chicken and mashed potatoes. There are vegetables from the garden, and Molly can make us a fresh apple pie. You girls can even pick the apples. How about that! Sound like a good idea?" Sarah really didn't expect an answer from Olivia.

Olivia stared at the woman who made such wonderful tasting food. I hope there is something just as good tomorrow, she wished to herself.

After it got dark, Olivia lay on her new bed, uncomfortable as all get out. Her back hurt, and she was too hot under the pile of blankets. She lay listening to the house creak and groan. There were no other sounds of the night; no owls hooted, no rustle of aspen leaves as the breeze lifted and tossed them. Olivia tossed and turned for hours. Finally, she slept soundly on the braided rug lying on the floor beside her bed.

* * * * *

Molly was excited about having a little sister. All the while Clay was gone, she had been busy making plans for things she and Olivia could do together. She hadn't fully realized that she and Olivia would not be able to communicate. Before he left, Clay had warned Molly that Olivia did not know their language, but she didn't give it a thought.

As patiently as the family tried to get Olivia to understand what they were saying, she would put her hands over her ears and turn away. Speaking more loudly only made it worse. Olivia constantly searched for Clay, the only one she trusted. The only one she chose to talk to.

It was a long first week for the family. They were so frustrated with Olivia, they wondered if she would ever understand anything. Sarah reminded her two youngest, who finally gave up and left her alone, this was not going to be easy. They paid no more attention to Olivia than need be. Olivia was relieved.

When Clay saw what was happening he sat the children down and asked them to make another effort. "You cannot ignore her," he said to Adam and Molly. "If Olivia is going to open up to anyone, it will be to you two. Try using more of the hand signals I taught you." Molly and Adam promised they would try harder to include Olivia.

Adam thought Olivia was the most beautiful girl he had ever seen. He never said so out loud. Even so, he could not get it out of his mind that she was an Indian. She refused to wear any of the dresses his mother made for her. Molly gave up showing Olivia more of her clothes. Adam complained about the stained buckskin dress Olivia had yet to take off. "And," he said, "it smells something fierce."

Molly said she had tried, but Olivia had no interest in clothes or any of the toys or books in her room. "She prefers to be outside," Molly told Clay and Ma.

"It's creepy when she sneaks from room to room touching things. She never asks what they are, but I have seen her picking up the forks and spoons. Candles are another thing that fascinated her. I'll try again with her. I promise," Molly assured them.

Ben had all the patience in the world with the girl, just like with his own children. Olivia liked the old man's face, and felt comfortable around him. "Will you say my name for me, Olivia? My name is Ben. I want you to call me that." She repeated his name several times before reaching out to touch his hand.

When the pressure was too much, Olivia would look for Ben. In his calm way, he told her he understood how difficult it was to leave behind her old ways and try to adjust to an entirely new life. "I don't think my own children could handle the same situation as well as you have, so far," Ben assured her. It seemed to him that Olivia was giving herself time, but he felt her frustration.

Olivia thought she could listen to his kind and gentle voice forever, even if she did not understand very much what he was saying. She knew everything would be all right as long as he was around.

* * * * *

Chapter 18

Ben gave Olivia a leg up onto her horse and they rode away from the ranch. He figured she had enough of people. "Let's ride over this way. I have a special place I want to show you. No one else knows about it. It's a quiet place where we can sit and talk. That is, if there is anything bothering you, or something you might like to ask."

Olivia smiled at the thought of spending time alone with Ben. She did need to get some answers to questions she was storing up to ask him. She had watched Clay teaching Ben the Indian words he knew and all the hand signals he and Olivia used. Ben was surprised how easily it was coming back to him.

Ben thanked Clay for spending time with him to refresh his memory. "The more we can communicate with Olivia, the easier it's going to be for all of us. I noticed that lately she is making more of an effort too."

The big man and little girl stopped along a creek winding its way along a fence line, then through the woods. They perched themselves on big rocks to talk and eat the lunch Sarah sent along. Olivia was in awe of this huge man who was so gentle. She liked him a lot and felt at ease for the first time in days, away from everyone else and all their activity. Some of the food they gave her still made her stomach queasy, but the jelly sandwiches today were going down just fine.

Ben asked Olivia if she missed the tribe and what her life was like in the Indian village.

"I miss my baby brother," said Olivia. "His name is Red Morning. I helped my mother take care of him every day. There are no babies here so I don't have anything to do."

Ben had taken Olivia away from the house on purpose. He knew it was time to explain a few more things to her, including her mother's journal. First, he told Olivia how he found journal. It was the first time anyone, other than her Indian family, told her what they knew about the raid and how she was taken away. She fully understood what happened to her; she was not really an Indian.

"I understand everything you are telling me," sighed Olivia. "Your family has been kind and patient with me, but I am so confused. There are questions I want to ask, but everyone talks at once. I don't know what to do!"

"I want you to take your time, but also," Ben advised, "try and learn your new language as quickly as possible. Life will be much more interesting once you understand all the words. Don't be afraid to say the words because you need the practice. We won't make fun of you if you get them wrong at first.

"I promise you one thing. Once you can communicate with everyone that lost feeling will go away.

"I don't ever want you to forget your native tongue," said Ben. "Learning a new language is not easy, but I know you can do it. You have to do it, Olivia. Clay and I can talk with you easily enough. If there is something the rest of the family doesn't understand, you just come to either one of us and we'll help you out. Just don't be afraid of something new."

* * * * *

When they returned to the ranch house, Sarah and Molly were busy doing laundry in the back yard. Olivia thought it a waste of time, spending all day making hot water when they could use the stream running through the pasture. She shook her head as she watched the women struggle with the clothes.

There are some things, she thought to herself, that I can teach these white people.

Little by little, day by day, Olivia and her new family began to bond. Olivia still refused to wear a cotton dress. Alone in her room, she never touched the colorful dresses and never once slipped one over her shoulders to see what it looked or felt like. She did try a pair of shoes and clomped around the room. They pinched her toes.

Adam happened to glance into Olivia's bedroom on the way to his own room. He watched her taking off the shoes. "Don't they fit?" he asked. Olivia shook her head. Adam dashed to his room and returned with a pair of outgrown boots. "Here, try these on. They are bigger than Molly's."

The boots were wide enough so her feet did not hurt, but they were too long. Within a few hours of clomping around Olivia had an enormous blister on her heel. She unlaced them and put the boots back in Adam's room. It seemed to Olivia that each day brought a new frustration.

Olivia was getting used to her bed although she still slept half the night on the floor. When she could not sleep at all she sat in front of the window, watching the moon rise and move across the sky. She wondered if Quaking Tree was watching the same moon. She wondered if Quaking Tree was missing her as much as Olivia was missing her Indian family.

Everyone in her new family was aware she seldom slept a night through, but prowled around the house. "Sometimes, said Molly, "I see her sitting in front of the window in her room. I wonder what she thinks about; probably her other family."

Sarah agreed that Olivia would always miss her Indian family. "I think she thinks about us too, wondering what is going to happen next. We spring surprises on her every day. It must be very frustrating for her."

Olivia conquered the stairs. She flew up and down just as fast as Adam and Molly. Sometimes she startled Sarah because she didn't clomp around the house making noise like the other children. Sarah always knew where they were. Olivia crept silently from room to room in her moccasins. She would stand staring until someone turned and saw her. Then she would speak or motion what she wanted.

Olivia developed a vocabulary big enough to communicate with everyone in the family. She went from one word statements to putting three or four words into a sentence. She understood most everything the family said to her. Sometimes, if it wasn't to her liking, she would pretend not to comprehend and shake her head or put her hands up.

If she did not understand something, she was no longer shy in asking questions. Olivia had taken it to heart when Ben told her that her life would be better the faster she learned the language. Everything he told her was coming true.

* * * * *

Leaves were beginning to change color and flocks of birds were darting here and there in search of the last of the berries and bugs before heading south. The creek was full of honking geese. Olivia's old habits could not be shed in just one season. She asked Clay, "When are we going to move south, out of the coming bad weather?"

"We are here to stay, Olivia," he replied. "Don't you remember that white people don't move for each different season? The cold weather won't hurt us because we keep the house nice and warm. We put a fire in that big iron box that sets in the living room, and the smaller one in the kitchen. If it gets too cold to sleep in your room, you come downstairs where it is warmer. We have plenty of food stored so we won't go hungry.

"There is one thing we must do before the snow flies. Let's go talk to Ma and see if we can go to town and get you a warm winter coat.

"When the snow gets deep enough, Adam and Molly can teach you how to build a snowman. And snow angels. I'll bet you have never seen a snow angel!"

Olivia was again mystified. "What is a coat and what are snow angels?" she asked.

* * * * *

Abigail and Olivia adored each other. The first time Abigail visited Clay at the ranch, she invited Olivia to take a walk with them down to the orchard. Abigail, or Abby, as she was often called, being the daughter of a school teacher, learned much from her parents. She knew all about patience when teaching someone to read, or write, or add and subtract. Olivia learned more proper English from Abby than from anyone in the family. Abby was thrilled to watch her student progress. Olivia was now eager to learn.

Abigail and Clay made tentative plans for a spring wedding. Abigail told Clay she wanted to be wed when wildflowers were in bloom and the fruit trees were full of pink blossoms. "Next spring is perfect," said Abigail. "It is a new season for the year, and a new beginning for us."

"How long does it take to plan a wedding?" asked Clay. "Seems to me we better sit down and figure out whom to invite, the food and drinks, so much to think about."

"You are right," said Abigail. "And, in the meantime, I want to go to Billings and do some shopping. There are more things available there I would like to have for our new home."

The seamstress in town, who was a good friend of Abby's mother, was impatient waiting for Abigail to choose a dress pattern. Like everyone else in town, she was looking forward to the wedding of this popular couple. She was sure Abigail would want to order special fabrics. There was not much of a choice at the local mercantile; certainly nothing appropriate for a wedding dress. Abby surprised her one day when she walked into the shop with a bolt of white fabric under her arm.

"Are you ready to begin sewing my dress?" asked Abigail. "I purchased this material when I was in Billings. I even have a sketch of the dress I would like you to sew for me. I saw it in a shop window. Each time I went back so see it I managed to draw in more detail. I hope the sketch is good enough so you can copy it."

The seamstress and Abigail spent hours going over the dress design, making sure each detail was included in the pattern. Finally, the day came when the paper pattern was laid out on the fabric and the first cut was made. Abigail tried not to make a nuisance of herself, but it was all she could do not to stop by the shop every day.

Clay just wanted to be married. He found it difficult to understand what all the women were going through; a crisis seemed to come up nearly every day. He was mostly concerned about building them a house. There didn't seem to be enough time.

Ben and Sarah assured Clay the ranch house was big enough to hold the married couple for the first year. After that, they would be on their own. It was something to think about.

In the meantime, Clay worked on a house plan. He wanted to surprise Abigail with the design. She often mentioned there were certain things she wanted included in the house. Clay made a list so he wouldn't forget to include her desires.

Ben asked Clay to meet him in the office in an hour. Clay stewed every minute wondering what trouble he was in or had caused, or even if it was bad news about the ranch, or horses.

Ben was waiting for him. As soon as they were seated, Ben said, "There are some things I need to discuss with you. Son, get that worried look off your face. It's nothing bad. In fact, you might like some of the ideas I have."

Ben continued, "Ma and I are thinking it's time I cut back a little and let you boys learn the horse business. The day after your wedding, you are going to be foreman-in-training of the -ABC- Ranch. We can't mix business with pleasure on Abby's big day."

Clay didn't know what to say, it was such a surprise. "Thank you, Pa. Thank you for putting a lot of faith in me. I know I can do the job. Thank you."

Clay was younger than most of the hands working with the horses. From that day on, he paid more careful attention to everything he could learn from them and his old man. He knew he could do the job. It was gaining the confidence of the cowboys he had to work on first. If he needed help, he knew Pa would be right there.

Adam was taking care of most of the paperwork. -ABC- Ranch had every operation on the ranch covered by the best they could hire.

* * * * *

Chapter 19

Christmas was an unforgettable experience. Later in life, Olivia would tell the story over and over again about her transformation that happened during this special time of the year. She attended church with the Hardistys often enough to understand their God. She liked him. She also liked the reverence of Mother Earth her Indian family held so dear. She never abandoned either during her lifetime.

Townsfolk knew all about the Indian girl whom Clay brought back from the wild. Naturally, they were curious and asked many questions. Eventually, the curiosity waned. It irked some people that she still wore that awful deerskin dress and her hair in a braid.

"She could at least dress up for the holidays," said one of the old biddies from town who happened to be shopping at the mercantile when Olivia was there.

"Time will tell," Sarah assured the ladies. "We are not going to force her. She has so much to deal with as it is. She'll come around one of these days. Maybe we should hope for a Christmas miracle."

* * * * *

A steady stream of friends and family visited at -ABC- Ranch during the holidays. Men congregated around the kitchen table and drank coffee while the ladies sipped tea and exchanged decorated Christmas cookies in the parlor. Many brought their special rum-soaked fruitcakes to share. Close friends brought small gifts to put under the tree.

Olivia was fascinated by the red and green decorations, and the iced cookies and cakes full of fruit. "What is this celebration?" asked Olivia. "Will there be much dancing and feasting?"

Ben explained his family Christmas traditions. "I imagine the young folks will do some dancing, and yes, there will be a feast, probably more than one. Some of it lasts for days and days, until we get tired of eating cookies and pies."

Olivia told Ben, "My mother taught me about our traditions, too. Festivals are in autumn when the crops are ripe and there is much corn. During the full moon, we dance and sing to honor Mother Earth for giving us food."

While Ben was reading passages from the Bible about Three Wise Men bringing gifts to the new Savior, Olivia suddenly understood.

She interrupted and declared, "This is a very important birthday but instead of Jesus getting gifts, we get them in his honor."

Everyone smiled and nodded in agreement, astounded at what Olivia had to say. "She knows more than she ever lets on," Ma commented to no one in particular.

At the beginning of the holiday season, Clay and Adam invited Olivia to ride with them into the woods to find a pine tree they could set in the living room and decorate. No matter how much she thought about it, Olivia could not imagine a tree in the house.

Adam let out a yell when he found the perfect tree. The boys cut it down and tied a rope around the trunk. They gave Olivia the rope so she could have the honor of towing the tree home behind her horse.

The family gathered around, watching Clay and Adam struggle to get the tree through doorways. They offered all kinds of advice. By the time they got it set up, the floor and carpets were soaked with melted snow. Green needles littered the path taken through the house to the living room.

Olivia stood back, watching the family having fun making such a fuss about the tree. Molly handed Olivia a red glass ball. "Be very careful with it," Molly reminded her. Hang it on a branch, like this."

Olivia joined in the fun, hanging beaded chains and more glass balls from pine branches. She thought it was more fun stringing popcorn and looping the ropes around the tree.

Olivia said to Sarah, "I have to remember to bring some of these special corn kernels with me when I visit my other family. What a surprise it would be for them. I can just see my little brother jumping back when the kernels began to pop."

Abigail and her parents were invited to Christmas dinner. Olivia couldn't get enough of the baked goose, corn and potatoes, the blueberry jelly, and pumpkin pie for dessert. She sometimes missed the simple fare that fed her tribe but Olivia's stomach had gradually adjusted to the rich food this family ate.

After dinner, Pa announced it was time to open gifts. "Oh no, not yet," exclaimed Ma. "We have to clear the table and do up the dishes before anything else happens. You men bring in more firewood and light the candles on the tree while we women clean up the kitchen. We won‘t be long."

Molly had carefully explained to Olivia that gifts would be exchanged on Christmas day. "After dinner, "she said, "all of us gather around the Christmas tree. Adam and I hand out gifts to everyone and then we open them. It is wonderful to get gifts," she went on, "but it's even more special if you make something special for each person. Let me show you what I mean."

Molly showed Olivia a pair of mittens she knitted for Adam and a new shawl for her mother.

All eyes watched Olivia as she opened her gifts one by one. She was embarrassed to have everyone watching her, but there was nothing to do about it. She took her turn, pulling on a beautiful red ribbon. Inside the wrapping was a small hand-tooled leather purse from Adam. "Thank you, Adam," Olivia smiled.

Adam twisted in his chair and ducked his head. Clay had braided Olivia a set of reins using the long lengths of hair from the tail of her pony.

Ben stood up, "I'll be right back." He returned carrying a miniature doll house made to look just like the real house where Olivia now lived.

Ben said, "I hope you like this, Olivia. I promise to make furniture for it this winter when it's too cold to work outside."

Olivia smiled at Ben as he set the house on the floor in front of her. She had never seen anything so wonderful. She hugged him around the waist. He hugged her back.

When Olivia opened her present from Sarah, tears came to her eyes. Olivia dashed from the room with the box under her arm. No one tried to stop her.

Olivia bound up the stairs to her room, slipped out of her deerskin and into the beautiful new red dress. She looked just like the ladies she had seen at the fort. She twirled around in front of the darkened window and smiled at her reflection. This is what she had been waiting for, something very special.

In the parlor, no one had moved or said a word.

"What have we done?" wondered Sarah aloud.

"I'll go see," replied Molly.

She met Olivia half-ways up the steps. They returned to the party together hand in hand. Everyone clapped their hands at the sight of Olivia in her new red dress. Olivia twirled and hugged Sarah. "Thank you, thank you!"

"I've got something for you too," said Molly. She handed Olivia yet another box tied with ribbons. Inside was a new pair of shoes and white stockings.

"Now your outfit is complete, Olivia. Let me show you how to button the shoes so they won't fall off." Olivia thought white people clothes could not be any more complicated.

Olivia stood up and twirled around again so everyone could see her. They clapped their hands together again. She felt ready to belong. This was her debut. Olivia knew she was ready to step into a new world. There was still much to learn, but nothing was better than this family and what was happening right now. Olivia had lost her shyness.

Then it was her turn to hand out gifts. Olivia had taken Molly's advice and made something for each member of her new family.

For Mary and Sarah, Olivia wove long dry pine needles into baskets. For Adam, she stripped bark from a birch tree and made a large basket to set by his desk in the office. Ben received a beaded watch fob, and Clay opened a box of agates she collected from the river beds they camped along on their way to the ranch. All of them expressed their delight at receiving such thoughtful gifts. Ma told Olivia they didn't know she could be so clever.

Olivia had a special gift for Abigail. During summer she watched Molly press flower petals between pages of a big thick book. Olivia asked Molly to help her press some flowers, too. They picked up beautiful colored leaves that fell during autumn, and also some leaves from a plant that could cure a sour stomach.

Olivia could not read, so it didn't make any difference which book she picked from the shelf to use for a flower press. Because the one she chose wasn't as heavy as the one Molly used, they found a large rock and set it on top to add weight.

Now it was time to give Abigail her gift. Abby wondered why Olivia handed her a child's story book. Olivia made a motion to turn the pages. Abby opened the book and with each new page she found a beautifully pressed flower.

Realizing there was nothing for Abigail's parents, Olivia walked over to the Christmas tree, and removed two birch bark decorations she had made; one in the shape of a heart, and the other was a spiral. She handed one to each of them.

From that point on, Olivia never again wore her Indian clothes. She carefully folded her deerskin dress and placed it in a big wood box in her room, along with the bead necklaces and moccasins she had worn into the house.

Every morning Olivia opened the closet door and chose a new dress to wear. Some days she even wore shoes. She felt sad about putting her past away, but at the same time she was excited about what was to come next.

* * * * *

Olivia thought Christmas would be over the next day and they would go back to doing what they always did, but Sarah had another surprise for her.

"Clay and Abigail are hosting a New Year's Eve party," said Ma. "They have invited all their young friends to the ranch to celebrate. We only have a week to make all the food and do some more baking. Are you ready for this? Everyone has to pitch in and help."

Sarah explained to Olivia that parties were held on this special day to welcome in a new year. "A year is equal to twelve full moons for your Indian family. Some people use the opportunity and promise themselves to try and do better; like promising to go to church every Sunday, or to not eat so much cake."

Olivia thought this was another strange idea white people had but after pondering it over she changed her mind. She thought about what she could promise to herself.

The night of the party was the most glorious thing Olivia had ever seen. This was far better than anything she had seen at the trading posts and Army forts. Clay's friends wore black suits and shiny boots. It wasn't often young people had an opportunity to dress to the nines, so everyone took advantage of the occasion. Most of the young men even wore a tie threaded through the collar of their shirts.

The young ladies wore long fancy gowns of every color. Some even had fur trim around the necklines and cuffs. Clay and Abigail waited at the front door to greet their guests as they arrived.

Olivia helped in the kitchen, placing cookies on fancy plates until Ma reminded her was time to go upstairs and change into her party dress. Olivia peeked around the corner into the living room where everyone congregated to admire the Christmas tree and dip from a bowl of red punch. It took Olivia's breath away to see the gowns in every color of the rainbow.

Although she didn't know any of their names, Olivia recognized many people from town. The young women looked so beautiful with their long hair pinned up off their necks, twisted into curls held in place by sparkly combs. The usually scruffy-looking neighboring ranch children were so dressed up Olivia barely recognized them.

Olivia dashed up to her room and slipped into her party dress. Sarah and Molly worked on it for a very long time. Olivia was impatient every time Ma said, "Come here, Olivia. You need to try on the dress one more time. We have to make sure it fits right. Next time you try it on we will check the length and then it will be finished."

The taffeta skirt rustled when she stepped into it reminding her of aspens shaking in the breeze. A wave of homesickness washed over her. She straightened up and stood still until it passed. This is what you wanted for me, isn't it my Indian mother? I miss you so much.

This is my new life, Olivia said to her reflection in the mirror. Tonight I make my resolution to leave the past. I know the family wants me to become one of them, but it is so hard not to think of the past. I promise to try. I also promise never to forget Quaking Tree, and Red Morning, and Sky In Water. This is my resolution for the new year.

Olivia pulled the leather thong from her braid and brushed her long, dark, wavy hair until it shone. Not being used to so much hair flying around her face, Olivia went to Molly's room for a ribbon to tie it loosely off her shoulders. Tiny curls sprung from the trap and framed her face. She looked in the mirror again. Olivia wondered who was looking back at her.

There is one more thing I must do, Olivia reminded herself. She opened the big trunk and took out the little deerskin pouch she had always worn tied around her middle. Olivia shook out the contents on her bed. She smiled. Everything was so precious and meant so much to her.

She picked up the little gold four leaf clover and tied it around her neck. I will never take it off, she promised. This little piece of gold has brought me to this place, and will take me even further.

Olivia quietly slipped into the living room where she perched on a corner of the settee. Adam looked at her twice before he realized it was Olivia. He poured an extra cup of punch and walked over to her. He could not get over how lovely she looked with those little spit curls framing her face. Adam was speechless when he handed the cup to her. Olivia did not look like an Indian any longer. It was all he could do not to tell her how good she smelled.

The fiddle players Clay hired to provide music arrived and settled themselves near the punch bowl. It went without saying that they were the guilty ones when it was discovered, late in the evening, the punch had been doctored.

It was so crowded in the parlor for dancing that before long couples were waltzing around in the kitchen and down the hallway. Olivia had never seen anyone dance while hanging onto each other. She went to find Molly.

Ben, Clay and Adam each asked Olivia to dance. She shook her head no. When the band played a slow tune, she finally relented. Adam held her and swayed to the music, still tongue-tied. Neither one of them knew the proper dance steps. Olivia felt she was once again being invited into their world.

It was very late before the last guests departed, and much later than usual before anyone in the house woke up the next morning. Over a steaming cup of coffee, Clay asked, "Olivia, what did you think about the New Year's Eve party last night? Did you have fun? I saw you dancing with Adam, but you didn't dance with me. Maybe next time you will?"

Olivia grinned and said she liked the party very much. "I promise to dance with you next time, Clay. Adam stepped on my toes!"

Clay laughed and promised there would be no stepping on toes when she danced with him.

Ma and Molly gushed over Olivia, complimenting her on how beautiful she looked with her hair undone from the braid. Pa said, "I have never seen a more beautiful girl than you were last night, Olivia. Except for my wife, of course, but you understand."

Everyone laughed and ate their pancakes and bacon.

While they were eating, Olivia told them about her New Year's resolution. Ma looked at her skeptically. Olivia thought the others seemed to be pleased with the promises she had made for herself, but no one said anything. They just nodded their heads in agreement. It made her unsure if she had done the right thing in telling them.

* * * * *

Sarah and Molly were so elated that Olivia gave up wearing her leather dress. It really did smell terrible. When Olivia appeared New Year's Eve with her hair down around her shoulders they knew she had made some important decisions. Neither of them pressed the issue or went on and on about how she looked; rather they began teaching her how to take care of her hair and clothes.

On a sleigh ride to town to do some shopping, Ma told Olivia, "I want you to pick out ribbons while we are at the mercantile. Pick one to match each dress. We need to choose some more yarn for caps and mittens too. The boys go through mittens so fast I can't keep up."

When they got to the store, Olivia took her time choosing colored ribbons. It was the first time she had ever purchased anything for herself. Before now, everything she owned had been handed to her by someone.

Right off, Molly knew Olivia was not interested in playing with dolls. Olivia told her, "I took care of my baby brother. It doesn't make sense to me to take care of something that never cries or has to be fed." The dolls disappeared from Olivia's bed to live on a shelf in the closet with glass doors.

With everyone in the house during the harsh winter weather, Olivia's English lessons intensified. The men folk were looking for something to do. They took it upon themselves to teach Olivia how to write her name, to tie a beautiful bow in her hair, and how to rub oil into the leather of her shoes and saddle to keep them soft and comfortable.

"I'm going to teach you how to read," said Adam. It was frustrating for both of them. "I think you better leave reading up to Abby," said Clay. Olivia nodded in agreement.

Adam and Olivia placed most of the books back on the shelf but Adam kept back one. "I'll read this one to you, Olivia," he said.

When Clay returned from the wilds with Olivia, he gave Adam the journal he wrote in every day while he had been gone. "Don't read this all at once," said Clay. "I don't know if I wrote enough to keep your interest. Sure hope so."

At the time, Adam glanced through it and then tucked it away in a drawer to read later. He savored the thought of curling up next to the fire and reading during the long, cold days of winter when he was stuck inside.

On a particularly stormy day, while lying on his bed staring at the ceiling, Adam suddenly remembered the journal. He jumped up to retrieve it from his bookshelf. He began turning pages.

* * * * *

Chapter 20

Traces of winter were nearly gone. The geese were returning and landing in the river. The only snow in sight was far off on the mountain tops. Abby told Clay it was time to make final plans for their wedding. “If we wait much longer, the apple blossoms will all be gone,” she explained. “I know we are taking a chance with it maybe raining, but I do want to be married outdoors while the orchard is blooming and the pastures are full of wild flowers.

“The air will smell so sweet,” she told Clay. “The dresses for my bridesmaids are pale pink to match the blossoms. It will be perfect. And, we can invite as many people as we want. There’s room for everyone outside. We will have chairs for our folks, but everyone else can stand. The ceremony won’t take that long.”

“All right,” said Clay. “We can use one of the barns for the party and dance afterwards. We need room for the whole town, right?”

“That’s right! Let’s get all this written down so we don’t forget details.”

Abby chose Molly and three of her friends from town to be her witnesses. She gave Olivia the special task of carrying a basket of apple blossom petals that she was to drop along the path up to where the minister stood.

Ma told Olivia, “In the bottom of the basket, on a tiny white, satin pillow, I am going to loosely stitch the gold rings Clay and

Abigail will give each other during their wedding ceremony. When it comes time, the minister will ask for the rings and you are to hand him the basket."

Olivia was curious about the rings. Ben explained to her, "The rings are a symbol of love. They are very special. Let's look at Sarah's ring. Do you see that it has no end? Just like love. It goes on forever."

* * * * *

The new Mrs. Hardisty moved some of her clothes into Clay's room just off the kitchen, but there was not enough space for everything. Abby groaned, "I can't wait now until we have our own house."

The room offered only a bit of privacy for the couple in a busy household. Ben didn't notice. He was so happy to have Clay and Abigail still in the house. "There's no rush," Ben insisted, "to get your house up right away. Take your time. Take a year, or two! There is plenty of room upstairs for anything you want to store."

At first, Clay thought nothing about it, but the longer they stayed in the ranch house, the sooner both of them wanted out.

"We need more privacy," moaned Clay. "I need more space, and a bigger bed! You need closets and a place for your pretty things. We can't even use the gifts people gave us for our wedding."

Molly and Olivia loved having a new sister-in-law. "No matter what," Adam kept insisting, "she is still the school teacher's daughter."

Each evening after dinner, Clay and Abigail walked to the site they had chosen for their new home. Clay pounded stakes into the ground and they used twine to mark off each room. "I want lots of bedrooms and lots of children to fill them up," said Clay.

"So do I," agreed Abby. "Promise me you will build the biggest kitchen anyone has ever seen. I want the dining room big enough for a long table and chairs for all our children, and all their grandparents, and aunts and uncles and cousins at Christmas time."

Clay disappointed her when he told her they couldn't start building until late summer. Abby was anxious to start a family.

"First," he said, "the cowboys and I have to spend a lot of time getting new horses broke and ready to sell. By then it will be time to bring in the hay to feed them all winter. It's going to be a busy summer, but once it's over, we will get to work on the house."

Each time Sarah and Abby and Molly took the buckboard to town, they spent hours looking at fabrics for curtains, table cloths and quilts. Abby had worked on her hope chest since she was a little girl, so there were lots of towels and antimacassars, along with embroidered night dresses and pillowcases.

* * * * *

"Ma," said Clay. "Will you make fried chicken, mashed potatoes and baking powder biscuits for dinner, with apple pie for dessert?"

"What's the occasion, son?" she asked. "Are you and Abigail celebrating something special?"

"No. No. It's nothing like that, Ma. This Wednesday is the anniversary of the day Olivia came to live with us. I thought we might do something special for her. She's come so far and learned so much. I think we should celebrate. Can we keep it a surprise?"

* * * * *

Ben and Olivia once again rode away from the ranch and into the woods. At times when she felt imprisoned, Olivia went looking for Ben. Since their first ride together she went to him whenever she felt overwhelmed.

As they rode along, Olivia asked, "Where do Molly and Adam go every day? Adam told me they go to school. What is that? Don't you like them? Why do you send them away? They don't come back for hours and hours."

"I love my children," Ben told her. "But you see, they have to go to school every day and the school house is in town. If we are too busy to take them in a wagon they have to get up a little earlier and walk. By the time they walk home again after school they are pretty tired. It's a long day for both of them."

Olivia figured out many things on her own, but his answer still left her bewildered about what went on at school. It didn't sound like anything she was interested in doing.

The family decided Olivia would begin school in the fall. If it didn't work out, they could always keep her home until the next year.

Sarah did ask Abby to talk with Olivia about it. "I don't want her to feel so much pressure about school. I know she will refuse to go. Maybe you can persuade her to at least give it a try."

Abigail was always a very good student. She was thrilled to tell the child about her wonderful experiences and the things she had learned. She tried to make it sound like the most exciting and interesting place that Olivia could ever hope to be.

Olivia wasn't buying it. "I already know lots of stuff," she told Abby. "All I need is for Adam to teach me some more how to read. Molly has been helping me practice writing my name. That's all I need, isn't it?"

School never started in the fall until all the farmers and ranchers had their crops in the barns. Every son was needed in the fields this time of year. There were no excuses. Not even school was allowed to interfere. Timing was all-important. The haying had to be done while the sun still rode high in the sky, before cold rain and snow were expected which would ruin the crops.

Ben and Sarah took the children to town on a Saturday afternoon to buy school clothes. Molly and Adam always got a new pair of shoes. Molly could pick out one store-bought dress. She could choose from several bolts of cotton for more dresses and dirndls that ma would sew for her. Ma picked out fabric to make shirts for Adam and Ben.

Ben helped Adam pick out socks, an extra set of boot laces, and a set of long johns, then piled several pair of trousers in his arms.

"We will get you one pair in each size for this year's growth, son. The rate you are stretching out, one pair won't last but a month. I just hope your feet don't grow as long as your legs have over the summer," he kidded.

Olivia poked at each bolt of cloth but didn't have much to say. She thought she had plenty of dresses. Sarah insisted she pick out at least two pieces of fabric.

"Look for simple cottons," said Molly. "These dresses will be for every day, not like the ones Mother made for you for the parties. Won't it be fun not to have to wear the dresses I have outgrown? These will be all your own." Olivia still was not encouraged.

Molly was warned not to mention Olivia going to school. It was all she could do to hold in her enthusiasm for the new school year. After the girls made their choices, Molly suggested, "Why don't you pick out a slate too, Olivia? You could practice writing her name some more on it."

Ben and Sarah looked at each other and thought, step number one. "How clever of you, Molly," Sarah said when they were out of earshot of Olivia.

Olivia rode home in the wagon holding her one package. The slate was all she wanted. There were no new clothes or fabric or shoes. Olivia sensed something was going on but she could not figure it out. She wasn't going to school, so what else could it be?

Over chocolate cake after supper that night, Ben brought up the subject of school once again. He asked the children if they were happy with their purchases.

"When do you think school will begin?" he asked. Adam thought maybe two weeks yet. "I rode over by Jacob's house two days ago and they were still working in the fields."

"They aren't anywhere near finished, Pa," said Adam. "They still have a lot of cutting to do. I just hope they finish up in two weeks. I want to get back to school and learn some new bookkeeping. I've been thinking about asking Mrs. Fisk if she will help me with balancing all the books. Clay says he would like to have more detailed accounting, but I don't even know what that involves. She can teach me, can't she Pa?"

Ben saw an opportunity to make school sound like a good place to be. He began by drawing everyone into the conversation with a wink of his eye. Olivia refused to even look at him. She stayed real quiet, hoping no one would pay any attention to her.

"Are you ready for the big day too, Olivia?" asked Clay, testing the waters.

"I'm not going."

"Not going?" said Ben. "Well, I hate to tell you this, Olivia, but it's the law. Every youngster has to attend school until they graduate from eighth grade. You are not old enough to not go to school."

It was very quiet around the table. They waited for her reaction.

Olivia sighed and said, "I told you. I'm not going."

Everyone looked at Abigail. Sarah mouthed the words, "Talk to her."

"Olivia," said Abby. "Once you get there you will discover what a wonderful place it is. You will learn to read and write. You'll learn about the oceans and other countries, and our president and the Civil War. Oh, there's just so much to read about and talk about. There will be lots of kids your age to play with, too.

"When you get to be sixteen, and if you really love going to school, you can continue. You can learn to be a teacher, or an accountant like Adam, or a librarian who is surrounded by more books. You could even go away to another town to a special school called college. It is your choice. Isn't it wonderful?"

"Why? I know lots already. I told you all I need is for Adam to finish teaching me about reading. I can already sign my name."

"I tell you what," Sarah suggested. "Let's go into town and talk to Mrs. Fisk. I saw her at the school house this afternoon, cleaning up the place, and getting it ready for the new school term. Maybe after you have talked to her you will feel differently about it. Let's give it a try."

Olivia knew there was no way she was getting out of it.

* * * * *

After a shaky start, Olivia found her place in school. It was hard going at first. Olivia was a quiet girl, not used to being in a room full of noisy strangers. She wasn't used to being cooped up. She missed being outside. Once the classes settled into a routine, Olivia began participating more and more.

This is nothing like the way Quaking Tree and Sky In Water taught me things, remembered Olivia. She decided she was going to ask Mrs. Fisk if she could teach for just one day. If Mrs. Fisk said it would be all right, Olivia would take the children outside and teach them everything she knew. And it wouldn't take a whole year!

* * * * *

Chapter 21

It came as no surprise to Mrs. Fisk how quickly Olivia learned to read and write. She had several conversations with Ben and Sarah about how to handle the child but her concerns proved groundless.

Ben informed Mrs. Fisk that he had stressed to Olivia the importance of learning the language and how much easier her acceptance would be once she could understand what was going on around her, and be part of it!

"Evidently, Olivia took what I said to heart," he told her teacher. "We've also helped her a little at home. The children taught her some reading skills and how to write her name. Simple things like that."

Olivia didn't like it when she was assigned to sit with the little first grade children. Before the end of the school year, she had learned enough to be moved up where she had a desk with schoolmates her own age.

It was Adam's last year of school. He was cramming as much information into his head as possible. He stayed after school two or three times a week to study advanced math books with Mrs. Fisk.

"I am going to be the best bookkeeper possible," he told Mrs. Fisk, "with your help, of course. I've got an office already set up. The more I learn, the more I can be a help to Pa and Clay. At least I won't have to be on a horse every day and out in foul weather. I'm not much of a cowboy." Adam laughed and said, "I'm more the indoor type."

On awards day, at the end of the school term, Adam was awarded a purple ribbon for best math student. Olivia won a red ribbon for most improved, and Molly won red ribbons for reading the most library books and best writing.

* * * * *

Clay and Abigail finally began construction on their log house. They built on the opposite side of the river from the ranch house, far enough away to have privacy, yet close enough to walk over to the barns and sheds, or to visit with Ma and Pa.

Pa gave the foreman reins to Clay. Ben told Sarah: "He's doing a good job of it so far. I'm going to take some steps back and let him make more decisions."

Sarah smiled. "Good luck," she wished them.

Pa accepted some decisions Clay made. Others were discussed many times at great length, with much shouting back and forth. Mostly, they agreed to disagree, then it was a toss-up whose decision would be final, and it started all over again.

The ranch hands laughed at the shouting matches. With each argument, Clay learned a little more about running the ranch and the horse business.

It boiled down to Clay running the physical part of the ranch, while Pa did the managing. Clay shook his head after an argument about working the cowboys.

"You still have the last word, don't you Pa? The day will come when that will turn around on you. Just wait and see."

"Son," Pa reminded him, "you have got to get a few more years under your belt working with the hired hands. They cannot be bullied into something they don't particularly want to do. It just takes time to learn how to get the best out of them. They got to be treated right, or they walk. It happens every time."

* * * * *

While Clay and Pa went off breaking and taming wild mustangs, on buying trips, or tied up in a difficult sale, Abigail started a new sewing project.

On one of the few times she had managed to get away by herself to go into town, she bought soft flannel cloth for sleepers and blankets. Abigail whispered to Mrs. Larson at the dry goods, "You have to promise not to say a word to anyone about my purchases. Not a hint to anyone in the family either." Mrs. Larson agreed to keep her secret.

Abigail had told no one yet, not even Clay, they were going to have a baby. She calculated it would be around Thanksgiving time.

Young Lee, as he would always be called, was born the second week in November. Mr. and Mrs. Clay were ecstatic over their baby boy.

Abigail insisted Thanksgiving be held at their house, even though construction was not totally completed. It was time to start some new traditions.

* * * * *

Adam, now employed full time by the ranch, moved his office from the barn into Clay's old bedroom off the kitchen and set up shop. Pa kept his old office space in the barn to meet with the hands and talk business with buyers who came through.

When Adam wasn't particularly busy, he read Clay's journal over and over. He wanted to know as much about Pale Moon as possible. Clay had written with great insight about the child he had led out of the forest.

* * * * *

Molly and Olivia were both ready for school to start again in the fall. This was Olivia's last year, as far as she was concerned. She wasn't shy about letting the family know it. Her new parents often expressed hope she would continue and then study literature at college.

Olivia thought about what she would do when she was finished with school. She didn't know what to do. The Haristys couldn't keep her with them forever. She was much too young to think about marriage and children. Olivia definitely made up her mind not to be a teacher. Being cooped up all day long was still not to her liking.

If Olivia had stayed with Quaking Tree, she never would have left the tribe. In this new life, it was expected that she would move on and take care of herself, or be married someday.

The folks often hinted to Olivia about her future.

"If, as you say, this is your last year in school, what will you do after that?" asked Ma. "As long as you are in school you are welcome to stay here at the ranch. And that includes the years going to college."

The subject of her grandparents in Boston occasionally came up. Ben felt an obligation to keep them alive in his conversations with Olivia, even though he had never met them.

"If you decide not to continue with school, maybe you would like to visit your grandparents back east," suggested Ben. Olivia had much to think about.

* * * * *

After surviving a childhood fever, Molly never fully recovered all her energy. She didn't have the strength to keep up with her friends at school, so she turned to books and writing. During a particularly bad spell, when the heat was too much for her, Pa gave her Mary's old journal to read.

"I think you will find this very interesting reading. I hope it will take your mind off your misery."

Reading the journal was a great inspiration for the budding writer. Molly asked, "Pa, do you still have the things you found in the pail? If you do, could I see them some day."

He replied, "Everything is still in the pail on a shelf in the bedroom closet. Come along and we'll take a look at them."

Pa had something to say about each item as he removed them from the tin pail. "I believe this is part of the arrow that struck Olivia's mother. The other half was stuck in her side when I found her. I know the buckle belonged to her husband because I had seen him wear it most every day. The little dress could only be one of Olivia's. As for all this money, some day, I will give it to Olivia. It is hers, after all."

Molly wrote a story about finding an old belt buckle out on the prairie and another about a broken arrow. She shared her stories with Abby, who then took them to her mother.

"Do you think they are good enough to be printed in the newspaper?" she asked. "It would be such good inspiration to the children to see their stories published."

Mrs. Fisk was always impressed with Molly's writing and replied, "Yes, I'm sure they are. These latest stories are much more mature than those she has written in the past. If she keeps up with it, she could be a very good writer some day. Wouldn't it be a thrill to read a book written by our own little Molly?"

Abby talked to Molly about taking her stories to the newspaper office. Molly was thrilled beyond words but admitted she was much too shy to approach Mr. Denison herself.

"I'll do it for you, then," said Abigail. "Choose your best stories, and I will take them with me next time I have to go to town. I went to school with Mr. Denison's son. I've talked to him lots of times."

They kept their plan a secret from the rest of the family, just in case. They had to wait a month before one of Molly's stories was featured in the newspaper.

On the last day of school, at the awards assembly, Molly was presented with the grand literary award along with her diploma. Because of her health, she had already decided not to go away to college. At the end of summer, she was hired by Mr. Denison to write articles and help edit the newspaper.

* * * * *

Chapter 22

No one knew for sure exactly when Olivia was born. They knew the year from reading Mary's journal but not the date. Sarah, feeling extra motherly, chose October 21.

On her next birthday, Olivia received a fine gold chain from Ben. He told her it was for her lucky four-leaf clover. His fingers were too thick and clumsy, but between the two of them they got the gold charm off the leather thong and onto the new chain. Olivia never removed the gold necklace.

The day after her birthday celebration, Ben once again led Olivia on her white pony to their favorite spot in the woods. They nestled near the rocks out of the wind to eat sandwiches and talk.

Olivia asked Ben, "Tell me again about when you were a scout for the wagon trains, just one more time." Olivia never tired of listening to him. She knew about the pail that held clues to her story.

Ben also talked about letting Clay go out on his own to hunt for her and bring her back. Each time she listened to Ben relate her story, Olivia learned a little something more, something new she had not understood before; like realizing how young Clay had been the first time he went looking for her.

"Why did you let Clay go such a long ways all by himself when he was so young?" she asked. "He could have been hurt or killed. You would never have known what happened to him. Your son would have been lost no matter how many times you went looking for him."

"It was something his mother and I decided he had to do. The boy had such a case of wanderlust, always wanting to see what was beyond the horizon. He would light out, never telling us where he was going or when he would be back. This time we knew. That trip made him into a good man.

"Olivia," said Ben, bringing up the subject of her family once again, "your mother wrote in her journal that she wanted nothing more for you than to be with our grandparents in Boston. That is, if you chose to come live among us. You are getting to the age now where you can make up your own mind. Make some of your own decisions. This will have to be one of them. Understand that we won't send you away if you don't want to go.

"At this point, we don't know if your grandparents are aware you are still alive. We aren't even sure if they were ever notified their son and his wife were killed in the Indian massacre and you survived. There just isn't any way to know until we talk to them. We haven't taken it upon ourselves to do that, seeing as how they are your family. Your mother made it pretty clear she wanted you making the decisions."

"This sounds like the same thing I had to go through when Clay came for me. It was my decision if I wanted to go with him or not," said Olivia. "I am glad I made the choice I did. I like being here with you and your family on the ranch. Abby is my best friend. I love every one of you. I'm just getting used to living here. I can go days now without thinking about my Indian family or missing them so terribly I think I will die.

'This is a much better life than I would have had with Quaking Tree and Sky In Water. I saw the things people did and said to my mother. A lot of them hated her for being a wife and not a slave. The same thing would have happened to me. This is much better no matter how much I miss them.

"And now you are asking me to leave again," she continued. "I like it here. Nothing bad ever happens. There is always enough food, and it is so easy to keep warm. I like it here, Ben."

"No, I didn't say you had to leave. Whether you stay or go is all right with us. If you want to go to Boston, you don't even have to leave right away. If you go now, we thought we would send Adam with you. You think about it. Take your time. When you decide what you want to do, let us know. Then and only then will we make arrangements.

"There is one more thing I need to talk to you about," Ben continued. "I still have the little pail that held your father's belt buckle, your tiny baptism dress, and some other things. Maybe, I'm thinking, you would like to take them to your grandparents. It's just something else to think about. Like I said, take your time and let us know. We haven't said anything to Adam about maybe accompanying you on the trip. If you decide, that is."

Olivia didn't know what to do. In the end, she chose to stay in school until she graduated.

"I've gone this long, so a couple more years isn't going to change anything," she told Sarah. "By then I will be nearly sixteen. I'm too scared right now to leave this place. I had never been any place out of the woods until I came to this ranch and then into Fort Benton. That's it. I don't know anything about anywhere else. I'll talk to Adam about going with me when the time comes. Until then, he can show me on a map where this Boston place is and how we get there."

Sarah could not wait to tell the family Olivia would be with them for a few more years at least. None of them wanted her to leave.

Adam and Molly thought that if she did get to Boston, she might like it too much and never come back.

Clay was especially happy with the decision. "Now," said Ben to Clay, "I feel like we have kept our promise to Mary. Well, almost.

Just a few more years and Olivia will be with her grandparents. I hope it will be for just a short time. I sure would miss that little gal if she decides to stay in Boston. You never know with Olivia. She's come a long ways from her past experience to who she is today."

* * * * *

Olivia enjoyed school more each year. Mrs. Fisk gave her extra projects that required extensive reading and writing. There was so much history her star pupil needed to catch up with if she was thinking about college. Mrs. Fisk was sure Olivia would continue her education.

It was all new to this brilliant child with an insatiable thirst for knowledge. Olivia told her teacher that a long time ago Ben said if she learned to read and write the whole world would be right at her doorstep.

"At the time," said Olivia, "I didn't have any idea what he meant but now I know. Book reports are my favorite thing. I can remember when I thought if I could write my name that was good enough. Ben knew what he was talking about."

Olivia was given an opportunity to teach her outdoor class near the end of the school year when the students were restless after so many months indoors. Mrs. Fisk hadn't let her do it when she was so young because the other children would not have believed anything Olivia told them.

On the other hand, if she were older, they would tease her about being teacher's pet, and who did she think she was to teach them anything? Now was just the right time and age.

When her big day arrived, Olivia was ready. She did her homework and marked a trail ahead of time through the woods with stops along the way to point out medicinal herbs and various trees and how the wood was used. Olivia was forgetting some of the Indian words that used to come so easily because she didn't use them every day.

She and Clay bantered back and forth at times in her first language, especially when they did not want Adam to know what they were talking about, or just to tease him.

Olivia tried her hardest to remember everything that Sky In Water told her about preserving the land, the rivers and forests. To Olivia, it just made good sense to leave something for the next generation of children.

The students spent most of their day long the riverbank learning how it sustained life. "This river," said Olivia, "will one day supply water for thousands of people. All of us have to take care of it now so it never runs dry and our cattle and horses die. I can teach you about irrigation so the crops will not shrivel up and die from lack of water. Water is life.

"Water can also be your enemy," she continued. "It can make you sick enough to die if you drink from where animals have been. It can drown you by pulling you under or flooding our homes. Water is like a god. It is to be respected."

Olivia asked the younger students to pick leaves from each tree and plant they were able to identify. She stressed the importance of taking only what they needed.

"Never take more," Olivia instructed. "When you come back, you want it to be there again. If too much is taken, the bushes, trees and animals all die. Think about the disappearance of the buffalo and why that happened. Too many were taken just for the thrill of the hunt."

When the students returned to the school house, Olivia showed them how to press their leaves and blossom petals between pages of a book. When the leaves dried they would be pasted into scrapbooks labeled by each student with its name, where it had been found and when, and a little something they had learned about the plant.

* * * * *

Chapter 23

Ben died when Olivia was sixteen. She had seen death before and accepted it as the way of nature. This was different. This was personal. This was between her and her spirits and she could not understand how any of them could be involved in such a tragedy.

Ben's death was simple and it was quick. He did not suffer. Ben was helping a ranch hand shoe a horse. One of the dogs came around a corner of the stable chasing a barn cat. The horse spooked and kicked out, landing his hoof right smack on Ben's right temple.

Sarah had always carried one great fear in life. She often thought about one of her men not coming home. Riding all over and looking for wild mustangs often took Ben and Clay into treacherous country. She just knew that, someday, either one of them would come riding in strapped across their saddle.

Sarah could year yelling and shouts for help coming from the stable area. She met the hands who carried Ben to the house at the bottom of the steps. "Ben, Ben, don't leave me. Please don't leave me. Open your eyes, Ben. I'm right here. Open your eyes!" she sobbed.

Toby, one of the older hands who had been at the ranch a long time, told Sarah that Ben had died instantly, before he even hit the ground.

"He took a good wallop to the head, ma'am. He just closed his eyes and sank to the ground. I don't think he felt any pain at all."

Olivia thought her heart would break. Clay had rescued her, but Ben was the one she went to in time of need.

"I loved that old man," she cried. "It isn't fair. I need to talk to him some more. Why did you do this, God? You are supposed to take care of people, not take them away."

Olivia got sick and tired of everyone hugging her and telling her it would be all right. She knew better. Things would never be the same for her.

I have to start all over again, thought Olivia. This time it will be different. Everyone I ever loved is gone. That will not happen to me again.

After the funeral, Sarah sat down with Clay and Adam to talk about the ranch. Molly and Olivia stood quietly listening at the kitchen door. Abigail was hushing her babies in one of the upstairs bedrooms.

Clay opened their conversation when he said, "Olivia is the only one you have at home anymore, Ma. Maybe it would be easier for you in town. You could buy a nice house and get away from all the hard work out here on the ranch."

Sarah would have none of it. "I've always lived in the country with your father. What would I do in town? Sip tea and gossip with the neighbors? That would drive me insane. I'm staying here, right where Olivia and I belong. That includes Adam, too. There will be no more talk of anyone moving away.

"We can manage. Between you boys and what I know about it, we can run the ranch the same as always. Our hands know the routine. I don't foresee any major changes to consider.

"Your father would want us to stay on the ranch. He was so very proud of all of you. Nothing was more important to him than being a family. So that's what we will continue to be; a family. And this is a family run ranch, right children?"

Clay and Adam both assured Sarah they would, and could, handle the responsibility of the ranch. "We want what's best for you, Ma," said Adam, speaking with tears in his eyes that he refused to let flow down his cheeks.

Over the years, -ABC- Ranch grew bigger and bigger. Hundreds of horses were bought, traded, tamed, and doctored every year. The race track was improved time and time again. The latest innovation was a small set of bleachers for spectators.

Ben and Sarah never charged anyone for the use of what they made available. Thousands of dollars had been raised at many charity events. The school children still came out for their annual sports day and picnic at the end of each school year.

Sarah would allow no changes. "Things were just fine the way they were, and they will stay that way. Clay, if there are problems you cannot solve come to me. I know how this ranch runs. Every evening, your father and I talked about what happened during the day. I doubt there isn't much he did not tell me. It's still the -ABC- Ranch and it's going to stay that way. We have a reputation to protect."

Clay shook his head and agreed, awed by his mother's tenacity.

* * * * *

Olivia stayed in school, but it took everything she had not to return to Quaking Tree. Ben was the closest to her; she missed his gentle ways so much it was often hard to make it through another day without him.

Late one night, when she could not sleep, Olivia opened the big chest at the foot of her bed. She took out the deerskin dress she wore when Clay brought her to the ranch.

She wanted to take off her cotton night gown and slip into the soft suede, but the dress was much too small. I guess that tells me something, she thought. If I went back to my other family, it wouldn't feel the same either. Her fingers traced the outline of the beads. I am grown up now. I can take care of myself.

Olivia folded the leather dress and laid it back in the chest. She touched the four leaf clover hanging around her neck. Ben told her she could go see her grandfather in Boston. She considered the thought that maybe now was the time.

* * * * *

"No," said Adam. "You cannot run away. It won't bring him back. Stay one more year. You will be out of school. Then you can decide what to do. We would like you to stay here but I know it's very important for you to meet your grandparents.

"Remember the part in your mother's journal where she asks that you be returned to your people in Boston? Well, we'll see that you get there, only not this minute!"

Clay came walking up the path to talk with Adam about ordering supplies. When he saw Adam and Olivia with heads together, he figured he was interrupting something so he turned to go.

"No, stay," said Olivia. "You need to be part of this too. I just wish someone would tell me what to do. I am so confused about everything. I miss Ben so much. How will I ever find my way without him?" she cried.

Clay took her hand and said, "We are all here, Olivia. Don't be afraid. You can stay here, or you can go away. I know Ma has talked to you about it, and Abby as well. We want what is best for you. It's just a matter of time before things get back to normal.

"Personally, I don't think you should leave with just a year of school left. If you are considering going to Boston to meet your grandparents, I don't think this is the right time. Do you want to spend your last year in a new school with all new people?

"Finish up here and you will be free as the wind. Go to Boston then. Go to college. Go to a big city and teach. Just never forget us, or your Indian parents, wherever you do go."

"You make so much sense, the two of you," Olivia told Clay and Adam. "I hadn't thought about going to school in Boston. It would be a waste of everything if I didn't graduate from here. I'll stay for another year. I'll stay in school."

"While we are talking about it, Olivia," said Clay, "there is something I have been thinking about. I can never find the right time to bring it up, so here it is. Would you like to see Quaking Tree and Sky In Water, and Red Morning before you go looking for your grandparents?

"I'm just afraid that, once you get back east, you won't want to return to Montana. It would mean so much to your Indian family to see you one more time. I would be more than happy to take you to them."

Adam was thrilled with the prospect of tagging along on a trip with Clay and Olivia, even though he had not yet been asked. After reading Clay's journals from his last trip, Adam wanted to experience life on the trail. "Say yes, Olivia. Let's all go. I've never been on a real adventure," pleaded Adam.

"So many nights I have lain in bed thinking of my other family and what I would say to them if we ever met again. Red Morning is nearly grown. I'll bet he is the fastest runner and has the best aim of all. Yes, I would like to see them, even though I am afraid I have lost the language.

"How will I ever be able to tell them everything that has happened to me and all that I have learned? Or to understand what they want to tell me? How will Red Morning and I manage? I want to know all about his life. I'm afraid I won't be able to understand him."

Tears welled in her eyes as Olivia spoke of her first family. Clay knew there was nothing in the world she wanted more than to see them again. He wondered why she had never once mentioned going back to see them some day.

"All right, it's decided," declared Clay. "You finish up here, and as soon as school is out, we begin our trip. Adam, if you can figure out a way the ranch can get along without both of us, you are welcome to ride along. Oh, and be sure to bring an empty journal so you can write down every day of your adventure."

Olivia suggested they go tell Ma and Abby what had just transpired.

* * * * *

The following year was not the easiest the Hardisty family had ever endured, but they managed to survive without Ben at the helm. Clay and Abby welcomed a new baby named Benjamin in honor of his grandfather.

To her mother's delight, Molly was being courted by a dashing young lawyer who had come west looking for adventure and a new life far away from his domineering parents. Both Sarah and Molly liked that about him.

Tad Wannamaker told Molly that if he had stayed in the city any longer, his father would have been in total control of his life.

"Of course," said Tad to Molly, "he would have insisted I work in the family law firm and eventually become a partner. That life is not for me. I'm here, in the west, raring to go."

Adam had his doubts about Tad. "If the guy would just wear a pair of boots," he moaned. "At least that would give the appearance he knew which end of a horse to ride."

Sarah could not make it through the holidays without crying herself to sleep every night for a month. It was Ben's favorite time of the year. He loved all the fuss. He loved having every member of his family in the house with him. The holidays would not be the same without Ben.

Olivia wove a necklace of beads and put it under the Christmas tree in a box. Ben's name was on it. Christmas Eve, she opened the box and told the family it was to hang on the cross over Ben's grave.

New Year's Eve, the entire family trekked across the snowy windblown field to the family cemetery near the edge of the woods. Olivia handed the Indian style necklace to Sarah who led them all in a prayer, then carefully hung the necklace over the arms of the cross.

* * * * *

Once the ranch had worked itself through spring and all the work that came with it, there was time for a breather. Adam was getting antsy. An adventure lay just ahead, and he wanted to get started. He had nearly memorized the journals written by Olivia's mother and Clay. He was anxious to write one of his own.

It came down to the day when Clay could not put him off any longer. He was sick and tired of Adam's constant pressure to make real plans.

"OK, OK." sighed Clay. "But we cannot leave until after Olivia is finished with school. That was the promise. There will be parties and whatever else they have planned she will want to attend. We won't be out of here till near the end of June."

The entire family attended Olivia's graduation. Half the town followed them out to the ranch for a barbecue party. Even though Ben was still missed, it was time for everyone to have some fun. Olivia told Sarah she could feel Ben's presence.

She said, "He's so happy that everyone is having a good time. This is the kind of party he always liked, lots of people and lots of good food."

Clay had the ranch hands clear out one of the barns for a square dance. They danced until midnight. No one wanted the party to end. Babies fell sound asleep in hay-filled mangers. The young children curled up in the back of their family buckboard when they couldn't keep their eyes open any longer.

Two weeks later, Clay bounded into Adam's office and asked if he had everything ready for the two of them to be gone for a while.

"I've got the ranch hands squared away and assigned who is in charge of what jobs, and everything that has to be done while I'm gone. They are ready and so am I. What about you, Adam?"

"If you can give me one more day," replied Adam, "we'll have confirmation of the delivery date for everything I have ordered from the mercantile. I don't want Ma and your family going without a thing while we're gone. I've talked to Scully at the feed store and Jake at the harness shop. The vet also knows we'll be gone. They all told me they would keep in touch with Ma. As soon as we hear from the mercantile we can leave."

"Okay, let's go tell Olivia."

The little band of travelers didn't get the early morning start they had hoped for. No one could say just one good bye. Clay's children whined and Abigail cried.

Searcher tried his best to trot along but his chicken-chasing days had caught up with him. He was in no shape for a long trip. He was up in years. His favorite spot was lying in the sun or next to the fireplace where he would be warm.

Adam ended up locking him in the barn, with instructions to the cowboys not to let him out. "I don't want to be looking back a couple days from now seeing Searcher struggling along the trail," he warned.

Olivia clung to Sarah. Her emotions were so high that she didn't know whether to laugh or cry, so she cried. Sarah said to her she knew they were tears of joy, not sorrow. "You'll be back before long, child. Go see your other mother and have a safe trip."

Finally, Clay told Adam and Olivia to mount up. "Let's get started. Adam has an empty book just waiting to be filled with his big adventures."

As the three headed out, Clay thought about where he was headed once again. He said to himself, *Even though I swore I would never go back, at least this time I'm not alone.*

* * * * *

For several days on the trail, everyone was thoughtful. Adam took in every sight and sound and wrote them all down in his journal at night around the campfire. Clay and Olivia rode together practicing what Indian words and signs they could remember.

They were both surprised at how easily it started coming back, once they got started. At night they taught Adam some basic words. Adam remembered that Clay had written Indian words in the back of his journal so he did the same. The language did not come easily to Adam.

The closer they got to their destination the more Olivia worried. "What if I do not recognize Quaking Tree after all these years," she cried. "For a long time now I haven't been able to remember the faces of my family. I don't even know what they sound like anymore. What if they don't remember me?"

"Well," said Adam, "I don't want to hurt our feelings, but Clay is the one they are most apt to recognize. He hasn't changed all that much, but you were a little girl when you left them and now you are a young lady. They are going to remember the child. I don't think you should worry so much. Don't make yourself sick over it. Everyone is going to recognize everyone else. It's going to be a big old family again. Just like ours back at the ranch. I just hope Sky In Water doesn't hate me as much as he does Clay."

That put a smile back on Olivia's face, while a shudder ran through Adam.

Clay told Adam and Olivia he was sure they could not be lucky enough to find the tribe camped in their usual spot along the river.

All along the trail Clay asked settlers and miners they met about the location of any tribes they had seen. They got back all sorts of answers. Clay decided they should go to the nearest Army fort and talk to the men in charge.

"I'm the commander here. What can I do for you folks? My name is Byron Carthage. I am pleased to make your acquaintance."

Clay let Adam take over. He was the one who could talk to anyone and get answers. Adam explained what they were about, and who they were looking for.

"Indian war parties are pretty much a thing of the past, but we do send out patrols to let them know we are still here. I believe the tribe you are looking for is camped closer to the headwaters of the river. I heard they were looking for fresher water, and more of it for their crops.

"Last winter was a hard one on them. We have been told they will plant more crops now in case this coming winter is another long one. They don't want to run out of food again.

"Why don't you folks stay here for a day, rest up, eat some good food? I can draw you a map showing you exactly where you need to go. We'll have a bonfire tonight so you can meet some of the people who live here at the fort. They might know something I don't know."

Sitting around the campfire that night, Clay was saddened to hear his old friend, Long Johns, had passed away. "He was old when I first met him," said Clay. "I guess he couldn't live forever. What about Percy? Does anyone know him? He made the best squirrel stew I ever did eat."

When they started out the next day, Clay took a long look at the map to get his bearings. It would be a few days ride to the camp they were seeking. He also noticed something else but waited until that night to mention it.

"Olivia," said Clay, "I want to ask you something."

Immediately, the hackles went up on the back of her neck. She hated it when someone said that to her because it was always something bad. "What is it?" she asked.

"Well, I noticed that, according to this map, we aren't too far away from where the massacre was that killed your folks. Would you like to go there?"

"No," she replied. "I have no interest in seeing that place."

Later in life, Olivia would change her mind. She would make a pilgrimage to the spot where her parents were forever together.

"Let's be on our way then," said Adam. He was filling in the pages of his journal every night and looking for something a little more exciting to write about than seeing huge bear and elk.

Adam was the first one to see smoke rising over the tree tops. They had ridden along the bank of the river far beyond where the tribe had previously camped. Clay was thinking maybe they had chosen another spot from what the commander at the fort knew about and moved on to better farmland. With a whoop and a holler, Adam goaded his horse into the river.

"Stop, stop, Adam," yelled Clay. "Come back here. You're going to scare everyone within miles. We'll never get close to the Indians at this rate. To them you sound like trouble. That is not what we need.

"We have to approach very carefully. Let them find us first. If we go charging in, we would be dead in minutes. Now come down off that horse. Let's make camp right here."

Clay remembered from his past trips how he had camped across the river and let the Indians find him. That's what they did once again. He chose a site with plenty of trees around so the young warriors could hide while spying on them. It was also back up-river so the tribe would not be intimidated by white people being so near.

"We'll just rest here for a few days. Let them find us," Clay explained. "The chief will send his young men into the woods where they can get near enough to see us yet not be visible to us. They will report back to him when they find we mean to harm. Then we just wait for the day we are invited to come across the river.

"So, this is home for the time being. It will be good not to get on a horse for a change. Spread your things out. Make it look like we will be here for a while. We have to let them know we are harmless."

Adam was beside himself. He still wanted to charge across the river to meet the Indians. Clay kept warning him of the consequences if he did so. Adam took to taking long walks in the woods, which also frightened Clay. He knew Adam was looking for those Indians who were looking for them.

"I just hope," he said to Olivia, "no one finds that boy. If they do, Adam won't live long enough to write about it in that journal of his."

The three of them settled into a quiet routine. Time hung heavily. They had all caught a flash of movement, now and then, off through the trees. They heard splashing in the river, but still no one came near.

One morning, Olivia awoke early, so she walked down to the river bank with a kettle to bring back water for coffee. No one seemed to be stirring among the tepees. Olivia perched herself on a large rock and sat there watching and listening.

It wasn't long before Clay went looking for her. "Beautiful morning, isn't it, Olivia? Do you remember anything about the river now? Has any memory of your camp, much like this one, come back to you?"

"I was just thinking about the river," she replied. "I remember playing in the river and my mother braiding my hair. I remember that part because she always cursed how difficult it was to tame this wild hair of mine. I think she even put bear grease on it once. I didn't let her do that again. It smelled so awful."

"Let's get back and have some breakfast. I think this is going to be our lucky day," said Clay. "We have been here long enough. They know we won't trouble anyone."

When the young brave came to fetch the campers and lead the three across the river into the Indian camp, they were ready. Each had stuffed beads and mirrors, and other trinkets into their pockets. Olivia carried several bolts of bright cloth under her arm, a gift for the chief.

The chief assembled his men around him. Clay took the lead with Adam behind, and then Olivia. Clay got quite close before the chief smiled and said, “I know you. Welcome. Welcome.”

Clay introduced his brother. Adam stared, not knowing if he should shake hands or bow. Finally, he held out his hand, which the Chief ignored.

Clay brought Olivia forward. Olivia was shaking so badly Clay put his hands on her shoulders to calm her down. “Chief, you probably will not recognize this young lady. This is Pale Moon. She’s all grown up.”

The look of shock on the old man’s face said it all. “No. I would never have known you are Pale Moon. Let me send one of the boys to fetch your mother. Red Morning is right here. Come meet your sister, Red Morning.”

* * * * *

Chapter 24

Red Morning stood at the back of curious onlookers. The more curious surrounded the white people who had come into their camp. When he heard the chief call his name, Red Morning shyly stepped forward.

“Red Morning, do you remember me?” asked Clay. Red Morning could not recall having seen this white man before. He had not met up with many of them. This face was not familiar.

“Red Morning,” said the chief. “This is your sister, Pale Moon. She has ridden many days to come see you and Quaking Tree and Sky In Water.”

Red Morning did not believe the chief. Backing away he shook his head, “I do not know these people,” he said to the chief.

Olivia was heartbroken. She remembered what Adam had said about no one knowing who she was because she was no longer a little girl. As Red Morning stalked away she looked for Quaking Tree.

Olivia spotted her mother walking towards the group. She seemed in no hurry. The man who had gone to fetch Quaking Tree did not know about Olivia. He only told Quaking Tree that the chief wanted to see her right away.

By this time, almost everyone in the village had gathered around the chief’s tepee. As Quaking Tree approached, they parted to let her through. Olivia stood between the chief and Clay. She held her arms out to her mother.

Quaking Tree recognized Pale Moon the second their eyes met. She stopped in her tracks, overcome with emotion.

"Mother," cried Pale Moon. "I have come to see you and Red Morning and Sky In Water. It has been a long time. Do you know me, Mother?"

"Yes, my daughter. I know who you are."

"Red Morning was here, but he ran away. He said he didn't know me, and did not recognize Clay. Will you bring him back to us? I want to talk to my little brother. Where is Sky In Water?"

Quaking Tree smiled at her daughter. "I will find the boy and explain to him who you are. I will tell him why the white people have traveled so far to see his family.

"But first, I have a surprise for you, Pale Moon. Follow me back to our tepee so I can show you. Clay, I recognize you too. Welcome. Would this be a brother of yours Clay? He looks something like you."

Adam was out of his mind with excitement. Here he was, standing in the middle of a tribe of Indians. He dug in his pockets and brought out a handful of mirrors and colored glass beads. He filled outstretched hands all the while talking a mile a minute to no one in particular.

Quaking Tree and Olivia walked together to the teepee where her family lived.

Clay and Adam followed. They were met by a little girl who came running towards them. "Here is your surprise, Pale Moon. You have a sister. We call her Fawn."

Pale Moon looked into Fawn's eyes. "You are beautiful, little sister. You look just like our mother. Oh, don't let me scare you. Let's sit down so mother can tell you who we are. I don't look anything like you, but I am your sister."

Sky In Water stood up from the campfire as the group neared. He had no idea who these white people were. They seemed to have Quaking Tree surrounded. He shifted his body closer to a weapon.

"Oh, no," moaned Clay. "Adam, do not, I repeat, do not open your mouth until I tell you it is OK. We are in big trouble here. Let me take care of it. Stand still. The man by the fire is Sky In Water. He does not recognize Olivia or me. Just be careful and stay quiet."

Adam was so scared he shook his head in agreement. For once he didn't have anything to say.

Quaking Tree called out, "Look who has returned to us, Sky In Water. Can you guess who this is, my husband?"

Pale Moon stopped walking so Sky In Water could get a good look at her. She held onto Fawn's hand for support. She was so full of excitement she thought she might collapse. No matter what, she told herself, I cannot let myself cry. I cannot let them see how emotional this is for me. It is not their way. Please let me be strong, she prayed.

Sky In Water, keeping his eye on the big white man, finally realized who he was.

As the years that passed, both Clay and Sky In Water had gotten over their bitter anger toward each other. It returned in a flash. Clay's anger at Sky In Water, who had taken the child from her parents in the first place, and Sky In Water's anger at Clay who, in turn, had taken the child away from him. Judging from the look on his face, Clay hoped all would be well, if no one made any sudden movements.

"Adam," said Clay, "now take your time. Do not start jabbering like you usually do. We are going to have to take this very easy. Right now I want you to meet everyone. I will tell them your name, say just a few words then back away and wait. Got it?"

* * * * *

Back at their own campfire that evening, on the other side of the river, it was hard to tell who was most excited about their day, Olivia or Adam. Olivia couldn't get over how easily she had been able to talk to her family. They understood her and she knew what they were saying in return.

"It was a good thing we practiced along the way, isn't it, Clay? Once I got here, it all came back, even though it has been so many years."

Adam's nose was buried in his journal, writing down every detail that transpired during their first day with the Indians. He kept his word and not talked very much the whole time they were across the river. Sky In Water had truly scared him.

Clay said he was very surprised when Sky In Water suddenly disappeared then came back shortly with Red Morning.

The young man was reluctant to accept who the white people were, even though he had been told many times about Pale Moon once being a part of his family.

Red Morning was finally convinced after Olivia began telling him some of the things that happened when she lived with them. She talked about things they had done together, like finding the honey bee hive and both getting stung.

He showed her a small scar on a finger cut while attempting to skin the first rabbit they had trapped. Quaking Tree assured Red Morning that Pale Moon was telling him all truths. After he understood and accepted this he did not leave Pale Moon's side.

For a week the whites and the Indians visited back and forth across the river. They often shared an evening meal.

Red Morning and some of his young friends took Adam into the woods to teach him many of their ways. They laughed at his clumsiness. They laughed at all the noise he made. They cheered when he finally, successfully, shot an arrow from a bow one of the warriors had made for him.

Adam came back late one afternoon all excited. “They gave me an Indian name today,” he boasted. “From now on I will be called Echo of Wind.”

Clay and Olivia laughed so hard they fell off the log where they were sitting. “What’s so funny?” asked Adam. “I think Echo of Wind is a very good name.”

“Oh, it is. It is, “said Clay. It fits you very well.”

“It is the perfect name for a young man who sometimes talks too much,” laughed Olivia.

Adam was not offended by her remark. He knew when he was being teased.

Olivia and her sister, Fawn, spent a lot of time together playing in the water along the riverbank. Fawn was not allowed to go to the river unless there were adults around. Her mother still carried the fear of losing another child to the rushing water.

Fawn wanted to know why Pale Moon was called Olivia by the men who were with her. “I will let Mother explain that to you,” replied Olivia. “It is a long story. It involves her, too. So I think she should be the one to tell you. Tell me why you are called Fawn.”

Clay spent his time tending camp and visiting with the chief. He was pleased to have been recognized after so much time had gone by. He also went hunting with the warriors so there was enough food for all.

Clay was interested in how the Indians irrigated their crops. How they kept the river so clean while they were camped along it for such a long time. He learned new methods that he could implement when they returned to the ranch. Clay especially saw the importance of keeping the horses downstream of where the families lived.

* * * * *

At the end of the first week all three agreed it was time to leave. They were ready to get home again. There was nothing left to talk about. Clay saw their presence was interfering with the tribe’s work. The gardens were not being tended like they should be. The young boys would rather be off exploring with Adam instead of doing chores.

The chief called for a celebration when he learned the visitors were leaving. Elk and deer were hung from spits. A wild boar was buried in the ground to cook for an entire day. The women prepared fresh vegetables from their gardens. They crushed fresh corn meal for biscuits.

Adam told the women he had never tasted anything so good in his whole life, especially the ears of roasted corn.

Later that evening gifts were exchanged between Olivia's families in front of the tepee. Clay brought along bowie knives and whetstones for Sky In Water and Red Morning. Adam presented them with the leather sheaths he made to fit each knife.

Clay had a huge ball of string for Quaking Tree. He gave her many packets of seeds Adam somehow managed to talk Sarah out of, including some of her precious flower seeds.

Olivia placed a box full of head pins and another of sewing needles in front of her mother, along with an even bigger box of spools of thread in every color of the rainbow.

Red Morning received enough fish hooks to last a life time. She gave Sky In Water several coils of rope. She had not forgotten to bring along the popcorn kernels.

Realizing there was nothing special for Fawn, Olivia took the ribbon from her hair and tied it around Fawn's thick braids. She also gave Fawn her set of watercolor paints and a sketch book.

Olivia had thought she would try to capture on paper some of the sights they had seen along the trail. Olivia demonstrated to Fawn how to use the watercolors.

"The next time I come for a visit I want to see all the pictures you have painted," she told Fawn.

In return, Olivia's Indian family gave them each beautifully beaded moccasins and enough dried fish and elk to last on their return trip home.

Quaking Tree gave her daughter Pale Moon a beaded suede dress tanned from the hide of a deer Red Morning killed. A hole in the leather, near the bottom fringe, was where Red Morning's arrow pierced the hide.

Red Morning, who remained so quiet all evening, disappeared into the tepee. This is so hard for him, thought Olivia. At first he didn't believe who I was. Now he doesn't want me to leave.

"Please tell him to come back, Mother," said Olivia. "I want to tell Red Morning I will come back some day. I will never forget him."

Red Morning returned carrying a small white puppy. "This is Snow," he said. "She is old enough to leave her mother. I would like you to have her. Dogs always remember where they come from. Maybe someday she will lead you back to us."

Tears rolled down her cheeks as Olivia held out her hands. "Red Morning, she's wonderful. Such a special gift you have given me. Yes, Snow and I will return one day. I promise that."

Quaking Tree held out her hand. She asked Clay if he remembered the ring he had given her so many years ago.

"It was my connection. One I never wanted to break with my child," she said. "Like the ring, with no beginning and no ending, that is my love for her. Take it, Olivia, and some day bring it back to me."

* * * * *

Chapter 25

The troupe was up at dawn to get an early start on their trip back to the ranch. Olivia spent a sleepless night thinking about all that happened during the past week. So much of her past life had come rushing to her. They were a child's memories. But they were all she had.

It was difficult for everyone to say good bye. Olivia clung to Quaking Tree. She looked deeply into her eyes. She ran her hands over Red Morning's face, hoping she would never forget the feel and scent of her brother.

Olivia reminded her new sister to fill the pages of her watercolor book with many pictures of animals and plants and all the birds she saw.

She stood in front of Sky In Water, "Thank you for saving me and bringing me to your tribe, and my family."

He smiled and looked lovingly at Quaking Tree. "You will always be ours, Pale Moon," he assured her. "Come back to see us again before we become separated and gone forever."

Tears flooded her eyes as she turned and walked to her horse. Clay and Adam had packed up camp. They waited patiently for Olivia to say her good byes.

Finally, Clay made a clucking sound to the horses and they ambled off along the river, looking back again and again. Finally there was nothing to see but trees and rushing water.

When the sun rose high, they stopped to give Olivia some time to herself. The men fixed food and coffee. She felt better afterwards and the rest of the day quickly sped by.

At campfire that night all three were able to laugh and repeat funny things that had happened during the week of their visit. Snow provided a good distraction when any of them got too sorrowful.

Clay had led a fast trip to the Indian village but he decided they could take their time getting back to the ranch. It was a beautiful time of the year. All the wildflowers were in bloom and berries were ripe. Some days were just too hot to spend much time in the saddle.

Adam could not get enough of the wilderness. When he spotted a bear on its hind legs scratching its back against a tall pine tree, he made Clay stop so he could write it down in his journal.

Olivia wished she now had her watercolors so she could paint a picture of the bear for Adam.

Adam discovered he liked to fish. He caught trout in the icy waters and, with the food the Indians had given them, they never went hungry.

Olivia thought Adam was going too far when he tried to teach Snow how to sit and speak. "I'll teach him," said Olivia. "He's my dog. He's not going to be a ranch dog. Snow is my personal escort wherever we go from now on. I will teach him anything he needs to know."

Adam backed off when he saw the look in her eye. He smiled and handed the puppy back to Olivia. "He's too young to learn anything anyway."

He understood Olivia needed something of her very own to love and care for. Someone who would never go away from her side, like so many had already done.

Olivia had been very quiet and a little touchy the first few days. Finally Clay asked her if something was bothering her.

"Something is bothering me, Clay. You must understand. I just left my family behind. I don't know if I will ever see them again. My heart is sad. I can't seem to stop crying. I am exhausted."

When it did not seem any better for Olivia the next day Clay suggested they stop and spend a day in camp, maybe two days. He used the excuse that he was trail weary.

"Adam and I need a rest before we make the last push for home," declared Clay. "I'm stiff and sore. You probably are, too. We'll talk about everything we have seen and heard, and about your two families, Olivia. If Adam gets started, time will go fast. I need to have a break from sitting in the saddle for so long."

They found the perfect camp site along the river in a clearing surrounded by trees and wild berry bushes. Adam and Clay went hunting while Olivia set up camp.

She was ready for them when they returned with a small buck and wild potatoes they discovered in an open field. She had picked berries and made a cobbler in a big iron pot over the camp fire.

Adam swore he could smell something good baking a mile off.

After supper they sat around the fire, reluctant to go to sleep. Clay and Adam had given Olivia the entire day to herself and, they hoped, had cried herself out. Neither one could take much more of a weepy woman.

"What kind of a dog is that you've got there?" asked Clay.

"I've been wondering that myself," Olivia replied. "Doesn't she remind you of a wolf? What do you think? I have never seen such a pure white dog before, but I have seen white wolves. Her hair is so long and silky. I also wonder why Red Morning and Sky In Water both gave me pure white animals. Maybe it has something to do with me being white, too. Or maybe it was just a coincidence. I do find it curious, though."

Adam could not believe what he was hearing. Could this trip not be any more perfect, he thought to himself. It's just been one exciting thing after another. He began writing in his journal again.

When he finished he tried on the beaded moccasins Olivia's mother had given him. They fit perfectly. He strutted around the campfire. Down along the river he looked back at his footprints in the sand.

It gave him an idea for a story he would write some day. Or maybe, he thought, I'll tell Molly and she can write it for the newspaper.

The second day of their rest along the river brought Olivia out of her deep sadness. She couldn't stop talking. She talked about their trip and her family, how they had changed, how she had changed, and anything else that came to mind. She took Snow for a long walk along the river. They returned with a pocketful of beautiful agates.

Adam tried his hand at panning for gold. When a smidgeon of gold dust sparkled in the pan, he let out a holler, "I'm rich. I'm rich!"

"I don't know how much you think you need to be a rich man, Adam. But this amount of dust won't come close. You better keep at it," teased Clay who recognized it as fool's gold.

Adam didn't care. It was all part of his big adventure.

Bright and early in the morning they were ready to ride again. There was nothing, or no one, to hold them up, even their selves. No sad good-byes this time. They kept up a steady pace until the ranch came in sight. Olivia reined up once again at the edge of the woods and looked at all before her.

"There is a lot more to look at than the first time I stood in this spot," she said. "Of course, then it looked huge to me. Now I realize there was nothing more than a corral, the barn, and the house. Now there are stables all over, and more fences. Remember how scared I was to follow you over the fence, Clay? I still won't do it."

Clay laughed and galloped ahead to open the gates for Olivia and Adam. Some of the hands had spotted them. By the time the trio got to the farm house Sarah was standing on the steps, waiting.

Someone had ridden over to tell Abigail and the children their daddy was home. They were on their way over too. It was a joyous reunion.

Clay couldn't get over how much his children had grown. Abby couldn't get over the length of Clay's beard.

Adam began talking the minute his feet touched the ground. "Is Molly around? I've got wonderful stories I want to tell her. Maybe she can put them in the newspaper."

Olivia looked deeply into Ma's eyes and smiled. How she loved this woman who had raised her and made her part of the family.

"It's so good to be home again, Ma. We had a wonderful trip. My other family was so excited to see us. It was sad to leave them, but it's good to be home."

"Home," said Ma. "I am glad you have come home."

* * * * *

Ma, Abigail, and all the hired hands managed the farm quite well while the boys and Olivia had been gone.

"No major difficulties," Sarah assured Clay. "Adam did such a fine job of arranging deliveries and alerting everyone in town you would be gone that we were taken care of quite nicely. No one got sick or injured, including the animals.

"We missed you, though. I missed the clump of your boots on the steps, Clay. I missed Adam's constant yakking, believe it or not. I just plain missed Olivia."

Summer chores were in full swing on the ranch. Some of the hay fields were cut and needed to be racked and hoisted into the haymows before it got wet. Horse trading was good. Between Sarah and the hired hand Clay had put in charge, they made some excellent deals.

"It's true, Ma," said Clay, you really do know what's going on around here. I sure am glad Pa shared everything about running the ranch with you. Thank you for letting us take Olivia away for a while."

Hot days faded into cooler nights and shorter days. It was time to make some more decisions. Olivia could not make up her mind if she wanted to leave again so soon. She really did want to travel east and meet her grandparents, but held back. Maybe it's because I'm not over my trip to the Indian camp, she thought. I just can't get my other family out of my mind.

Adam, more or less, made up her mind for her when he started talking about the distance they were going to travel by stage coach and then train. He tried to explain to her how big the city would be. It was beyond her imagination. He was scaring her with all this talk. She needed more time to convince herself.

"I tell you what," she told Adam. "I want to spend Christmas with this family. Not with strangers. In the spring we will start planning. A year from now we can go. That will give you time to train someone for your job and the summer work will be done. It's the best time to leave, not now. I'm just not ready."

* * * * *

Chapter 26

On a beautiful, bright Sunday morning in the month of April, Molly and her friend, the attorney from back east, Tad Wannamaker, called at the ranch. Ma knew they were coming. She invited the whole family over for her fried chicken dinner.

After apple pie and coffee, Tad took Molly's hand and pulled her to his side. "We have an announcement to make," Tad grinned. "Molly has consented to be my bride."

No one said a word. Then it was pandemonium. Adam swallowed hard before holding out his hand to congratulate Tad.

A tenderfoot for a brother-in-law, and the teacher's daughter for a sister-in-law, he thought to himself. It can't get any worse than this.

He smiled, kissed Molly on the cheek. "You are a lucky girl, Molly."

Olivia was stunned by the announcement. She was quite naïve when it came to adventures of the heart. No boys in school or young men ever approached her. She had developed crushes on friends of Clay and Adam, but they didn't last long.

She could not wait to get Molly alone to discuss what all this meant and how it had happened.

When they did talk, Molly's answers really didn't satisfy Olivia's curiosity. Molly assured her, "You'll know when it happens. There is no simple way to explain when you fall in love. You just know.

"In the meantime, if you do want to get married someday, one thing is for sure. You have to let them know you are available. Right now, boys your age think you are stuck up. To them that means you won't have anything to do with them.

I have heard them talk about how pretty you are, so they are interested. You just have to let them know you are interested in them too."

"But I'm not," replied Olivia.

She mulled over this new information about boys for days on end. Finally, she went to Abby.

"Yes," said Abby. "I agree with Molly. We do know some of the boys know you exist. It's pretty much up to you to turn things around."

"And how do I do that?" asked Olivia. She wasn't sure she was ready for a boy in her life. Clay and Adam had always been enough for her.

"You'll know," laughed Abby. "You will know."

* * * * *

Molly and Tad said they planned to wed during late summer. Molly didn't want a big wedding, because she knew she would be exhausted for weeks afterwards.

Tad understood. His family wired that none of them would be attending his marriage. Tad held out hope that maybe his older brother might show up.

Molly and Tad were married at the little white church in town with Molly's family and close friends in attendance. Afterwards, Abigail and Clay hosted a picnic at their house.

The newlyweds sneaked out early. They went back to Tad's house so Molly could move her things into closets and drawers.

Tad loved taking care of Molly. He knew how fragile she was but that did not make any difference to him. For the first time, he felt in charge of his life. He was determined to make the most of it.

He often thought of his tyrannical father and how difficult it was just being around him, never able to please. Tad was just the opposite, humble and appreciative of everything he had. He thought maybe he ought to thank his father. In a curious way, it was because of him he had found Molly.

Tad had the last laugh after all.

* * * * *

Clay and Abby announced they were going to have another baby. They hoped for a girl this time. Her name would be Amanda. They refused to pick out a boy's name. Young Lee and Ben thought a sister might be nice but would not be much help around the ranch.

Once again, Olivia was struck by all the things in the family happening around her. She felt like nothing. She wasn't contributing to the happiness of the family. There were no engagements or babies, not even a new friend to introduce.

No one in the family asked about living with the Indians anymore. They didn't seem to care. All at once, it was like that part of her life never existed. No, all of a sudden, it was like *she* ceased to exist.

It's time to move on, Olivia told herself. I cannot bear to sit here another day with absolutely nothing happening in my life.

* * * * *

Olivia told no one her plans. She was ready to meet those she now thought of as her third family. At least I have some place to go, she told herself.

I'm too old to go back to Quaking Tree. If I stay here, I'll probably end up the spinster school teacher. I have to get out of here. Now is the right time to go, she convinced herself.

Olivia told Ma and Adam about her plans one evening while sitting on the porch, refreshed by a cool breeze.

"Adam," she began, "I know it's earlier than when we had planned on leaving go to back east, but I have to go now. You can come along if it can be arranged on such short notice, or not. I can go alone if I have to. Of course, I would much rather have you with me."

Ma and Adam were both so shocked at what Olivia just said neither one could immediately reply.

Then Ma asked, "What brought all this on? Did something happen that changed your mind about waiting for fall to take your trip? If so, maybe we can fix it. That would give you a little more time to get organized."

"No," said Olivia not wanting to hurt Ma's feelings. "Lately everyone has been telling me that I will just know when certain things happen. Well, I just know that now is the time to meet my grandparents. I want to go before it's too late and they, too, are gone. I want to go now, right now."

"Well," said Adam, "this is short notice but I'll see what I can do. I'll talk to Clay in the morning. We'll try and set it up so I can be gone for a while. It worked out well enough last time. I think we can do it again."

Clay was happy to hear that Olivia wanted to be on her way. He worried deeply about the girl's destiny. He did not want her to stay with his family any longer than necessary.

It was time for her to get out and into the world. If she stayed, it would be a lonely life on the ranch. He thought that Olivia didn't appear to be interested in marriage. She never talked about having children.

Clay and Adam worked it out, just like before. The merchants in town were alerted that Ma would be alone again. Supplies were ordered early.

The hired hands reassured them they would be happy to pitch in and help out in any way they could. They all knew they were fortunate to be working at the -ABC-. No one resented doing extra work in exchange for their well-being.

* * * * *

The whole family was at the livery when the stagecoach headed to Helena pulled in to take Adam and Olivia away. Tears and good wishes flew back and forth between the travelers and those who stayed behind.

Ma took Olivia's hand in hers and said, "I understand if you do not come back. There is so much more to offer in Boston. You can go to school, meets lots of new interesting people, and be with your real family. Of course, we would love to have you come back to us some day. Just know that we love you no matter what you decide to do.

"I can't make any promises, Ma," said Olivia as they clung together." I love you with all my heart. This isn't the last you will ever see of me."

Neither Olivia nor Adam had ever ridden in a stagecoach. They were totally unprepared for the long, jolting, dusty ride between way-stations. By the time they got to the railhead they were stiff and sore and hungry for a decent meal.

The train proved to be a smoother ride but the cars were stifling hot. Passengers quickly gave up their clean clothes in exchange for a breath of fresh air and lowered the windows. The soot that came back from the engine stacks through the open windows quickly covered them in black dust.

Adam was again in his glory. Another adventure and this one was so different from anything he could have imagined. The scenery was constantly changing. After a day of travel he realized there were no mountains off in the distance. He saw nothing but blue sky. He talked with all the passengers, reported everything back to Olivia, and then wrote it all down in his journal.

Olivia was taking the time to think about what Molly and Abby had told her about meeting people. The passengers provided a golden opportunity for her to practice talking with strangers. It wasn't long before she was acquainted with all the ladies and their children. There were no men her age in the car other than Adam.

Olivia and Adam talked and talked about everything. When their conversation waned they talked about themselves. Adam began by telling Olivia his dreams, what he wanted to accomplish and do for the rest of his life.

It surprised Olivia he was so interested in writing. She thought he was the bookkeeper for the ranch. Adam didn't see himself in that role much longer. "I'm not a rancher," he said. "I hate horses."

"What I really want to do is write stories. I read all the dime novels. I think I can tell a story as good as any of those writers. I have all my journals full of notes. Someday, I am going to write a book."

Olivia got up the nerve to ask Adam about his friends. He realized she was trying to find out if any of them ever expressed an interest in her.

She is so naïve, Adam smiled to himself. He did tell her, in so many words, that yes, there was interest. What he didn't say was that he had been a little jealous when her name came up.

Olivia sensed he wasn't telling her everything. Adam took Olivia's hand in his. He held it for a long time. And so did she.

When Adam and Olivia arrived in Boston they were totally exhausted and ready to walk on firm ground. They were used to wide open spaces with lots of room to move around. Neither one had enjoyed being confined to the railroad car for days on end.

Adam got them rooms at the Eastern Hotel so they could rest for a day before beginning their search for her grandparents. All Olivia knew about them was that their last name was McCreedy.

Olivia was afraid of the city. On the ride from the train station to the hotel she was surrounded by buildings and people with no way to escape. Buildings blocked out the sun, parts of the city reeked and there were beggars.

"This isn't the place for me!" she exclaimed. "I hate it here already. There is no place to move without bumping into someone. The streets are mud, full of horses and carts and buggies, all going in different directions. How can anyone stand this mess?"

During dinner, Olivia said to Adam, "I want to find my grandparents, maybe have tea or a meal with them, and go home to the ranch. I hate this place. It's big and dirty and noisy. I could never live here.

"How do people do it? How can they live like this? It's like there is no place to be alone. There are people everywhere you look."

Adam lent a sympathetic ear. He tended to agree, while on the other hand, he was so excited about being in a big city. Adam loved the hustle and bustle of people going about their business. He could not get enough of it, at least for right now.

Adam began their search for the McCreedys, asking the hotel clerks if they were familiar with the name. One man said he had heard the name but wasn't acquainted with any of the family. He recommended they go to the newspaper office and inquire there.

"Over on Washington Street is where the *Boston Globe* is located. They cover news about the entire city. I'm sure they would be familiar with the name."

At the newspaper office Adam explained who they were looking for. It was suggested they speak with the society editor. The man knew all about the McCreedys.

"Pillars of society," he explained. "Old man McCreedy is on his way to becoming an industrial magnate.

"Mrs. McCreedy is always available to help various charities. She is on several charitable boards in the city. She's also very involved with the new Red Cross, and the city library."

Adam explained that Olivia was their granddaughter and they had come to Boston to meet them for the first time. "We live out west," said Adam. "This is our first trip to the east."

"This is a nice thing to do for your wife," said the society editor. "Titus and Olivia McCreedy live in a big house in Back Bay. Hire a driver and tell him who you want to see. He'll know where to take you. And good luck. I think you will enjoy meeting those fine people."

"He thought we were married," giggled Olivia the minute the office door closed behind them.

"Yes," smiled Adam. "How about that?"

* * * * *

Adam and Olivia stood in front of her grandparent's house. Olivia was shaking so badly she couldn't stand still. The door was answered by a black man who invited them into the foyer. He said he would be right back.

When the butler reappeared he was followed by an older, tall dignified looking man.

"May I be of any help to you?" he asked not knowing this strange couple.

Adam stepped forward and made the introduction, "This is your granddaughter, Olivia, daughter of your son, Micah, and his wife, Mary."

Adam paused, waiting for a reaction from the gentleman who stared at Olivia

He continued, "My name is Adam Hardisty. Olivia has been living with my family since she was a child. My brother Clay brought her to us after rescuing her from the Indian family she was living with. They stole her when she was a baby, after killing everyone in your son's wagon train."

The old man sat down heavily on a nearby chair, gaping at the young couple. He was unable to draw a breath or utter a word. He motioned for the butler to go find his wife and bring her to him immediately.

"My goodness," shouted Mrs. McCreedy when she saw her deathly pale husband slumped on the chair. "Are you all right? Is it your heart? Who are these people?"

Adam began again to explain who they were. McCreedy thought he was hearing a tale. He would have none of it.

"Our son and his family are dead and have been for many years. Who do you think you are coming into our home and upsetting us with this wild story? It is time for you to leave."

While Adam kept trying to talk to McCreedy and explain the situation, Olivia had reached into her bag and gripped her father's belt buckle in her fingers.

When they were asked to leave the second time, she held out her hand to her Grandfather and asked, "Do you recognize this?"

Olivia walked over to Mrs. McCreedy and leaned down in front of her. Olivia touched the little gold four leaf cover lying in the hollow of her throat.

"Does this look familiar? Do you know why I have it hanging around my neck?"

The McCreedys continued stared at her, speechless.

Quaking Tree and Sky In Water had told Olivia often enough how she had come to be with them. She began repeating their story to her grandparents.

"Well, now that I have somewhat recovered, let us move into the parlor. We can sit there to discuss this matter," Mrs. McCreedy announced. "You can continue your story there."

As soon as they were seated Mrs. McCreedy rang for the butler to tell cook to prepare tea for their guests. An uncomfortable silence followed before Adam spoke up. He began revealing an incredible story of survival.

The McCreedys found it hard to believe Adam and Olivia. They had been informed many years ago their son and his family had not survived a massacre. They had put their son to rest.

Mrs. McCreedy interrupted when the butler returned with the tea tray. "Go on with your story Olivia while I pour. How old were you when you were finally found and taken away from the Indians?"

The McCreedys were saddened when Olivia told them she could not remember her parents at all. There was nothing she could tell them about her mother or father. Her history began with Quaking Tree.

"I do know I was baptized before they were killed," she told them. "There is a description of my dress in the journal my Mother wrote in every day.

"She wrote that the fabric was taken from a favorite dress of hers she often wore to tea with her mother and aunts. I did not bring it along because it is so very fragile. If you would like to have it I can send it to you.

"It is also when my father tied the four leaf clover around my neck. When I was taken by the Indians they didn't know what it was, so Quaking Tree took it off me and hid it.

"Several years later I found it and stole it from her. I kept it in my cache. She knew it was there all the time. When Clay came to find me she made me show it to him. It is what convinced him that I truly am your granddaughter, Olivia.

"My mother also left her journal that Adam's father found, so we have that too," said Olivia. "She wrote in it, asking anyone who found the journal to promise to bring me to you. Here is a copy I made of the last page in her journal.

"We didn't bring the real journal either, because the pages are beginning to tatter. I copied the last words my mother wrote so you could read them for yourself."

The McCreedys excused themselves and went to another room to read the page. They took a few minutes to discuss what they had just been told by this young couple. "It's so far-fetched it could be the truth," said Titus to his wife.

"Oh, I agree," she replied. "I believe Olivia is our granddaughter. Her hair is exactly like Micah's, so dark and wild. She has his coloring. Her face is more like her mother's though, rather serious and thoughtful. I am certain she is who she says she is."

The couple returned to the table and sat down. Mrs. McCreedy said to Olivia, "Please read again the page from the journal. It does sound like Mary, always so concerned about family and doing the right thing. It's just all so very sad." She began weeping again.

* * * * *

After ten days in the city, Adam decided it was enough. He spent his time visiting every museum and library in the city. He even checked out the waterfront and ate some very strange fish.

"I'm ready to get back to the ranch. Are you coming with me, Olivia, or are you going to stay? It's your decision. Whatever you say is fine with me. It would be nice to have some company on the way home."

"I'm staying."

* * * * *

Chapter 27

Adam had prepared himself for Olivia's reply, but that didn't mean he liked it. "All I can do then is hope for your return to the ranch, and me," Adam sighed. "We are your family, too. We don't want to lose you."

They endured a sad good bye at the train station. Olivia's grandparents accompanied them to the station and quietly stood by. Olivia could not give Adam an answer to his question of when she would come back to the ranch.

"All I know," she told him, "is that I have to stay here for a while. Until I know who my real family is, I cannot do anything else. I know you don't understand any of it. You have always had your family with you, Adam. I have three families now. These people are my roots. I need to know about them. I need to know about me. Then I promise to come back to you."

With tears in his eyes, Adam tenderly kissed Olivia on the lips. She kissed him back. She held his hand so tightly he hoped she would never let go.

"Thank you for your hospitality, Mrs. McCreedy, Mr. McCreedy. It was an honor to bring your granddaughter to you."

"Thank you, my boy," said Mr. McCreedy. "There are not enough words to thank your family for saving our granddaughter and getting her away from those Indians."

* * * * *

Grandfather Titus brought home a map so Olivia could show them exactly where she lived with the Hardistys and the route she and Adam had traveled to Boston. She kept track, day by day, of where Adam was on his return trip to Montana.

Olivia had no idea she would miss Adam so very much.

Olivia's grandparents were not interested in Olivia's life with the Indians. Titus declared more than once, "I hold no truck with those people."

His wife was just plain afraid of them, not that she saw many Indians in Boston. She read enough newspaper articles about them going on the war path when things didn't go their way.

Given even the slightest bit of opportunity, Olivia talked about her Indian family. She told her grandparents that her Indian name was Pale Moon because of the color of her skin when the moon was full. She told them about her Indian brother and sister and her pure white horse and dog.

They listened mostly without comment.

It came to an end when Olivia told them that on her last visit with her Indian family, before coming east, her mother had given her a beautiful suede leather dress and new moccasins.

"I wish you could see the dress," she said to her grandmother. "The beadwork is so intricate and full of meaning."

"That is enough, Olivia. It is bad enough your clothes are made of homespun. Do not tell me you ever wore leather clothes. After all the years with those people, I am afraid of what they have done to you. You talk of nothing but wild animals and wild people. No more, please. No more.

"You are with us now. We shall see to it that you become a proper young lady. One who can go out in society without a trace of shame because of your misbegotten past."

"I agree," said Titus. "We would like you to meet our friends, Olivia. There isn't much of the family left. I have a brother and your grandmother has one sister who lives here in Boston.

"When you are properly attired, we shall have a party so you can meet some of your relatives. There are a handful of cousins, but I haven't kept track of their whereabouts. I'll see if I can locate them, too."

Well, thought Olivia, another lifestyle for me to experience. Am I supposed to choose the one I want to live? I thought my Indian parents were strict, but they were nothing like these people. If I stay here, I won't be me for very long, that is for sure.

There was one relative Olivia was very pleased to become acquainted with, her Aunt Josephine, Grandmother's sister. Josie, as she liked to be called, was a free spirit who took Olivia away from the formality of the McCreedys on several occasions. They became best friends, much to the dismay of Titus who was not exactly fond of Josephine and how she lived her life.

Josie called for Olivia at least once a week, sometimes more, for a day of shopping, or maybe a tea party. Her favorite afternoons were spent listening to Olivia's tales of the west.

Josie was fascinated with anything other than Boston and Boston society. She told Olivia she had been born in the wrong part of the country.

"I, too, should have been a pioneer and been on that wagon train with Micah and Mary and you. My parents would not allow it. Here I am, still stuck in Boston with no hope of ever getting away. I'm too old now to do anything drastic, like run away from home. I have no proper suitors. None that my sister approves of, anyway. I'm just lost."

Olivia laughed and hugged her aunt, "You should return to the ranch with me when I decide to go back to Montana. I won't be here forever. I hate Boston. There's too much of everything and never enough peace and quiet."

* * * * *

The scent of fall was in the air. It wasn't quite there yet but one could feel the sharpness in the air. People were getting the urge to finish up projects before it got too cold and snowy.

All summer, Grandfather McCreedy tried to convince Olivia to stay and live with them. "We can well afford it," he assured her. "Surely you do not want to go back to that rough and tumble life you have described to us, do you? That's no place for a young lady."

Grandmother tried even harder to convince Olivia to stay in Boston and live with them. "You bring such brightness to our lives, Olivia. After we heard that Micah and Mary had been killed, we thought we would never smile again. But here you are, nearly the spitting image of your father.

"Haven't you enjoyed the life we have shown you while you have been with us, the balls, the dinners, even the opera?"

Olivia stood firm. "Grandmother," said Olivia, "I have told you all along that I was going to return to Montana and that I had no intention of living in Boston. Now that you have brought up the subject again, I have decided it is time for me to go home, to Montana."

She saw the look of disappointment on the faces of her grandparents when she called Montana her home. To them, it was out there someplace in the wild. Montana meant nothing to them.

"I wish you would reconsider, dear girl," pleaded her Grandmother. "We love you so much. We only want what is best for you. Couldn't that be Boston as well as any other place?

"Already there are several young men who have expressed their interest in you to your grandfather. You could marry, become part of society. You could use that position to do so much good for others through charity work."

"I thank you again for your kind offer, but no. I have already wired Adam that I will be returning soon. If I decide to go to college, I have enough money. Before mother died, she found an empty lard pail and put all their life savings in it. They were going to use it to build a new home for us. Sarah told me there is plenty money to use for my education."

She continued, "I will tell you that I plan to live in Montana. I promise to come back and see you now and then. I hope that you come and see me some day too. The West is not wild and woolly, as you have been led to believe. Actually, my family is quite ordinary."

* * * * *

Chapter 28

When Adam received the telegram from Olivia that she was coming home he was beside himself with happiness. He had missed her something awful.

He couldn't make up his mind if he should make the return trip to Boston and bring her home, or if he could meet her at the end of the train line in Helena and accompany her back to Fort Benton on the stage.

"She couldn't get into much trouble on the train traveling by herself, but I don't trust some of those pikers who travel by stage," he told Clay. "What do you think I should do?"

The consensus was that he should return to Boston and accompany Olivia home again. Adam then planned to leave early so he could spend a few days in New York or Washington D.C. before picking up Olivia.

The first thing he did was to purchase another journal to write down everything he saw and did on this trip. Rattling across country on the train day after day he wrote about the people he met, the food he ate and, of course, his daily adventures in the big cities.

Adam had thought Boston was extraordinary but New York and the Capital made a lasting impression.

On the appointed day, Adam knocked on the door of the McCreedys. This time he was greeted by the butler who invited him inside, "I'll fetch Miss McCreedy for you sir."

Adam's heart did flip-flops when Olivia entered the foyer. She was prettier than ever. She was dressed in a beautiful traveling suit and handmade leather boots. Obviously, her grandparents had been very generous.

Adam held out his arms as Olivia stepped towards him. He kissed her on the cheek, pulled her to him, and kissed her on the mouth. It surprised both of them.

"I have missed you so much, Olivia. I didn't think this day would ever get here. You are beautiful."

"I love that you came for me, Adam. I'm so happy to see you. I can't wait to be with the family again. Shhh, here come Grandfather and Grandmother. I don't want them to hear me say that. They are still insisting that I stay here with them."

"No, darling," smiled Adam. "You are coming with me."

Olivia blushed when Adam called her darling. She looked him in the eye. Neither one said another word as they turned to join the McCreedys.

After a light lunch it was time to leave. Titus arranged for a cab to take the young couple to the train station.

At the last minute, he handed Olivia an envelope and said, "Do not open this until you get to your home in Montana."

Grandmother kept wiping tears from her eyes, still trying to convince her grand-daughter to stay in Boston. She realized it was to no avail when Adam arrived and she saw the look in Olivia's eyes.

She smiled and thought to herself they were obviously in love, at least Adam is. Olivia would need more time to understand what she was feeling. "I remember when Titus looked at me like that."

"I wish you both well, then. Have a wonderful trip home. Don't forget about us child. We want to hear from you. Remember, you are always welcome in our home."

Olivia's grandparents stood in the doorway, waving good-bye until the carriage was out of sight.

* * * * *

"Adam," said Olivia. "I have never been so happy to see anyone in my life. I thought I was going to explode if I stayed in that house one more day. When you wired that you were in New York for a few days, all I could think of was wanting to be with you. Thank you again for coming all this way just to take me home."

"It wasn't just for you, Olivia. I did it for me, too."

As the train clicked and clacked its way westward the young couple had eyes only for each other. Adam knew he had fallen in love with Olivia ages ago. He had no idea how she felt about him. Oh, he knew she loved him like a brother, but that wasn't good enough anymore. He wanted her to love him the same as he loved her.

Olivia studied Adam when she thought he wasn't looking. What's wrong with me? she wondered. Every time I look at Adam my heart feels like it is going to burst and my hands are all sweaty.

"Adam, I think I must be coming down with something. My heart is racing and my hands are cold. Could it be something I ate, do you think?"

He looked at her and placed the palm of his hand just below her shoulder so he could feel her heartbeat. "No, Olivia. It's not something you ate. I feel the same way. Let me explain and see if you agree."

Adam took a deep breath and looked into her eyes. "I love you. I love you with every heartbeat, and have for a long time. Ever since the New Year's Eve party when you unbraided your hair for the first time. I fell in love with you right then and there."

"Oh, Adam," whispered Olivia. "How can this be? I do love you. I love you, too." She raised her lips to be kissed.

Adam told Olivia they needed to get off the train in Chicago, as he had some business to attend to. She could either come with him or wait at the train station for his return.

"I won't be long," Adam assured her. "What I have to do won't take more than an hour."

"I'll stay," said Olivia. "I saw a little park not too far away. I would like nothing better than to just sit quietly and enjoy the colored leaves. Breathing some fresh air will do us both some good."

Olivia had just finished a sandwich when she saw Adam striding towards her with a huge grin on his face. "Looks like your business was successful," she commented.

"Oh, it was. It was," grinned Adam. "When we get back to Montana I'll tell you all about it, but not before. Don't even ask."

* * * * *

Luggage was transferred from the baggage car to the stage line office for the last leg of their journey. "I never want to travel that far away from home again," swore Olivia, "especially on a train."

"What about the promise you made to your grandparents about going to see them again?" asked Adam.

Olivia saw the twinkle in his eye and knew he was teasing her. "I'll handle that when they pressure me to visit. Not before."

It was late afternoon when the stage pulled into Fort Benton. Molly and Tad were there to meet Adam and Olivia.

"We thought you would be exhausted from our trip so we told the family you would rest with us overnight. Tomorrow we'll take you out to the ranch. They are planning a welcome home party for you, so act surprised," Molly explained.

Olivia woke just before noon the next morning. For the first time in days she had enjoyed a deep peaceful sleep. Adam said he felt better after having slept where it was quiet for a change.

After breakfast they loaded up their luggage one more time and headed out to the -ABC- Ranch. Home, at last. Because there was only room for three on the buckboard seat, Tad said he would follow on his horse.

"Horse?" questioned Adam. "You are on a horse? Welcome to the west, brother. Where are your boots?"

Everyone had gathered at the ranch for welcome home hugs and kisses. Olivia was overcome with emotion. She needed a moment to herself. She needed to breathe in the country air, to feel the open spaces she so dearly loved. Snow was so happy to see her he almost knocked her over.

"You missed me, didn't you? Well, I missed you just as much. Let's go for a walk, just you and me."

Olivia and Snow were halfway across the pasture, going towards the woods, when Adam spotted her.

"Back in a minute," he said to his mother. "I'm going to see if Olivia is OK."

Adam knew just where Olivia was headed. He ran off to his left so he could get there before she did hoping Snow wouldn't spot him and give him away. Adam stood up as Olivia neared her favorite sitting rock, the place where Ben used to bring her when she needed time away from everything and everyone.

"Adam, I didn't expect to find you here. I thought I had snuck away without anyone seeing me."

"You can't get away from me," said Adam. "Come here. I have something I want to give you. But first, will you answer me this?"

"What is it, Adam?" she asked as she held out her hand to him.

Adam bowed his head and kissed the palm of her hand. Olivia had never felt such a thrill in her entire life.

"Olivia," said Adam. "Will you be my wife? Will you marry me? Will you be the mother of my children? Will you marry me?"

"Yes, I will. When?"

"First things first, my darling." Adam smiled and reached into his pocket, "I promised I would tell you what I was up to when we were in Chicago once we got back to Montana. I knew I would never find the perfect ring for you in Fort Benton, so I went shopping."

Adam took Olivia's hand and slipped a ring on her finger. Olivia couldn't catch her breath she was so surprised. She sat down on rock next to Adam.

"I wish your father was here to share this moment with us. Did you plan all along to ask me at this spot, where Ben used to take me when I needed some space?"

"Not really," laughed Adam. "My only plan was to ask you as soon as possible. You made it both soon and possible coming here by yourself today."

"Actually I did want to be away from everyone just for a minute or two. I have been carrying grandfather's letter with me. He told me not to read it until I got home. Can you believe he actually called Montana my home? I thought I would read his letter here, where it's always so nice and quiet."

"Go ahead and read," said Adam. "I'll just sit here and wait for you. Then we can get back to the party."

Olivia opened the letter and began reading. Tears slid down her cheeks. "Adam. Listen to this."

"'Dear Granddaughter, Your grandmother and I are so grateful to you for making the trip to Boston. We didn't even know you were alive when suddenly you appeared at our doorstep. It was heart stopping when I looked at you that first time. I saw the face of my son.

"'Enclosed are a few photographs of your parents, taken before they left for the West. You can see that you have the same dark wild hair as your father. You have your mother's smile.

"'My offer to pay for your education will always stand. We would prefer you attend college in Boston so you could spend more time with us. But, of course, it is your choice of where you want to live your life and how you want to live it. Your mother made that very plain in her journal. Decisions were yours to be made.

"I have enclosed some papers for your signature. Since I have only an elderly sibling, as does your grandmother, we would like you to inherit our property when we are gone. We want it to stay in the family.

"We send our love.

"P.S. It was obvious to your Grandmother and I that the young man, Adam, clearly has intentions to marry you. We think you love him in return, even though you might not know it yet. Marry him if he asks you, Olivia. He is a good man."

* * * * *

More guests from town and neighboring ranches had gathered in the side yard by the time Olivia and Adam walked back out of the woods.

"They will notice my ring," said Olivia. "We have to make the announcement."

"You are right. Let's just gather everyone around when we get there. You grab hold of Ma's hand and I'll find Clay and Abby and Molly and Tad. I want us all together when we do this. "I'm a little nervous, Olivia."

"I am, too. In fact, I'm more than a little nervous."

By the time the roasted pig had been dug out of the ground and the side of beef taken off the spit, every lady guest had told the happy couple how their wedding should be staged. Each idea was gracefully received.

Late that night, after everyone had gone home, Olivia told Adam she knew exactly the kind of wedding she wanted.

"Just like Clay and Abigail had in the spring when all the blossoms are in full bloom and the air is sweet. Spring is always a new beginning, and next year will be a new beginning for us. I want our wedding to be so special."

* * * * *

Chapter 29

Now that she was back home Olivia didn't know what to do. It was time to make decisions again but she had no idea which way to turn. She was upstairs in her room going through the old trunk at the foot of her bed. Olivia hoped maybe she could find some answers in there, maybe a clue from Quaking Tree.

Olivia returned Micah's belt buckle to the leather case Ben had made for it. She took it to Boston with her thinking grandfather would like to have it, but he told her to keep it.

"You need something of your parents even though you do not remember them, Olivia," her grandfather had told her.

She held up the tiny dress she wore when she was christened in the river so long ago. I wish I could remember something, anything, about my real parents, she thought. I have so many mothers and fathers and brothers and sisters but I don't even know my own real parents.

Sometimes, she said to the walls in her room, I feel so lost among all these people. Will I ever feel like I actually belong in once certain place, and it's where I should be?

Olivia picked up the broken arrow. She was staring out the window when Sarah walked by and saw her, "What's troubling you, child?" she asked.

“I don’t know what to do with myself,” answered Olivia. “I can’t stay with you and do nothing but eat your food and wear clothes you make for me. I’m not a child any longer. Adults earn their own way.”

“You have come such a long way,” said Sarah. “You are welcome to stay here as long as you want. You are my daughter. I have never thought of you any other way. You are not a guest in this house. This is your home as much as it is mine. If he were still here with us, Ben would never want it any other way either.

“If you want something to do, Adam is making noises about not wanting to keep track of the books anymore for the ranch. Says he has bigger fish to fry. Would you like to take over his job?”

“No, his job sounds too boring to me, just adding figures all day long. I don’t dare say that to him though. He tells me the ranch couldn’t get along without a bookkeeper as good as himself,” replied Olivia.

“He also told me about wanting to find something else to do. In his heart I think he is a city boy who just happened to be born in the country,” laughed Olivia. “He wants to do some writing in the meantime.”

“Well,” said Sara reassuringly, “stay with me. This house is big and cold at night since all the children have grown up. They don’t have as much time for Ma as they used to. I would appreciate your company. Now don’t worry about not knowing what to do. Have you investigated any schools yet? There’s the money from your parents that will pay for any kind of education you want.”

“That reminds me,” said Olivia. “Grandfather gave me a letter to read when I got back to Montana. Adam and I read it together. They want to pay for my education and would like it to be in Boston. He also included some papers for me to sign. When they have both passed on I will in inherit their mansion in Boston. Can you believe that? What am I going to do with that big old house in Boston? I never want to see another big city as long as I live.”

"Adam knows about this?" asked Sarah. "Don't be surprised if he tries to talk you into moving there some day. You just said how much he likes city life."

"Believe me," replied Olivia, "I have thought about that a lot. If it ever comes down to it, I don't know what will happen. One of us will have to give in. I can say it will not be me until I am blue in the face. Adam would probably do the same thing. I guess it's just another one of those things we will have to face when the time comes. Meanwhile, here I am, your permanent house guest, at least until our spring wedding."

* * * * *

Sarah and Olivia made several trips to the mercantile stores in Fort Benton and Helena to buy fabrics for her wedding dress and the bridesmaids and little flower girl dresses. They cut and sewed every day.

Olivia missed Quaking Tree, wishing she could share the happy time ahead with her. There wasn't time to travel to the Indian village, either now or in the spring. No one could travel over the mountains and through the forests during winter. Olivia would never forget her Indian heritage.

She told Sarah that somehow she wanted to include it in her wedding.

Sarah thought for a moment then suggested they outline a favorite Indian design with seed pears on the small train of her dress. "And we could serve something at the reception that would be typical at a feast of celebration."

Adam heard them discussing Olivia's wishes. He asked, "Is there an amulet we could exchange along with the traditional wedding rings?"

"Let's do all three," said Olivia. "I do have a favorite tribal symbol for the dress. We can serve stoneground cornbread at the reception in honor of Quaking Tree. She spent so many, many hours at that rock grinding corn.

"There are all sorts of amulets. Some keep away evil spirits. Others are for good health or good hunting. I'll draw out the design for good health and you can carve them, Adam. Oh, this is wonderful. I feel much better knowing we are including my first family, at least in a small way. I just wish they could be here."

* * * * *

Olivia hosted a Halloween party for all the children at -ABC-Ranch, including boys and girls whose fathers worked for the Hardistys. There were prizes for costumes and apple bobbing, lots of food, and candy to take home.

This is what I want to do, Olivia told herself as she said goodnight to the last little ghost. I want to be with children. Maybe I should be a teacher after all. I know it would make Adam happy if I went to college.

It was the time between Thanksgiving and Christmas when word came from town that the teacher wasn't feeling too good. Mrs. Fisk had missed a few days of school before it was closed for the holidays.

Olivia was surprised at the news. She asked Abby about her mother. "As far as I know," said Abigail, "Mother is fine. She did have a bad spell. The doctor came to see her but she said he couldn't put a name to it. Just told her to take a few days off and get some rest."

Abby and Clay discovered her mother had not been completely honest with them and had sworn her husband to secrecy. She didn't want to burden her daughter and grandchildren with the knowledge she did not have much time left.

There was a name for her illness but there was nothing anyone could do to help her. It was too advanced for medical help. Mrs. Fisk passed away just before the new school term began.

The school board thought it prudent to allow the children an extra week of holiday vacation while they sorted out what was to become of the school. Obviously, they couldn't ask anyone to come any great distance in the middle of winter to take a job that would last only a few months.

Overhearing a conversation at the stable in town one day, Clay interrupted and said he had an idea.

"Let's go see the president of the school board," said Mr. Larson after listening to Clay. "The school board is willing to listen to anyone who can help us out of this situation. It isn't good for the children to be away from their classroom for such a long time."

"I know she doesn't have a college education," said Clay, "but Olivia would make an excellent fill-in teacher. She's very bright, knows a little bit about everything. Plus that, she does have a way with children. She would be perfect. If you give her a chance, I'd even bet she goes on to college to earn a regular teaching license."

* * * * *

"Who is that coming up the lane in the middle of a snowfall like this, Olivia?"

"Did you invite someone out for tea, Ma? Oh, listen. Can you hear the sleigh bells?"

Sarah opened the door to find three members of the school board shaking snow off their hats. "Come in, come in, gentlemen. To what do we owe the pleasure of your visit on a day like today?"

"Is Olivia here? We need to talk with her, if you don't mind."

Olivia went into the parlor, and perched on the edge of the settee. She had no idea what this was all about. Neither did Sarah. "Hello gentlemen. Please sit down. Sarah is making some hot tea for you. It looks cold and miserable out there."

"Thank you, Olivia. That would be nice. Olivia, you look worried. No need to be, you aren't in any trouble. Let's get right to the point of our visit. We have come to ask you to fill in, as teacher, for the remainder of the school year. We can't ask anyone from the outside the area this time of year to come and teach. Your name came up as the perfect candidate. What do you say?"

Olivia was speechless. She stared at the three men, absolutely stunned.

"We would like an answer, as soon as possible, if you don't mind, Olivia. We have to get the children back in their classroom before too much more time goes by. We have talked to Mr. Fisk and he said he would make all his wife's books and supplies available to whoever takes the job. That should be a big help to you."

Olivia was nodding her head in agreement even before Mr. Hess had finished his request. "Oh yes, yes. Of course I will do it. I don't know what to say, gentlemen. Thank you. Thank you for this opportunity."

While Sarah served tea the group worked out details of a contract. The school board was very generous with the amount of salary she would receive. They had even arranged for a room in town where she could stay, if she so desired. Members of the school board thought of everything.

One thing they would not tell her, when she asked, was who had suggested her name to them.

"That," chuckled Mr. Hess, the board president, "is for us to know and you to find out."

Olivia was glowing when Clay and Adam came in from the barns a short time later. "We saw sled tracks in the snow. Who was here in such foul weather?" asked Clay. "It must have been someone important, with something special on their mind, to come out in the weather."

"A bunch of gentlemen came to see Olivia," smiled Sarah. "No, Adam, she's not in any trouble with the law. Olivia, tell them what happened. Why did you have gentlemen sitting with you in the parlor just a short time ago? What went on in there?"

"Adam, Clay," said Olivia, "you will never in a million years guess what happened to me. I got a job! Some members of the school board rode out in this awful weather to offer me the teaching position at the school in town. Can you imagine?

"Adam, I'm sorry, but they needed an answer immediately so I couldn't wait to talk to you about the offer. I told them yes, yes, yes! We even had the contract all ironed out before they left. I will sign it in the next day or so. The position is just for the remainder of the school year. They will put an ad in the newspaper announcing the re-opening of school next week, and I will begin teaching my first class."

Adam was speechless. Clay pretended to be.

* * * * *

Before going home to his wife and children after his day in the barns, Clay stopped by the house.

"Ma, will you and Olivia come over to our place tomorrow for supper? I think we should celebrate Olivia's good news," he said. "I know Abby will be happy for Olivia when I tell her the good news. And then I will tell her we are having company for supper.

"I hope this will distract Abby a little from everything that has happened with her mother. She needs to find herself something else to think about. Planning a celebration will brighten up her spirits, I'm sure.

"See you tomorrow night for supper, then. Oh, I already talked to Adam about this so he knows where his next meal is coming from," laughed Clay as he banged back out the door.

* * * * *

Chapter 30

Olivia had only a few days to prepare teaching a room full of children. Abigail suggested they go to her father's house in town. There, they could go through her late mother's lesson plans, texts, and supplies.

"That way," Abigail told her, "you can pick up where Mother left off. You can do it, even if you do have to fly by the seat of your pants in a couple of subjects.

"It's been only a few weeks since Mother left us. I still cannot believe she is gone. You have taken on a huge responsibility, Olivia. I hope you enjoy teaching as much as my Mother did."

Olivia assured Abby she was looking forward to teaching the children. "It's something I have always thought I would like to do. With this experience, I will find out for sure if it's the job for me."

They loaded up the wagon with supplies, lesson plans and books Olivia would need right away to get started. They stopped by the house where the school board had arranged for Olivia to have a room while she was teaching. She had reluctantly moved into town after everyone had convinced her it was too dangerous to travel back and forth during the winter months. "Too much could happen along the road," said Adam.

“Besides that,” Adam pointed out, “you will have to get to the schoolhouse early to get the stove going. The building has to be warmed up before your students arrive.”

“OK. I do not like it, but I will do it. Mother, would you help me pack my clothes?”

By the time Olivia was ready to leave there wasn’t much left in her room. The old trunk, full of her Indian clothes, still held its place at the foot of her bed.

With confidence and assurance she could do the job, the only thing that really worried Olivia was how to discipline her students, especially the older boys. After moving her things into her new room in town Olivia stopped by to see Mr. Fisk. She explained how concerned she was about keeping control of the classroom.

“If I am defied by them, what am I to do?” she asked Mr. Fisk. “What did your wife do when a student failed to do as he was told?”

“Well, Olivia,” said Mr. Fisk, “I think the best thing for you is to state your position right off. Maybe ask them for some help. Give them responsibilities. If they understand what is expected, the school day will go much faster without disruptions. They will cooperate. I’m sure of it.”

“What a good idea. I hadn’t thought of that. I had planned on assigning a chore to each child so we would have something to work on together other than just daily lessons. Depending on how many students return I hope we can come up with enough jobs. I’ll need help with everything from cleaning erasures to hauling out ashes. I’ll even have to assign help with getting the little ones into their mittens and boots when it’s time to go home.”

* * * * *

The time had been too short for Olivia to get everything organized at the school house to her liking. She left early Monday morning hoping she could get through the first day with no major problems. Olivia thought it best to be prepared for her first day rather than take time to unpack and hang dresses in the armoire or fill dresser drawers.

Olivia's landlady provided a quick breakfast, handed her a lunch pail as she flew out the door, and wished her a good day. On the way to the school house Olivia was joined by two little girls headed in the same direction. It was a pleasant surprise to open the doors of the school house to find it warm inside.

"Welcome, Teacher," said a voice from the front of the room. The president of the school board, with all the other members and their wives, were lined up in front of the chalk board. "We came to welcome you and your students back to school. When they are all here, may we take a minute to explain to the children what has happened? We hope you don't mind."

"No. Of course I don't. I'm really glad you are here to make introductions. I think most of the students recognize me but don't really know who I am. Everyone should be here in just a few minutes. I'll ring the bell and we can begin our day."

Olivia thought she was ready for anything, but not the quietness when all the students had returned to their desks after an extra-long winter vacation. Things changed during the afternoon session when everyone was feeling more comfortable with the new teacher.

Olivia took advantage of their good humor and began assigning daily tasks. It appeared the most coveted task was cleaning erasers. Lots of hands waved in the air when she asked for a volunteer. Olivia explained this particular job had to be done after school when the blackboard was no longer in use. The best part of the job, each child knew, was that you got a chance to be alone with the teacher and ask all kinds of questions.

By the end of the second week the students and Olivia had all settled into a daily routine. There had not been any discipline problems other than reminding students to be quiet while another grade was being taught. Because all the students were seated in one room Olivia had arranged the desks by grade. She soon discovered those at the back of the room were missing out on too much. She tried several different arrangements including those suggested by the children. Half circles seemed to work the best for everyone.

Olivia missed being at the ranch with Sarah. Weather allowing, Adam picked her up every Friday after school let out and took her home for the weekend. Since becoming engaged, they were careful about appearances. Sleeping in the same house during this time could lead to gossip. Sarah assured the couple that if anyone got the wrong idea she would be glad to straighten them out.

Weekends were spent busily sewing on Olivia's wedding dress. She sketched her favorite Indian design on the train. She was anxious to begin outlining the meaningful design with tiny seed pearls, then filling it in.

Adam had been warned about sticking around when Sarah and Olivia worked on the dress but he could not help himself. "You can't see the dress until our wedding day," cried Olivia. "Go away."

"I'll stay completely away when you start sewing on the pearls. I haven't seen the dress on you, even during fittings. I want to see you in it for the first time when you walk down the aisle towards me. You are going to be the most beautiful bride this county has ever seen.

Clay told me he is so honored that you asked him to walk with you down the aisle and give you to me."

"There is no one else to even consider," replied Olivia. "He is the one who saved me and brought me to you. He is my hero," she laughed.

* * * * *

The church sponsored a Sweetheart's Dance in February, which was always held at the schoolhouse. The children helped push their desks back along the walls. They hung red and white streamers from the ceiling before they were excused for the weekend.

Saturday morning the church ladies set up food tables while the men hauled in wood and made sure the fire didn't go out in the woodstove. Then they stood around figuring out where everyone could sit. If people weren't dancing most would want to sit and visit. Families, including all their children, were invited to the dance. Everyone brought food and drink to share.

When plates had been filled and it was quiet, Clay stood and proposed a toast to the Olivia and Adam. "Here's to my brother and sister," he laughed. "May they enjoy wedded bliss. Here's to being as happy as Abby and I are. And here's to babies, lots of babies."

The couple blushed for the crowd while accepting congratulations from all their friends. It was a night of memories.

* * * * *

Meanwhile, the ranch had been pretty much shut down once again for the winter. All but a handful of cowboys were given time off to return to the homes of their youth, or to their own families, for a long visit. They left with the promise of a job when they came back in early spring.

Clay kept his skeleton crew busy repairing harnesses and saddles, ordering new equipment for what could not be repaired, and tending to the few horses that had not been sold off or traded.

Abby liked this time of year best in spite of the foul weather. It meant Clay would be home early nearly every day. The children loved having him around. He had always told Abby he wanted lots of babies. She was doing her best to provide them.

Sarah was secretly working on a wedding quilt for Olivia and Adam. It would be her wedding gift to them. Sarah's health was declining, not as good as it used to be. The children noticed she had slowed down a lot. When it had been suggested she leave the ranch, Sarah insisted she was staying even if she was alone most of the time.

Olivia came home weekends if the weather allowed. Adam was there in his office but it wasn't like having a daughter in the house. She set up a quilt frame in an unused bedroom where she disappeared for hours. Sarah kept reassuring Adam she was OK. "I'm working on a project you can see when it was finished, and not before."

Adam teased Sarah, "I know what it is already. It is something for our wedding."

Sarah teased back, "Maybe, maybe not. You can't be sure about it. Just have to wait and see."

Adam worried constantly about Ma. He wondered if she was lonely.

* * * * *

Olivia stuck to Mrs. Fisk's original lesson plans as best she could but she had a problem teaching students the same lesson plans their former teacher used from year to year. Olivia remembered the exact same lessons, and tests, from when she had gone through the grades.

"There is so much more for children to learn," she moaned to Molly. "I want to teach them about trees and the air we breathe. I want to teach them about animals and how to keep our rivers clean. I want to teach the children things I learned about nature from my Indian parents. Nature and surviving are just as important as arithmetic!

"Even though I was only a small child, Sky In Water and Quaking Tree stressed the importance of keeping Mother Earth pure for future generations. They watched the buffalo disappear. They do not want that to happen with anything else that means life to them. My students should also learn that.

"I have to figure out a way to introduce those subjects without mentioning Indians and what I learned from them. Some of the parents refuse to have anything to do with the redskins, like they are called. Makes me furious when I hear some of the comments they make. But, I have learned to hold my tongue. My turn will come."

The students loved their new teacher. It was hard for the little ones to get used to the idea that Mrs. Fisk would not ever be returning. Olivia fretted over what they had been told by well-meaning parents. If the children asked questions, she answered as best she could, making sure she did not encourage the subject of death and dying.

Olivia had been very leery about teaching the older boys. They sometimes did give her a bad time. After a few false starts, she figured out the only way to keep them from turning totally hostile was to treat them as men, not little boys. She used the opportunity to teach them responsibility while doing their daily assigned tasks, and how they could delegate without being bossy.

She encouraged the children to form clubs to study subjects they were particularly interested in. The science club was soon studying the formation of snow flakes and bubbles formed in ice. The boys got together a wood carving club. All the girls sewed, or knitted and crocheted. The little ones read to each other and kept track of the number of books they borrowed from the meager school library.

Olivia made every effort to make school as interesting as she had wanted it to be when she was attending as a student. She tried every day to take away the boredom and to replace it with extra credit assignments or book reports children could work on while she was teaching another grade. Mr. Fisk stopped by occasionally after school, when he saw she was staying late to correct assignments and tests, to see how she was getting along.

Molly kept encouraging Olivia to have the students write more themes and essays. She told Olivia that she would see to it that some of them were printed in the newspaper.

"It would be a real incentive for the children see their words in print and read by everyone in town," exclaimed Molly. "I want stories from all the children, first grade included. And that means from the boys, too!"

* * * * *

Time was flying by for Olivia and Adam. They still had final wedding plans to work out. All the dresses were just about finished. Sarah insisted they save the hems for last. The little flower girl was still growing. The length of the bridesmaid's dresses depended on the height of the heel on the shoes each friend wore.

Adam's new suit and shoes hung in the closet. "Is there anything else you would like me to do? I feel like you and Ma are doing all the preparations. I don't want to be left out."

"Yes," Olivia answered. "There is something I must do. I need you to take me shopping one more time."

"Oh, no," said Adam. "What else could we possibly need?"

"You'll see."

The next weekend Olivia had to stay in town because of a snowstorm. It was impossible for Adam to get to her so Olivia went shopping by herself. Even though she was a grown woman, living on her own, shopping by herself was a relatively new experience. Olivia now had her own money to spend on whatever she wanted. No one could tell her otherwise.

Olivia's first stop was the mercantile. She knew the good jewelry was kept in a big safe at the back of the store. She waited until the owner's wife finished with a customer then approached her. "I would like to buy a wedding band for my soon-to-be husband," she said. "Could I see what you have to offer, please?"

After she made her selection, Olivia asked to see a variety of gold watches. "For yourself, ma'am?" asked the owner's wife as she withdrew another case from the safe. "We just got in these ladies watches that are so dainty and beautiful. Something like this would look very nice pinned to your blouse."

"No. Thank you. I am looking for a man's watch. Adam's brother inherited their father's gold watch so I want to give him one as a wedding gift. He can then pass it along to our son someday."

Olivia left the mercantile with a big smile on her face, happy with her purchases, and that she had done it all on her own.

Unbeknownst to her, Adam too had visited the mercantile a short time before. He had purchased a cameo pin to give to Olivia on their wedding day.

* * * * *

The stretch from March to May seemed interminable for Olivia and her students. The weather was so terrible the children were forced to have recess inside the school house most days. Tempers flared. Best friends changed on a daily basis.

The older boys could not resist teasing the little ones. Teasing was an intolerable situation for Olivia. She remembered what Quaking Tree had to suffer and the little bit of it herself before she left the tribe. Teasing made her younger students cry and say hurtful things. She could not get it stopped, until the day she finally turned the tables on the boys.

"If you promise to behave and be polite, I will send all you boys to the mercantile to buy some things we need for our next crafts project. Caleb, you are in charge. If any one of the boys acts out I want his name. Understood? OK. Kindly ask that the items be charged to the school account. Here's the list, be on your way. I expect you back in less than thirty minutes."

While the big boys were gone Olivia spoke to the rest of her students, particularly the ones who bore the brunt of teasing, about remaining passive when the teasing started.

"There is nothing more irritating than being ignored. You all know that when I don't call your name when you have your hand up, you don't like it, do you? So, when someone starts picking on you, ignore them. Don't look at them. Don't talk to them. Hum a tune if you have to, but do not direct any attention to the person who is doing the teasing. If someone is picking on a friend, all of you gather around and start talking to your friend. Ignore those big boys."

The children were so excited about having a solution to their problems they couldn't wait for the boys to return so they could try it out. It almost seemed as if one of the big boys had stayed behind and listened at the door. No one did any teasing all afternoon.

The children got their opportunity to practice being passive, more than once. The big boys did not like it one bit, just like teacher said. When teasing didn't work, the boys gave up and looked for other ways to entertain themselves. Olivia suggested a chess club. It became an obsession with them.

Nearing the end of the school year, time for the annual school outing was fast approaching. Sarah went to the school and invited the children out to the -ABC- Ranch for the annual day of fun, games, and picnic. "We'll have everything all set up for you. All you have to do is show up and have fun!"

Sarah took over, as usual, and organized the entire day. She bought prizes for everyone. No child would go home without a prize or trophy in hand. She organized duties for the mothers and fathers, arranged for food, even set up a first aid station. There were always bumps and bruises, scratches and cuts that needed tending.

Adam worked with the hired hands to set up all kinds of races and games. They made sure there was something fun to do for every child.

Clay dusted off several old saddles and picked out a few horses he thought the children might like to ride around the pastures. "Little kids never get to ride so we'll have a real treat for them this year," he promised Olivia. Three cowboys were assigned to help the children on and off the horses and to dry any tears if they got scared.

Since Ben's death, the once popular racetrack didn't get used as much. Folks knew it was Ben's project and missed seeing him there, cheering on the riders.

Clay decided to do something about it. "Let's get the track cleared off," he said, "so the boys can do some horse racing. Let's pull out the two sulkies so the girls can race them if they've a mind to. Let's make this a fun school experience those students will never forget."

* * * * *

The night before play day, as he called it, Adam hitched up the buggy and went to town to bring Olivia out to the ranch. She was as excited as the children.

"It was all I could do to keep them in their seats today," she said to Adam. "It is going to be wonderful. After tomorrow, it's just a short time until the end of the school year, and then, then, our special day. Right now I have to take one thing at a time. I've been so busy with everything happening at once my head is beginning to spin."

Throughout play day, many of the children, including the older boys, would run to Miss McCreedy and say, "This is the best day of my life," then dash off to run another race or play another game. By lunch every child had ridden a horse, run in a race, and dunked for an apple or pinned a tail on the donkey.

The boys could not believe they were allowed to race horses on the track that only rough cowboys and visiting ranchers had used for years.

"Lucky it's lunch time," said Clay, "or those poor horses would be run right into the ground. Joe, run them over to the far pasture for a while so they can rest up and drink from the stream."

The bleachers were packed with mothers, fathers, younger brothers and sisters, aunts and uncles, friends and neighbors. They all cheered for every one of the students. They stood up to applaud the winners.

After lunch, and eating too much, the younger children found a shady spot to nap while their mothers cleaned the picnic area. Clay and Adam challenged the boys to a game of horseshoe. The girls sat, quietly talking about boys.

Everyone was raring to go again in the afternoon. After the final race had been run it was time for the awards ceremony. True to her word, Sarah called every student to the front of the grandstand. Each one was applauded for their win and presented a winning ribbon.

“What a day of memories for these children,” Olivia said to Clay. “You made it so special for them. I can never thank you enough.”

“It was my pleasure,” he said. “Wouldn’t Pa have loved this day, too? Hope I did right by him.”

Olivia couldn’t help it. Tearing up, she said, “Yes, I wish he could have been here. But Clay, you are taking this ranch back to his original concept. I love you for that. We lost it for a few years after he died. I think you have found it again.”

* * * * *

Chapter 31

A week before school dismissed for summer vacation, Mr. Hess sent a message to the school asking to meet with Olivia one day after school.

"Members of the school board, and I, would like you to return in the fall and teach again, Olivia. You have done an excellent job with the children. The parents can't say enough good things about you, too.

"Of course this means you would have to start working on a getting a teaching license. That shouldn't be too difficult for you. There is a Normal Teaching School in Kansas now. Maybe you could go there. I know it's a distance to go and what with you getting married in just a few days…"

"Thank you for the offer, Mr. Hess," Olivia replied. "I did enjoy teaching and getting to know the children these past months. I also learned about myself. I must admit something, and you are the first one I have said this to. I don't want to be a teacher. It's not something I want to do year after year. It's too structured for me. I need the freedom to pick up and choose what I want to do without having to answer to anyone."

Mr. Hess was taken aback. He didn't know what to say.

"Adam and I will be married very soon. I want to spend my time with him. We have talked about all the choices open to us. We are looking for something we can do together. I realize I am passing up a wonderful opportunity, Mr. Hess, but teaching is not for me. I'm sorry."

Mr. Hess stood up, still not believing Olivia's answer. He and the school board were all convinced she would want the job. "Well, Miss Olivia, you have surprised me, to say the least. If you are positive you have made the right decision we will go ahead and look for a new teacher. I will ask the board to hold off for a while to give you some extra time. In case you change your mind."

"I won't change my mind, Mr. Hess."

* * * * *

When Adam picked up Olivia after school on the last day she told him what had transpired. "I'm sorry I never talked to you about my decision, Adam. It never occurred to me they wanted me to stay. When Mr. Hess asked me to return in the fall he insisted I give him my answer right away. As much as I like children, I know that teaching is not for me. Well, I do like teaching, just not in a stuffy classroom."

"Your decision does not surprise me," said Adam. "What has surprised me is how long you were able to stay in the classroom. I know you are much more comfortable in the outdoors, free of walls, surrounded by your trees and river.

"Ma planned a family supper tonight. It would be a good time to tell everyone about your offer from Mr. Hess, and your answer."

It turned out the little ones were most disappointed that Olivia would not be teaching anymore. They all thought it would be fun to have Auntie Olivia as their teacher.

Then it was Molly who had a surprise for the family. "Tad has something he wants to tell you," she announced.

Tad stood up next to Molly, tightly holding her hand, shifting from foot to foot. He was becoming more a part of this big boisterous family but he still felt challenged by them.

"I'm going to be a father," he said. "We are going to be parents. All you little ones are going to be cousins. Think of that, someone new to play with."

Blushing red, Tad sat down and kissed his wife on the cheek. "I have something else I want to tell you," said Molly when everyone had settled down again. "The doctor has told me that because of my precarious health I must not continue at the newspaper. The last few months I will have to stay in bed to ensure having a healthy baby.

"It appears that everything is falling into place. The newspaper is being sold so I will be out of a job anyway."

"Why is it being sold?" asked Adam out of curiosity.

"Mr. Denison wants to buy a bigger newspaper in a bigger city," replied Molly. "He's already looked at two of them. It's just a matter of making up his mind which one to purchase. He's been asking around town if anyone is interested in buying the paper but no takers yet."

Adam looked at Olivia, and Olivia looked at Adam. They both held the same thought. A smile slowly spread across Adam's face. He said nothing more about the newspaper. He couldn't wait to be alone with Olivia. They needed to talk in private.

* * * * *

As much as Adam loved his sister and Tad he could not wait for the party to be over. When the last congratulations had been shouted into the night, and goodnight hugs were given to Clay and Abby and the children, Adam let out a yell. Olivia gave out another one. They clung to each other and danced around the kitchen table.

"Whatever in the world has possessed you two?" asked Sarah. "I know we are all happy about Molly and Tad having a baby. Something else is going on with you two. What is it?"

"Ma, Olivia and I haven't even talked about it yet, but I think Molly just opened up the future for us. What do you say, Olivia?

Want to sit down right now and have this conversation, or do you want to sleep on it and talk in the morning?"

"Let's do it now. Right now." yelled Olivia. "Ma, join us. We would like to have you, and Clay too, involved in any decisions we make. We need your guidance and experience."

"Ma," said Adam, "you have known for the past few years that I want to do more than keep books for the ranch the rest of my life. I want to spread out. Do something on my own. I'm not a rancher like Clay. Never was, and never will be.

"When Molly said the newspaper was for sale, Olivia and I looked at each other. We knew this was our chance to move on, to do something on our own. This is our opportunity of a lifetime. It's my opportunity to do some serious writing. The one thing I have always wanted to do."

"I have spent my whole life relying on someone else, never on myself," said Olivia, "except for the past few months when I taught school, of course. Adam, I know we haven't discussed it, but what do you think? Could you run the newspaper? I'm sure Molly would be more than willing to guide us. We would have to be careful not to push her too hard and go against doctor's orders."

"Together we can do anything we want to, my dear. Let's do it. We don't need to talk it over. Our future is falling into our laps. We need to take advantage of it. We'll talk to the owner on Monday and go from there."

Adam and Olivia were up half the night talking about buying the newspaper. Ma was awake, too, hoping the best for her young son. He does love to write, she thought. I hope he's good enough so people will want to read his stories.

Early next morning Adam walked out to the barn to tell Clay what he and Olivia were planning. Clay was happy Adam had finally found something that would keep him interested for more than just a few weeks.

“I know you’re fed up with keeping the books for the ranch. Good luck with the newspaper, little brother. Maybe now you can publish all those journals you have been keeping over the years. They make some mighty good reading.”

Clay asked, “What will Olivia do? You will have a new bride, plus a new business. Be careful, Adam. Don’t neglect one for the other.”

* * * * *

The McCreedy’s money Ben had found a lifetime ago in the little tin pail was in the bank. Olivia knew it was there. She never took any out, thinking she would someday use it to further her education. She offered it to Adam to buy the newspaper.

“I have some savings put aside too. Yes, we can use some of the money to buy the newspaper. Not all of it, though. Clay will probably buy out my share of the ranch so that will give us even more. We’ll need to buy a house in town, plus everything else a newlywed couple needs.”

Olivia made Adam go by himself to talk to Mr. Denison. She was beside herself by the time she heard the horse and buggy returning. Rather than stopping at the house, Adam went to the stable, unharnessed the team, and walked back. Olivia took it as a sure sign the news was not good. She ran out to meet him, “Adam, do not make me wait one more second. What happened?”

“Well, Olivia, I don’t know if this is good news or bad news. The good news is yes, the newspaper is for sale. The bad news is that Denison told me it takes years and years of experience to get publishing right. There is an awful lot to learn. He reminded me that we don’t even know how to ink the presses, let alone write an unbiased news article or editorial. He was not encouraging at all. Even when I offered a cash deal, he still expressed doubts we could run the business.

"On the other hand, he wants to leave town so badly he can taste it. He's willing to take a chance. All we have to do is not let the newspaper go under. If we realize we cannot make a go of it, Mr. Denison wants a promise that we will talk to him first. He'll help us sell the newspaper to an experienced editor. He doesn't want either of us to lose any money."

Olivia threw her arms around Adam, "What else? What else did he say? I know there is more."

"Now let me see. There are so many details. We came to an agreement on the sale price. I did manage to talk him down a little bit. I assured him the money is there. He said he wasn't worried about that. He knows the reputation of the Hardisty family."

"So, the deal is done?" asked Olivia. "We are the new owners of the newspaper? I cannot believe it! My head is spinning. Oh! Will we have to get a paper out the day after our wedding? I was hoping we could get away for a few days at least."

"No, no, no," laughed Adam. "Denison knows we are getting married soon. He promised to stay awhile to show me the ropes. We can go away for as long as we like. It will just shorten the number of days we have to learn anything from him.

"But, like you said, we do have Molly. Denison takes over the newspaper in Kansas City he's buying in July. It looks like everything is falling right into place."

* * * * *

It rained during the early morning of Olivia's wedding day. By the time tables and chairs had to be arranged out by the orchard the grass had nearly dried off. The air smelled of sweet apple blossoms.

"Rain has always been a sign of good luck for newlyweds," Ma said confidently. "The sky is blue and will be for the rest of the day. Now go get yourself into your dress. Abigail is here to do your hair. Clay is going to take Adam for a buggy ride. Man talk, you know."

Adam stood under a branch of apple blossoms that matched the colors of the dresses in the wedding party. As Olivia and Clay approached him, Adam could not believe the beauty of his soon-to-be bride in her white gown. This is right, he said to himself. So many new beginnings are happening right now. I can't wait for us to get started.

Right behind Olivia, before the bridesmaids, was Snow. From the day Red Morning had given her the puppy Snow never left Olivia's side. He was not about to leave her now. The white dog sat on his haunches next to Olivia during the ceremony. Snow led them back down the aisle when it was over.

"I wish your Indian family could be here to celebrate with us," said Adam. "I'm glad you included some of their ways into our party. I see the Morning Star design you sewed on the train of your wedding dress. Does it have a special meaning?"

"Yes. It does," replied Olivia. "It means new beginning."

* * * * *

As much as both Olivia and Adam would have liked to spend their honeymoon returning to her Indian family, they knew they couldn't. Again, there was not enough time. Within a few short days they would be responsible for publishing the town newspaper.

Instead, they chose to go to nearby Billings. The newlyweds reveled in the city. They ate at a different restaurant every night, stayed at the best hotel, and saw what there was to see.

Adam insisted they visit the local newspaper office. The editor was more than willing to share his expertise with Adam. Olivia definitely felt left out. She sat and chatted with two reporters who were working on stories for the next edition.

When Adam and Olivia returned to Fort Benton the first thing they did was buy a house. During the winter Olivia lived in town while teaching, a certain house had caught her eye. Adam found one similar and they purchased it. They made many trips back and forth between the house and the ranch, moving all their belongings from one place to the other.

While they were gone, Mr. Denison had the bank draw up all the papers required for sale of the newspaper. Olivia noticed her name was not included on the deed. She didn't question it at the time, not wanting to delay ownership.

Finally, there came the evening Adam and Olivia sat down together after supper with nothing to do. They could enjoy each other for a change. For the first time, Snow curled up next to Adam and fell asleep with his heavy head resting on Adam's shoes.

* * * * *

Adam spent his days at the newspaper office gleaning as much information as possible before being left on his own. Olivia had purposely stayed away after she realized she intimidated the former editor. He was much more comfortable talking business with a man.

Olivia stayed home and put their new house in order. When that was finished she spent her afternoons with Molly who was getting bigger and moving more slowly.

Molly knew her own health well enough that she took lots of naps and saved energy for when she needed it. Tad was busy with his law practice. Olivia and Molly had always enjoyed visiting with each other.

The day Adam officially ran the newspaper by himself not much was accomplished. The owners of every business establishment in town managed to stop by sometime during the day to welcome him to their fold and, of course, invite him to join the Merchant's Association.

Six months later, Olivia spent part of every day at the newspaper. When Adam was busy on a story, or had to be elsewhere, she attended meetings for him taking copious notes so he could write a story for the paper.

The government was coming down hard on the Indians. There was much unrest in the countryside. Tempers flared, armies patrolled. Indians balked at having to move, sometimes hundreds of miles away from their home lands. It was an outrage to Olivia. She wanted to write plea after plea, on behalf of Native people, to be left alone.

"Why can't I use the newspaper to write about how poorly Indians all over are being treated," she cried. "People need to know what is happening."

"Not now," Adam told her. "This is a very touchy subject. There is little sympathy for Indians right now. If you can write something short, something that will not offend anyone, of any color, maybe I can find a spot in the paper to print it. No promises. You write something first, not too long, and we'll see.

"I do agree the government making them move from their lands is newsworthy. It's just that our readers far outnumber us. If they are offended and stop reading the newspaper because of our agenda, that is the end of our livelihood. Let's just take our time. This is a subject we have to ease into, little by little."

Olivia finally agreed with Adam. She backed off and did not bring up the subject again. She worked on two articles she had written until she was satisfied with them. Still she did not present them to Adam. He's right, she thought. It's too soon for new owners of the newspaper to get on the bandbox.

Adam was learning how to write editorials and to accept criticism that often came from disgruntled readers of another opinion.

"This is good," he explained to Olivia. "In their own way, people of this town are letting me know what they want to read about. Maybe the day will come when we can broach the injustices of the government toward the Indians. We just have to be patient."

Olivia helped at the newspaper office as much as possible. The young Hardistys were becoming well-known around town. Both

Adam and Olivia developed many new friendships. Their days were full, their social life busy. They were thrilled living in town, while at the same time, missing being at the ranch with Ma. They drove out to see Ma as often as possible. Always, before they returned to their house in town, Olivia walked out to the rock pile she and Ben had shared so many years ago.

* * * * *

On their first wedding anniversary, Olivia told Adam that he was going to be a father. "What does the word father mean to you?" she asked.

"Means the world to me," said Adam, not getting the gist of her hint. "My father was the most special person in my life. I can only hope I mean that much to our children some day."

"Well, you will soon find out."

Their daughter was born in June. Adam and Olivia spent hours agonizing over what to call their new baby. Finally Adam said, "You name her. We can't seem to agree on a name both of us like. You name our daughter. I will name our son when he gets here. Is that a good compromise?"

"Yes," said Olivia. "I can call her any name and you won't be offended?"

"I will not be offended or disappointed. I will love any name you choose for our daughter."

Faith Dawn Hardisty was baptized in September. The entire family was invited back to the house for lunch after the ceremony. Each little cousin held the baby while Aunt Abigail sang lullabies.

While the women were getting the children ready for the buggy ride back to their ranch house, Clay and Adam waited in the sitting room, quietly talking. Adam held his little girl in his arms and gently rocked. Olivia walked into the room to tell Clay his family was just about ready to leave.

"I have to ask you something, Olivia. I think I have figured it out. Tell me if I'm right. How did you come to name your baby Faith Dawn?"

"Adam and I could never agree on a name we both liked. He made a deal with me. I could name our daughter and he will name our son."

She reached over and took the baby in her arms. "Faith is for my mother. For the faith she had in her journal that I would be rescued," she said looking into Clay's eyes.

"Dawn is for her Indian grandmother, Quaking Tree, who gave me a second chance. And last, but not least, Hardisty is our family, for Grandmother Sarah. All three women have led us to where we are today. What do you suppose is next for us, baby girl?"

After Adam and Faith fell asleep, Olivia crept down to the baby's room. She opened the old wood chest that had been in her room at the ranch. It still held her leather dresses and moccasins, her baptism dress, and the rest of the items Ben had found in the little tin bucket. She picked up the belt bucket and the broken arrow. She felt no kinship. She had never known her real parents.

She looked for Mary's journal but it was missing. Adam has it, she said to herself. That book is such a fascination to him. I don't know how many times he's read it and then re-read it. Olivia thought Adam could probably quote pages, he had read it so often.

Before Faith was born, Olivia had purchased a leather-bound journal from one of the traveling salesman who always stopped at the newspaper office whenever he came through Fort Benton. She sat down in the rocking chair, opened the journal and began writing.

"Today, you were baptized, Faith Dawn. Everyone in the family was here for the celebration. You were named for your grandmothers."

* * * * *

Part III

Chapter 32

Faith kept Olivia fairly housebound during her first two years. After that, Faith went wherever her mother had to go. Often she was bundled up in warm horsehide blankets, perched on a sled, and pulled along to various council meetings. Olivia took notes and wrote up the proceedings for the newspaper.

Adam appreciated every hour his wife dedicated to making the paper a success. They now had a firm standing in the community. Adam was getting bolder with his editorials, which riled a few, but there were others who congratulated him for speaking his piece. "We are all entitled to our opinion," those readers reassured him.

Olivia always made sure he presented both sides of every story. If anything, she thought everyone should be able to express their opinions. Every letter to the editor sent to the office was printed, no matter what opinion was expressed.

During spring and fall, when most of the fund-raising activities were held, mother and daughter were there reporting for the newspaper. News slacked off during summer so the family was able to spend more time together. Of course, their favorite place to go was the ranch.

"I'm just not a rancher," Adam told his brother Clay. "Sometimes I feel such a disappointment to our Pa, especially after he gave me the opportunity to be part of the ranch and keep the books for you guys. That was the best day of my life. I'll never forget it."

"Don't worry about it, Adam," Clay reassured his brother. "We are all different. Each of us has to find what it is we want to do with our lives. After I brought Olivia out of the woods here, to our home, I knew I never wanted to leave again. And I'm the first one who wanted to leave and never come back when I was younger. You just have to find your own place in the world. To not settle for anything less than what makes you happy.

"That reminds me of something. I keep hearing good things about how you have changed the paper around. Local folks appreciate what you've done so it's a real hometown newspaper now. They like your stories too, especially those from all the journals you kept during your many adventures. Folks around here haven't had the opportunity to travel far away like you have."

Clay never did buy out Adam's share of the ranch. He and Ma thought it best to keep it in the family so everyone would have a little extra spending money, including the newlyweds.

The ranch had been profitable from the beginning. None of them had been left wanting. Now with all the grandchildren, who had to be fed and clothed, Sarah remembered how hard it had been when Ben took up scouting because it paid so well. Even then there never seemed to be enough. She didn't ever want any of her children, or their children, to have to struggle as hard as she and Ben had for many years.

Olivia read everything she could about Indians being mistreated. She was very concerned for her tribe. They were not a large group. She felt they might be easily pushed around by the government.

The United States decreed Indians would sell their land to the government and in return move to designated areas reserved by treaty. Most often the land was barren and far from their homelands. This is so unjust, she said to herself. She kept pestering Adam to let her stand up for them in print. He still managed to put her off. She made copious notes for the time it would be right to have her articles published.

At bed time, when Faith insisted on yet another story, Olivia always told about her life with the Indians, about the people and how they lived, what her Indian family meant to her.

"You'll meet them one day, Faith. When you are a little older we'll ride for days through the woods, over the mountains, and along rivers until we come to their camp. I can't wait for you to meeting Quaking Tree and Sky In Water, and my brother and sister.

* * * * *

Molly and Tad welcomed their child, a boy nicknamed CB in honor of Molly's brother, Clay, and her father, Ben. "C.B. Wannamaker," said Tad. "Sounds like the name of an attorney if ever I heard one. That is, if he chooses to be one," he quickly added, remembering how his father had pressured him.

Sarah welcomed all her new grandchildren with open arms. She had always had a special place in her heart for Molly who had gone through such an awful illness in her childhood. How she had survived to bring babies into the world was a miracle. Sarah moved to town to take care of her and the baby until Molly was strong enough to cope.

Tad was talking about moving back east again. "Not to where I came from," he stressed. "Not anywhere near my parents. It would be so easy for father to take over my life again. I will not allow that to happen. I like living in the west, but if I am to be the lawyer I want to be I need to defend more than drunken cowboys and greedy land barons."

Molly quietly listened to him, rarely offering an opinion. She did want to encourage her husband to be his best. At the same time, the thought of leaving her close knit family, moving hundreds of miles away, was more than she could imagine.

"Maybe when the children are much older," she finally told Tad one evening. "Shepherding two small children half-ways across the country is more than my health will allow right now. When they are older, they can more or less take care of themselves. It's something to think about. Later."

Clay and Abigail's family grew nearly every year. All the bedrooms in their house were filling up. "There's only one empty room left in the house," Abby told her mother-in-law. Adam thinks we should turn it into an office for Clay. When I told him, Clay just laughed. He said he expected as much from a man who likes to be inside all the time.

"Clay said he wants a houseful of happy children, and that, as much as he hates all the paperwork involved, he and the foreman do just fine using the old office out in the barn."

Thanksgiving had shifted from the old ranch house to the river house, as the family called Clay and Abigail's home. Abby made sure there was a table long enough to sit everyone during the holidays. Over the years, each person had kept his own place next to the same little cousin, or an aunt or uncle. The most revered chair to sit on was next to Grandma Sarah. It was rarely traded off.

Olivia and Adam hosted Christmas dinner for the family at their house in town only once. It wasn't the same as at Ma's house at the ranch, even though it was beautifully decorated for the season. The food was the same, there were presents to open, and carols were sung, but there was something missing that only Ma could provide.

Sarah's health had been failing a little as each year went by. "I'm nearly sixty years of age, and that's old," she declared at her last birthday celebration. "Look at how many friends of your Pa and me have passed on. You are just lucky I'm still here. Don't know what you will do when I'm gone and those grandbabies are on their own. I just don't know what you'll do!"

"Stop talking like that," said Abigail. "You have many more birthdays to look forward to and many more grandchildren to welcome. Don't quit on us now just because you have a few bad days now and then. What would Pa say if he heard you talking like this?"

"You're right. I guess I'm just feeling sorry for myself with this big old house creaking and groaning around me. It's so full of memories. Sometimes it drags me down and I can't get up until I get one of my kids or grandkids in sight. Let's talk about something else. CB, have you roped and tamed any broncos lately?"

* * * * *

Chapter 33

Olivia and Adam welcomed their son, Micah Adam, on a cold wintery day. Adam trudged through the deep snow over to the doctor's house just two days before a massive snow storm hit to remind Doc Marten that his baby was due any day now.

Adam delivered his son, while snow banked against the doors and wind rattled windows in the house. It would be another day before anyone in town could get outside. As soon as it was possible, Doctor Marten made it a point to go see how Olivia and the baby were doing.

"Your son is the spitting image of Ben," the doctor commented. "Faith looks like your family, from what I hear, but Micah is definitely a Hardisty."

"Do you like the name I chose for him, Olivia?" asked Adam. "I wanted it to be a surprise. That's why I would never tell you until he was born. Look at Faith watching the baby. I hope she's prepared to handle a little brother."

Grandma Sarah once again moved to town to take care of the newborn while Olivia got her strength back. By then, she was only too happy to get back to the ranch and recuperate herself.

* * * * *

Olivia did not know why, but she had been thinking of Quaking Tree a lot lately. Images of her Indian family flashed in her mind's eye at odd moments. She caught herself wondering if something was wrong or if they were in some kind of trouble.

"I just have this odd feeling," she told Adam. "It's as if Quaking Tree is trying to tell me something. I can't figure out what it is. I just hope and pray this past winter was not too hard on them. It's always a struggle. When some winters are worse than others a few never survive."

Adam assured Olivia he would try to find out any information he could about the tribe. Being a popular, outspoken kind of guy, he had formed many friendships during their time in town, many through owning the newspaper. Anyone who passed through, from tinkers to soldiers, rarely forgot the talkative, curious-as-the-day-is-long editor of the local paper. Most made it a point to seek him out on their next trip through. Consequently, Adam always had a handle on what was happening in and around the surrounding territory and beyond.

* * * * *

Adam signed for a telegram delivered to the newspaper office. After reading the short message he sat down to think about the possibilities it opened up for him and his family. Adam had to go home and tell Olivia her grandparents had both passed away, within weeks of each other.

Grandfather McCreedy had caught the influenza. In taking care of him, her grandmother also succumbed to the deadly disease. The house in Boston now belonged to Olivia.

Olivia wept a few tears when Adam told her that both grandparents had passed. "I wish now I had known them better," she whimpered. "I know your people. They are my real family, not those strangers in Boston.

"Now I am saddled with a huge house in Boston that will probably cost a huge fortune to keep up. Grandfather never wanted it sold. What are we to do? I do know that I am never going to live there. That is for sure. Maybe we can turn it into something useful for the community, like a museum, or a small private school."

"I do not think that is possible, Olivia," said Adam. "That house is located in a very affluent section of Boston. I'm sure the people would not allow anything that would bring strangers into their neighborhood.

"Personally," he continued, "I would love to live there. Think of all the culture, the music, the art and plays we could enjoy. The excitement is there. Boston isn't far from Washington, the seat of our government. Our children would receive the best education available. Won't you please reconsider?"

"No," she said adamantly. "I will not leave this place. This is our home. Why don't you take the trip back east and tend to what needs to be done about the house. If there are papers to be signed, I give my power of attorney. I do not want to go."

Olivia began the process of talking her husband into making the trip to Boston without her. "I know how to run the newspaper. We can get along for a couple of weeks without you. I won't write anything drastic, like an editorial bemoaning the trials and tribulations of the Indians. I told you I would wait until you said it was the right time for that. I will continue to wait.

"Please go. Have yourself another taste of life in the big city, then come home and tell me all about it. You can even write about it for the newspaper. Don't forget to take a new journal with you. I love you, Adam. Now, go pack."

* * * * *

Olivia was nervous when she unlocked the door to the newspaper building and entered, all alone. I don't know if I can do this. What was I thinking, she asked herself.

Tim Riley, Adam's assistant, came through the door just then and asked, "Don't you just love the smell of ink when you first open the door?"

Adam went over all the stories and advertising that was scheduled to be printed while he was gone, all the while assuring Tim he was capable of doing a fine job.

"Tim, you are in charge of advertising and calling on merchants. If Olivia gets herself into trouble writing up any daily news you can figure out what to do. You are also capable of writing anything that needs to go into the newspaper.

"You will do just fine. Don't worry about it. Take it day to day; just make sure everything is done when you lock the door at night. We want to always start fresh again in the morning. That system works best for me and you are used to it, too. Good luck."

Olivia and Tim were into their second week with no major catastrophes. They were taking a break, drinking coffee, and feeling pretty smug.

The bell over the door rang as a loud blustery voice boomed, "Where is the editor of this so-called newspaper. I've got a bone to pick with that man."

Olivia stood up, ready to defend her husband. Tim sat still, a big smile growing on his face. Olivia turned and saw that it was one of the tinkers who stopped by every time he was in Fort Benton.

"Welcome, Homer. What brings you this way? And no, you can't chew on my husband this time. He is out of town, in Boston, in fact. You will just have to deal with me."

"Oh, no," laughed Homer. "There is a woman in charge. I have to deal with a woman! Where's Tim?"

Homer grasped Olivia's hand and said, "I'm afraid I have brought you sad news, darlin'. Adam always asked if, in my travels, I would keep an eye on the whereabouts of your Indian family. He gave me the area where they usually stayed, which was very near my route.

"Well, my dear, I hate to tell you this, but they have been moved to a reservation. They held out as long as they could. They managed to evade the soldiers for many years. They were finally forced to leave. I don't know exactly when it happened but they should be well settled in by now. I haven't heard anything else about them at all."

Tears came to Olivia's eyes. She sat down. "That is why Quaking Tree has been on my mind for so long. I knew something was wrong. I just knew it. I was afraid they would be forced onto a reservation. It finally happened."

"I am sorry to bring you this information," said Homer. "I know you never have forgotten your family. I admire you for it. Maybe you can go see them more often now. I think they are living much closer to Fort Benton."

That brought a smile back to her face. Olivia thanked Homer for relaying the information. She had much to think about.

* * * * *

Adam was gone a total of three weeks, one of them traveling to and from by train. When he arrived in Boston Adam immediately went to the office of the lawyer who had sent the telegram. He presented himself and the letter from Olivia giving him the power to sign her name on any legal papers.

The lawyer told him everything was in order. It would only be a matter of a hours before the legal work was completed. "In the meantime," he said to Adam, I have arranged for a horse and carriage to take you to the McCreedy estate.

Adam roamed from room to room, duly impressed with the grandeur of the manor. He was saddened by its silence.

No, I could never see Olivia living in a place like this, he thought. She's much more comfortable on a smaller scale and being outside as much as possible. She definitely would not like it here.

But I would, he said to himself. There are bedrooms enough for a big family, a sewing room for Olivia, a study for me where I could write to my heart's content, and playrooms. There are rooms for every use we could think of, and then some. It's only a dream, he realized.

Adam returned to the lawyer's office to pick up all the signed documents. He headed back to the train station. He planned to spend a day in Washington and another day in New York before traveling west once again. Before he left the lawyer inquired as to their use of the house.

"None for the present." replied Adam. "If you could arrange for the same household help as the McCreedys had to go by the house every now and then to keep it clean and repaired, inside and out, I would appreciate it. When I get back to Montana I will wire money to your office to pay their salaries. Of course, we will keep you on a retainer to take care of these details for us."

Adam filled his journal with the sights and sounds of each city he visited. His plan was to read to his children, each night at bedtime from the pages, hoping to instill in them a sense of adventure.

* * * * *

Olivia reviewed all the legal documents Adam gave her when he returned. She expressed little concern. She had no interest whatsoever in the house in Boston. "Frankly, she said, "I don't care what happens to it."

Adam was shocked to hear about Olivia's family being moved by the government.

"At this point," she told him, "no one seems to know for sure where they were sent. Most likely, it's to the north of Fort Benton, bordering Canada. If that's the place it is a huge territory. A small band, like mine, could disappear up there."

Adam vowed he would find out for sure where they were. He knew Olivia was yearning to see her family as soon as was possible. It was up to him to find them.

Three years passed with no word about Olivia's family. Rarely did anyone from any tribe leave the reservation for fear of getting into trouble with the government. Traveling salesmen never went near the Indians other than dealing with them when they sold their wares at a fort or outpost.

Soldiers sometimes had to ride in to quell arguments and settle disputes. They were not curious about the identity of anyone. There was no one to help locate Quaking Tree.

* * * * *

Olivia gave up hope of ever finding her family again. She no longer talked about the day when she would take her babies to see them.

She never forgot about Indians and their culture. "There is so much to be learned from them," she insisted over and over again. "Please let me write something about their agriculture or their cures for maladies that occur. I promise not to write anything negative about the government attitude towards them or what more could be done for them. I'll write about simple everyday things."

Adam agreed but limited her to two hundred words. Olivia immediately set to work on her first article. She had thought enough about the subject so the minute Adam gave her permission she went to her desk and wrote an explanation of how the Indians plant different crops in different fields or patches every other year. That way, she explained, the soil is not worn out. She wrote in detail so maybe some of the local farmers could see the point of rotating their crops rather than wearing out their farmland.

There were no negative comments when the first article appeared. Adam let her write a second one, again limited to two hundred words. This time she explained the prudence of watering cattle and horses downstream of where a family would take water into their houses for daily use.

Two farmers who had read the articles stopped by the newspaper office. “Who wrote those Indian stories,” one of them inquired. “There was no name. We thought maybe someone from back east is here doing research for one of them there colleges.”

Adam laughed and said, “No. It’s a local person who knows a little about a whole lot of stuff. He could not wait to get home to tell Olivia her articles had raised some interest.”

Now, Adam thought, I will have to rethink my stand against Olivia writing more stories and articles for the paper. Maybe she would enjoy putting together profiles of local business owners. I think she would enjoy doing the interviews.

* * * * *

Chapter 34

In the spring, Olivia knew she had to find her Indian family. There was rarely any good news coming out of any reservation. Disease was decimating every tribe in large numbers. Guns and alcohol brought more tragedy.

Adam and Olivia planned to make the trip themselves but, if need be they would hire guides along the way. Clay was much too busy managing the horse ranch and taking care of his big family. He would be missed too much if he made the trip this time.

After a long discussion with both of them, Clay said he felt confident Adam and Olivia could make the journey themselves.

"Because of your experience on the last trip you will know, more or less, what to expect. There is always one thing to remember, though. If you go looking for trouble, you will find it."

Olivia and Adam talked at length about what to do with the children. Olivia wanted to at least ask Molly if she felt up to looking after the children while they were gone. She knew, full well, Molly was not in the best of health but felt she should ask anyway.

Molly's health had deteriorated more after giving birth. She became more fragile as time went on. Olivia was relieved when Molly suggested they take the children out to Clay's place.

"Clay and Abby won't even notice there are two more little ones in the house amid that crowd of kids they have," laughed Molly.

Ma was not too happy with Adam and Olivia riding off into the north, not knowing exactly where they were going.

"I know this is something you have to do. It is time you see your family again. I have a feeling time is running out for them. So go. Be careful. Promise to keep Adam out of trouble, will you? Adam, promise to keep out of trouble!"

* * * * *

Once again Adam and Olivia began the long ride in search of her Indian family. After the third day on the trail neither one was sure they had made the right decision. They missed the guidance Clay could offer.

Olivia teased Adam about getting lost several times. "I just don't know where I am right this minute," laughed Adam. Beginner's luck stayed with them. They always managed to find their way back on the trail and a river to camp next to. They searched the sky on cloudless nights for the North Star, marking a tree so they headed off in the right direction each morning.

* * * * *

Days dragged by with no sign of the tribe Olivia had lived with so many years ago. Both Adam and Olivia were growing more and more frustrated, the weather was not cooperating, still they trudged on.

After one particularly bad day in the saddle, they stopped to make camp earlier than usual. Olivia went to the effort of making their supper extra special. During a rest stop that afternoon she had picked wild berries and made a cobbler for dessert. She brewed a second pot of coffee as they settled in for another night under the stars.

"I think we need to talk about where we are headed," Olivia said as she poured Adam another cup of coffee.

“I’ve been thinking the same thing,” replied Adam. “It’s been such an awful day, let’s talk about it in the morning when we aren’t thinking about how much we are missing our warm, soft beds.”

“OK,” she agreed as she laid her head down using her saddle for a pillow. “I’m just going to lie here on my back and watch the stars. Maybe I can find one that will lead us to where we need to go.” Olivia was sound asleep before she finished her coffee.

While Olivia slept, Adam pulled a large log up near the fire and sat down using it for a backrest. By the firelight, he began writing in his journal.

> *Many years ago, there was great unrest between the Indian Nations and the United States government. It became mandatory that all Indians must live on reservations, free land set aside for them where they would be safe. But, in fact, the government in so doing sucked the very life blood from the Indians.*
>
> *The Indians, convinced that if they could amass enough repeater rifles, the white invaders could be obliterated, much as the pale face had wiped out their buffalo herds. No farmer, rancher, or wagon train was safe from Indian raids. Armies were sent west to protect settlers. Most often they were too late. The Indians were stealthy and quick to retreat.*
>
> *After one particularly devastating raid only two survived. The scout for the wagon train the Indians circled and plundered survived only because he had scouted ahead and was on his way back.*
>
> *The second survivor, a baby girl, was snatched from her mother’s arms and taken back to the Indian village.*

The scout was my father. The baby grew up with the Indians. She was eventually rescued by my brother. She is now my wife. And this is her story.....

~ The End ~

ABOUT THE AUTHOR

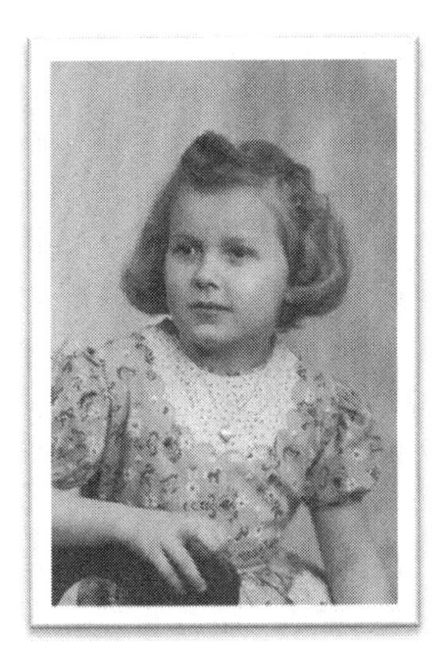

Kay Larson

When she was a child, Kay Larson realized that when she was gone her family name would go with her. Her father had six sisters and she was the youngest of his six daughters. Even if she married and had children it would be highly unlikely their last name would be Larson. A book was the only thing Kay could think of to leave behind bearing her family name.

Now, many years later, here is that book. It was the first entry on her Bucket List, most of which have been accomplished. One item still remaining is a 1941 Chevy pickup.

CONTACT GREAT SPIRIT PUBLISHING IF:

… you want to learn more about publishing with Great Spirit Publishing's traditional line of spiritual and inspirational material, or would like to learn about *GSP-Assist* and other alternatives to an author's "self-publishing" route to publication.

Feel free to visit our website to browse our growing selection of books. All items are available for purchase through PayPal, or online through CreateSpace and Amazon.

Send e-mail inquiries to greatspiritpublishing@yahoo.com.

FIND MORE ONLINE AT:

http://www.greatspiritpublishing.yolasite.com/book-store.php

independent and assistive publishing technologies

Great Spirit Publishing is proud to bring you entertaining and mind-expanding literary works from known and unknown writers. We help writers make their publishing dreams come true!

Contact Great Spirit Publishing directly by sending an e-mail to: greatspiritpublishing@yahoo.com.

Visit us online at www.greatspiritpublishing.yolasite.com/book-store.php.